WICKED BITE

THE ROYALS: VAMPIRE COURT BOOK ONE

MEGAN MONTERO

CHAPTER ONE

GRAYSON

$\mathcal{M}$isty rain settled like a cold blanket over Boston. It was the kind of rain that didn't actually fall. It seemed to hover in the air, soaking everything through and chilling me to my bones. My leather jacket barely provided a reprieve from the freezing rain, but I'd grown used to it. Though the rain was lighter here and the air even colder, the damp dreariness of it all felt like a familiar place I'd been trying to avoid: London. Even so, getting lost in a bigger city was the plan for tonight. At least until the Royals called upon me once more to perform my duties protecting the Witch Queens of Evermore. Until then, the world could piss right off, along with every other expectation held over me.

There was something seedy about Boston. It was a

mix of both culture and danger. Signs of the nightlife were all around me: people roaming in drunken packs up and down the streets, one girl screaming at her boyfriend for looking at another girl, a bachelorette party climbing into a limo while holding each other upright. Pubs were scattered along the roads and overflowing with people and noise. I just had to pick the right one to get lost in.

The light scent of something sweet and fresh tingled my nose, and I turned the corner, following that honeyed fragrance. Then the scent of something dark and coppery overtook it, ruining the sweetness and forcing me to halt just outside a narrow alley. It was a familiar smell, one I both loved and had grown weary of. Blood. It was both delicious and worrisome, depending on the context. I turned my gaze down the alley, allowing my senses to take over.

To the human eye, there would be nothing there. Maybe the lingering eeriness would cause a shiver down their spine—an instinct that would save some of them from the danger that lurked in the shadows. But I was no human, and shadows held no danger for me. I took a step from the glow of the streetlights and let the darkness fall around me like a cloak. I bared my fangs and hissed into the alley. Like animals in the night, three sets of eyes reflected back at me. At the center of the group was a single human with a slow, lagging heartbeat. Shaggy hair fell over his face as his head lolled to the side, losing consciousness. His skin was sickly pale, and I could tell from here they'd taken too much blood already.

"And what do you lot of amateurs think you're doing?" I strolled farther into the alley, stepping over one young human male, who was unconscious and barely clinging to life, while three fledgling vampires held another one up against the wall, feeding like uncontrollable vultures.

They hissed in my direction, and the female farthest from me spoke. "Move along, this one is ours."

I tilted my head to the side examining her features. Hair pulled back tight to her head, heavy dark makeup, bright red lipstick . . . or was that blood? It trickled from the corner of her mouth.

Blood then.

"And you're about to kill him. You do know there are other ways to feed without this kind of . . . disaster? Places to go."

The female closest to me popped her fangs from the guy's wrist and hissed in my direction. *Ballsy little sod.* She too had her hair pulled back tight in a high ponytail and wore dark makeup. "Ours. Leave."

Adorable.

I rolled my eyes. So typically, movie vampire. It was like they all lost their sense of self and decided this was who they were going to become. Horrible little night predators. Untrained and untamed.

"You're aware of the laws, yes?" I looked them up and down.

The third one backed away from the man and stared at me. His mouth fell into a little O-shape, and his eyes went wide. Strands of dark hair fell into his face as he nodded but said nothing.

Ah, that's more like it.

"What's it to you?" the woman with the darker hair snapped. She put her hands on her hips and swung her head with all the attitude of a young naïve vampire living in Boston.

"M-Mandy." The male vampire smacked her arm while never taking his eyes off me. "Sh-shh. Shut up."

He dropped to his knee in front of me and rested his arm on it. He bowed his head and glanced up at me. "Yes, we know the laws."

Mandy wrinkled her nose at him. "What are you doing?"

He grabbed her arm and yanked her down beside him. "The House of Shade."

She jerked free of him. "Yeah, what about it?"

"He's the heir you, moron." The young male jerked his chin toward me.

I arched my eyebrow, and chuckled. That was me, the reluctant heir to the most powerful line of Vampires the world had ever seen. And yet, here I was in the dredges of Boston, policing baby vamps and stopping murders in the street.

"I had no idea, your maja-highness." She awkwardly ducked her head while the other girl tripped over her own feet to drop down next to her.

"All right, come off it." I waved for them to stand up. "No need to be flopping about on the ground."

She staggered to her feet. "Your maja-highness—"

"Grayson. The name is Grayson, love." I glanced at the two nearly dead humans. "Right, so you've made a mess, and before the Royal Vamp Police show up to, well, you know, kick your arses, you should clean it up."

The young male vampire glanced around. "But how?"

"First, I'd cover up the fang marks you lot have left behind. Then I'd get these two to the hospital for a transfusion."

His face paled. "A human hospital?"

It was appalling to bring made vampires into this

world and not teach them how to live properly. I pulled a card from inside my jacket pocket. There were many layers to the Vampire world, the least of which was finding ways to keep our indiscretions a secret. "Call that number. Tell them what's happened. They'll come and help clean it up. Even Vampires know how to help the humans out occasionally and keep our secrets."

He snatched the card from my hand and smiled down at it. Blood coated his teeth and ran over the side of his lip. "Thanks."

I pointed to my own teeth. "You've got something . . ." I sighed and motioned to my whole mouth. ". . . well, everywhere."

Before they could say anything else I turned away from them and darted from the alley. The last thing I needed was to be cleaning up dead bodies and drawing the attention of my uncle. Instead, I once again locked on that sweet scent and followed it. I was here to get lost in the oblivion of mundane nothingness, not to make a political statement for my family.

I turned another corner and crossed a street toward a shady pub. The doors were thick dark wood that stood wide open. The entire front wall was made of windows that allowed people on the street to peek into the bar. Booths were set up along the side walls and closer to the windows. High-top tables were spread throughout, and big screen TVs hung over the bar facing outward. A warm light glowed from behind the bar, illuminating the many bottles on the shelves.

I wove my way through the heavy crowd of people gathered around the tables and paused, staring at the beauty behind the bar. Her fragrance was intoxicating. She was sultry, with wild midnight hair that fell nearly to her hips and bangs that framed her face perfectly. It was the kind of hair that was meant to tangle around my fingers in a night spent together. Her eyes were dark green with flecks of brown in them that matched the warm tan color of her skin. A waiter came at me, and I easily stepped around him heading right to the bar . . . right toward her.

Her words flowed together like a song I'd never heard before but sounded like heaven to my ears. She hadn't noticed me yet, but she had my full attention. When she turned toward the other bartender with her, I glimpsed a tattoo below the hem of her white crop top. It was a little bumblebee dressed up like a ghost with the word boo written under it. When the other girl faced her, I saw that she, too, had the same tattoo except under her bee it said bees.

Boo bees. I chuckled to myself.

Besties then. Interesting.

"So, there I am, buying into his usual line of bullshit. You know how they do. Painting that pretty little fairytale of happily ever after. I'd love to spend my days with you, just hanging out, watching TV. I mean, it's not like I was asking for a ring or anything."

She reached into the bin of half-melted ice in front of her and pulled out an ice-cold bottle. She popped the top and slid it across the bar to the guy waiting. "That'll be six dollars."

He slammed a ten down on the bar and smiled at her over the rim of the bottle before he took a sip. "I won't give you that line of bullshit. Give me your number and I'll let you keep the change."

"Right, like I'm only worth four dollars, Stew. Can I call you Stew?"

His mouth dropped open to answer but she continued. "Had I accepted your four dollars and given you my number, there are a few possible options here. One, you would think I was worth the four dollars you have spent and treat me as such, and let's face it, Stew. I'm worth way more than your four dollars and the inevitable two pumps it would take for you to get there in a night full of passion."

"But—"

"Now, Stew. I'm doing you a favor here. I'm saving you from embarrassing yourself while at the same time giving you enough material to fill your spank bank just by wearing this outfit alone. So, your four dollars just got you four minutes of conversation from me. A whole four minutes that you have spent staring at my bellybutton. We all win here, Stew. Now go back to your table and tell them I was oh, so nice to you."

Sassy little creature. So much life to her. I found myself drawn to it.

She glanced at her friend. "What is it with guys these days? They love to lay down that same old song and dance." She made change in the register and shoved it into her tip jar. "Do better, Stew. Just do better."

I pressed my lips together to stop from laughing at the poor sod while I leaned my elbow on the bar. I watched as her hips swayed with each of her steps. A smile played on my lips, and I took in every bit of sassy attitude she had to offer. *How refreshing.*

"You know I love you." The guy made a show of reading her name tag for a little too long. "Piper, darlin.'"

He winked and turned to head back to the table of guys he was with.

"I love when you do that." The girl next to her chuckled and scooped ice into a glass. She was the same height as Piper but the opposite in looks, with blond hair, milky skin, and pale blue eyes. "Yeah, so then what did the other bozo say? The one you were *talking* to."

I found myself getting comfortable just listening to her voice and watching the way she moved. There was an underlying rhythm to it that was nearly irresistible.

"So, then he texted me and says I shouldn't have built things up in my head. Like I'm the one over here painting pretty pictures in my own mind. Meanwhile, I was thinking we could just hang out and have fun. I wasn't asking for forever. I was asking for a little dependability, though."

"Dependability is a four-letter word to some guys." She rolled those big blue eyes of hers and finished off the drink she was making with a lemon. "Typical."

"Right? They hear the words foster kid and it's automatically talking about the family we never had." She leaned over the bar to the guy across from me. "What can I get you?"

He just stared down her crop top without saying a word. She snapped her fingers in front of his face, getting his attention. "Eyes up here, princess."

The guy licked his lips and eyed her up and down. "Um, rum and Coke."

I chuckled and shook my head. "Not very subtle, mate."

Her head whipped around, and she smiled at me for the briefest of moments. "I've got this."

I held my hands up in surrender. "Yes, and I'm finding it quite entertaining."

"Happy to entertain . . . *mate*." She rolled her eyes and turned back to her friend.

The friend, whose name tag read Dice, served a drink to the girl in front of her then moved to Piper's side. "So, where should I send the flowers?"

Piper threw her head back and laughed, sending those wild waves flying around her face. "Send them to the graveyard in my heart for the men I've killed there before."

"Roses or black dahlias?" Dice poured another drink and handed it to the customer in front of her.

"It's not a funeral if there's nothing black." Piper winked at her before turning toward me. "Now, my sexy Brit. What can I get for you?"

"Sexy Brit?" Laughter burst from my lips. "That's a first, I can assure you."

"Oh, happy to be your first." Her eyes flashed and she grabbed a glass off the rack and filled it with ice. "Let me guess, Jack and Coke."

I frowned. "How disappointing, and here I thought you were a professional."

She tapped her lip with her finger. "Hmm, not a Coke kind of guy?"

"I'm more of a purist."

"No Coke then." She flashed me a smirk and turned for the bottles. I let my eyes roam over the curves of her body. She was beautiful, and not in the modern chic sense of the word. There was a wild, untamed air about her that I couldn't put my finger on.

I leaned back, watching her every move when, from the corner of my eye, I saw the door to the men's room open, and a familiar sense of foreboding settled over me. *Always with the distractions.* "Excuse me for a moment."

"Don't go too far. You wouldn't want the ice to melt."

I smirked. "Don't ruin a good bourbon with ice, love."

She leaned on the bar. "You like things neat?"

I mirrored her pose and leaned in closer to her. "A mess every now and then never hurt anyone."

Piper looked like the kind of *mess* that could ruin a lesser man. The kind of mess that would be perfection for a guy like me. I turned away from her and headed right toward the men's room. Shoddy stalls lined one wall, and a single mirror stood across from them. I waited a moment for one last patron to leave then I flipped the lock on the door. When I turned back toward the mirror, it had already begun to undulate.

"All right, out with you." I leaned against the wall and waited.

The mirror rippled and stretched outward to a needle point. Then it slid back, and a raven soared from within. It circled around my head, dropping thick dark feathers that fell in slow circles. I didn't move. Then a hand came through and the mirror peeled back from it. Then a leg and the rest of the body followed. He stepped onto the sink and stood tall, staring down at me. Too many people, that raven was a harbinger of death and the man that followed was the executioner. To me, he was a lifelong friend.

He was slightly taller than me at a towering six foot four inches with a muscular frame. His hair was down to his shoulders and ghostly white, with dark black strands that ran back from his temples. A loose-fitting black linen shirt hung off his frame and was wide open at the collar down to the middle of his chest. Dark leather pants and thick shitkicker boots rounded out the outfit. When he met my eye, a wide grin spread across his face. He jumped down from the sink and landed in front of me.

I gave him a single nod by way of greeting. "Atlas Savage."

"Grayson Shade. The House of Shade beckons."

I rolled my eyes. "As if I don't already know. Uncle Titus has a far reach. Every bloody acquaintance he's gained over the years has offered me a lift home."

"That he does. But a greater man does not exist."

"You'll get no argument from me on that front." He wasn't lying. My uncle was a great man: annoying but great, overbearing but great, a pain in my ass but great.

"It's good to see you." He offered me his hand and I took it. "Done playing with the witches?"

I shrugged. "For now."

He dropped my hand and crossed his arms over his chest. "Do tell me what a two-hundred-year-old vampire gains from the follies and challenges of running around with the young, dramatic, and magical?"

"Let us not judge the dramatic. I do recall you have a flare for it. And I'm one hundred and ninety-nine to be exact." No one ever asked a vampire their age. They just assumed I was young, or I might have lied about it. Either way the job got done . . . for now. "And it's not for me to gain. Alataris had to die and one of us had to assure that he did. Pressing in on the vampires was his next move, and we all knew it."

"And now The House of Shade is aligned with the Royal Court of Witches."

I gave a humorless chuckle. The truth was I adored them all. I'd made friends with the lot of them and respected the hell out of them. "Rather brilliant, I do believe."

Atlas nodded and the Raven soared toward him and perched himself on his shoulder. "Still, posing as an eighteen-year-old baby vampire just to help the world . . . I wouldn't have done so."

"We both know that to be a lie. Had Titus commanded it, you would've done so." Atlas was all things to the crown for The House of Shade including an assassin, an enforcer, and one of my best mates for the past hundred years.

"Fair words." He shrugged and started for the door.

"Um, Sav?" He froze and glanced at me over his shoulder. I sighed and pointed toward the raven. "Can't go wondering about with Poe on your shoulder."

"Right you are." He brushed his hand between the lapels of his shirt, and the raven jumped up into the air and spread its wings wide. It smacked into his chest then stretched and flattened out over his skin, turning from a real-life raven into a detailed tattoo that stretched across his skin from shoulder to shoulder.

"Sav, what are you doing here?" I headed toward the door and flipped the lock. "Honestly."

He let go a heavy sigh. "Like I said, The House of Shade beckons. This is the year of the prophecy, and we all need to be there."

I groaned and yanked the door open. *Don't remind me.*

CHAPTER TWO

PIPER

"*U*mm, what was *that?*" Dice gave me a huge smile then turned to another customer to get their order.

When she spun back to me, I played innocent. "What are you talking about?"

"Oh, you know." Dice whirled around and grabbed a bottle of beer from the ice bin in front of her. "You flirted . . . with the tall, sexy Brit."

There were three things in life I was sure of: one, I'd make a shit ton of money—tonight the place was packed. Two, that British guy was hot as hell. And three, I could hide nothing from my bestie. She knew me inside and out. "I mean, did you look at him?"

She scoffed. "Psh, yeah, I did."

"He looks good." He was tall, with damp, wild,

wavy hair that fanned back from his face. His shoulders were broad, but the rest of him was trim and fit. Dark pants, a dark shirt, and a dark leather coat equaled my kind of fun . . . or trouble. It depended on the day. I gazed at the door to the men's room. "And that accent."

"Yeah, I noticed that, too. I also noticed he looks like trouble wrapped up in a nice package that you find on the road toward heartbreak."

I moved in closer to her and whispered, "Or on the road toward multiple org—"

"Have you figured out the drink then, sassy creature?" He seemed to appear out of nowhere, startling me.

I glanced at Dice. *Did he hear me?* I grabbed a chilled glass and poured Jack over the ice in the shaker.

He met my eye and gave a smile. "Very good."

"I know." There was something about the way he didn't come on so strong but at the same time, I felt like he would take me at any moment.

"Allow me to introduce you to my friend here." He pointed to a tall, dangerous-looking guy who seemed to be as still as night but everywhere all at once. "Atlas Savage. Sav, for short."

Dice slid in front of me and bumped me out of the

way with her hip. She offered her hand to Atlas. "Dice."

He leaned in close and took her hand in his. He turned it and hovered over it and caught her eye. He held her gaze and gave her barely a smile. "Lovely to meet you."

When he let his lips brush over the back of her hand, her cheeks lit to a bright pink, and she shook her head. "Oh, you are trouble, aren't you?"

"I haven't got the slightest intention of bringing trouble to your doorstep. If it happens to follow, then I suppose I'd be the one to blame for that, too. But you'd never catch me admitting to my own sins." He kissed the back of her hand.

I looked him up and down. "You're going to have to up your game with me."

"I believe actions speak louder than pretty words." He took the drink I handed him and sipped it.

"Ah, but the man with pretty words holds the keys to the kingdom." Atlas dropped Dice's hand. "I'll have what he's having."

"Piper might not be into that . . ." Dice took a cherry from the fruit tray in front of her and popped it into her mouth. "She doesn't like to be shared. You know?"

Sexy Brit chuckled under his breath. "As if I'd be

the type to share, love. I find I require undivided attention when it comes to certain things."

My eyes widened, as did Dice's. I leaned my elbows on the bar. "Oh, I don't know—" I motioned for him to offer an answer.

"Grayson, love. The name is Grayson."

"Grayson." I shared another look with Dice. "How do you know you could keep my attention?"

He ran his hand through his thick, wavy hair, and when he met my eye, I felt enthralled. His eyes were a deep mahogany color that seemed to hold all the secrets of the world and yet, he'd never tell a soul. When he took another sip of his drink, he fought not to smile. He placed the glass on the bar in front of me.

"Oh, sassy creature . . ." He gave a light chuckle that sent shivers over my body. ". . . I already have."

He took a small step back and motioned to the crowd of people waiting for drinks that had gathered around the bar. My pulse jumped and I shook myself. "Oh, shit."

Dice and I scrambled back to work, pouring drinks, taking orders, and cutting the line down. All the while, he never took his eyes off me, and I barely looked away from him. Even while his friend murmured to him, he didn't look away. It was a heady feeling of being watched and liking it. The sounds of the bar fell away. There was no music, or TVs, or even people around us. There was only me and him. Sure, I was working and slinging beers as quickly as I could, but the heat of his gaze traveled over my skin, and I couldn't help from being distracted.

When I went to the register, Dice moved to stand next to me. "Careful with that one. He looks like he bites."

I glanced over my shoulder at him, and the two of them were chuckling like they'd just heard some inside joke. I turned back to her and rolled my eyes. "Like I'd trust anyone to get close enough to let them."

"Touché. Because, girl, those emotional walls are high." She bumped me with her hip. "Except for me."

It was true, I didn't let people in. Because generally, people tended to disappoint, except Dice. We'd grown up in foster care together and when we both aged out of the system, we became our own little family. "Yeah, well, you know how it goes."

"I do." She made change in the register.

"Besides, I don't need drama. I need fun. And Grayson over there looks like the type of fun I'm looking for."

"Yeah, well, we know your picker is broken. So don't get too attached."

I nodded. "That's for damn sure. My picker of people is really broken."

It was an ongoing joke between Dice and me. If there was a disappointing guy within a ten-mile radius, I would be attracted to him and pick him to date. I would fall for him, give him everything I was, and inevitably, he would disappoint me and break my heart. It happened time and again.

My picker is seriously broken.

Dice chuckled under her breath. "But the other one could be fun. At least in a serious fun to poke at kind of a thing."

"That one has drama written all over him." I took the change from the register.

"Hey!" a gruff voice yelled from the corner of the bar

We turned in unison toward the voice. A man stood there, towering over the rest of the crowd. He was slightly older and swaying on his feet. "Can I get a drink around here or what?"

I loved this type of customer, the type that knew they were bigger and louder than everyone else. The type that thought the world owed them something. I held my finger up. "Just a minute, sir."

This was the type that would either pipe down with one good "Sir," or he would continue along his merry little path and end up with the bouncer's foot in his ass. But when I looked over the crowd, the bouncers were on the other side of the room breaking up a different fight.

The guy shook his empty beer bottle at me. "Been waiting long enough, sweetheart."

He dragged his arrrrrr out, like they always did with that harsh Boston accent. *Masshole.* "I'm working my way to you, *sir.*"

"You're working your way to pretty boy over there." He shoved his way closer to the bar, knocking people out of his way. "Now do I get my drink or what?"

Dice glanced from me to him and back again. She took a step toward him, and I grabbed her arm and yanked her back. She might've been tiny, but she had no problems cutting a dude like this. I pulled her to me then pushed her toward the patrons in the other direction. "Go help them."

We didn't need a bar fight on our hands, not on a crowded night like this. Not when there was a sizzling undertone to it all. "I'll get to you in a moment."

Three other people glared at him, and I knew they, too, were getting annoyed with his sweaty body hovering close. "What, like you're getting to him over there?"

"Oi, that's hardly necessary there, mate." Grayson took a sip of his drink and placed it on the bar. "The lady said she'd get to you. So stop acting like a stroppy cow and piss off."

The guy's arm whipped out and he hurled the empty beer bottle at Grayson's face. Without blinking an eye, Grayson caught the bottle before it hit his face and a collective gasp sounded. Grayson tossed the bottle up and down, repeatedly catching it. "Have we forgotten our manners?"

The guy snatched a bottle from the woman standing next to him and chucked it toward me. Beer flew from the bottle in a circular arch, spraying every-one. Grayson's arm shot out and he leaned across the bar, catching the bottle a moment before it hit my cheek. I froze, staring at it for barely a second before taking it from his hand. I pointed the bottle at the belligerent guy.

"You, out now!" I waved toward the door.

"Not till I get my drink." He slammed his fist down on the bar. Patrons all turned toward the two of us, watching me go back and forth with this man, and I wasn't going to do it.

"It'd be a pleasure to escort *that* out for you." Grayson's smile was relaxed and composed. Like taking on someone who was a good five inches taller and sixty pounds heavier wasn't a problem.

I glanced from him to the guy and back again. "Nah, I think the bouncer would be better."

I went up on my tiptoes trying to spot them through the crowd and couldn't. It was madness. They were turning people away at the door now, and there wasn't a place to stand. The hum was something out of a movie, and I felt the shift in the air. I looked to the left then to the right and couldn't pick out one of my co-workers. Grayson followed my gaze then caught my eyes.

"Don't worry. I won't let anything happen to you." His words were so calm, so sure, like he'd done this a million times before.

"You in the habit of starting fights?" I nodded toward the guy as he banged on the bar once more.

"I'm in the habit of finishing them."

The man snatched a glass off the countertop, and suddenly Sav was right next to him. He wrapped his hand around the man's wrist and pulled it back. His face was deadly serious as the man lifted his other hand into a fist. Sav didn't miss a beat. He slammed the man's hand onto the bar, breaking the glass in his fist. Blood poured and the man hollered in pain.

Grayson clicked his tongue and shook his head. "Pity, he beat me to it. Shame that is, really."

Sav shoved him back from the bar and the man crashed into a table, knocking several people to the ground. They fell like dominoes one after the other. Drinks spilled, and people cursed as they shoved each other away. The shoving turned into fists, and suddenly the crowd erupted into chaos. Grayson dove on the other side of the bar to stand next to me. Bottles flew toward us. He was some kind of ninja, catching them and tossing them in the trash as if it were his job. I stepped in front of the cash register. This wasn't my first bar fight, and I knew where they went next: after the booze and after the cash.

Dice hurried to my side. "And we were going to make a killing tonight."

"I know, right." The sound of shattered glasses filled the air, and people ran for the door while others joined in the brawl. Chairs scraped the ground, and alcohol soaked the walls and floor. Two college-aged guys began to climb over the bar, and Grayson stepped in front of them.

"Oi, what do you lot think you're doing?"

They kept coming. His hands shot out and he shoved them both in the chest at the same time. They tumbled off the top of the bar and fell back into the mayhem. "Piss off."

From the corner of my eye, I spotted Sav leaning

up against a table with a drink in his hand. He took a sip and watched the melee with a bemused look on his face. If anyone came toward him, he just shoved them to the side or stepped away, only to go back to the same spot.

"Your friend seems fine."

"He's seen some things." Grayson turned to a girl who reached over the bar for a bottle. He gave a sharp whistle. "Don't make me come over there."

She dropped the bottle back into the bar rack and ducked into the crowd, disappearing. Three men hopped over the bar at the same time. One grabbed a bottle and smashed the end of it on the bar and held it as if he was going to charge Grayson.

"You might want to rethink that one, mate." He shook his head. The guy charged, and Grayson sighed. "Or not."

The man thrust his arm forward aiming for Grayson's ribs. Grayson spun to the side and ducked under the man's arm then threw his elbow back. Air whooshed from the man's lungs, and he flew off his feet and slammed to the side of the bar. Before the second one could even move, Grayson shoved his shoulder into his ribs like a defensive end tackling a quarterback. He rammed him back then threw him over his shoulder. He turned and tossed him over the bar at two other guys trying to climb over. They all fell to the ground like bowling pins.

He was so strong and yet didn't have the bulk of a body builder. He was sleek and muscular yet so easy-going. Like this was nothing: the alcohol flying every-where was nothing, the fight was nothing, and another guy charging at him from behind was nothing.

"Look out!" I grabbed the plastic jar of cherries and hurled it past his head.

Grayson stepped to the side and the jar smacked the guy right in the forehead, knocking him to the ground. Grayson bent over the guy and smiled. "Bet that hurt."

All he did was groan and rub at his head. Grayson glanced up at me and winked. "Good aim."

I shrugged. "Been in a fight or two."

Sirens wailed just outside the bar as the blue and red lights flashed through all those front windows. Dice cursed under her breath. "And the night was going so well."

I glanced at our full tip jar. "We made some bank."

She grabbed the jar and held it tight. "Yeah."

"Are you girls all right?" The owner, Jake, ran over to the bar and leaned against it. He stood there with a bat resting on his shoulder and out of breath.

"We're good." I glanced toward Dice, and she gave me a nod. "Sorry about the fight."

Jake was a good boss. He was fair to all of us and treated us right. He was older, with thin gray hair, a dad bod, and a hard-ass attitude that came from growing up on the streets and making something of himself. "Nah, it was bound to happen at some point."

He looked Grayson up and down. "Good looking out for the ladies and my bar."

"My pleasure." He ran his hand through his hair. "Been a while since I've had a good bar fight."

"Looks like the cops are breaking this one up." He glanced around. "Why don't you two head out before they make you stay here all night. I'll close up shop."

"You sure?" I was already backing away from him to grab my purse from a cabinet behind the bar. If we stayed, it'd be an all-night affair, and I wasn't trying to do that, either.

He chuckled. "Yeah, go."

I grabbed my bag and jacket then tossed Dice her stuff. I shoved my arms into the sleeves and turned toward Grayson. "You want to get out of here?"

A smirk spread across his lips, and it sent a shot of excitement over my body. He motioned for me to lead the way. "Where you go, I will follow."

CHAPTER THREE

PIPER

I didn't know what came over me. Perhaps it was the adrenaline from the bar fight or the way he watched me like I was the most fascinating thing in the world. No matter what it was, I liked it. I liked him. There was an instant familiar connection between the two of us. It sizzled under the surface of my skin and made me feel alive down to my soul. I wrapped my hand in his and tugged him to follow me. I flipped the door to the bar up and pulled him through behind me.

I glanced at Dice. "You coming?"

She pursed her lips. "Depends."

I paused just outside the kitchen doors. "On?"

"On whether or not he's coming." She nodded in Atlas's direction.

A slight smile played on his lips, and it sent a chill down my spine. Where Grayson seemed warm and alive. Atlas seemed like bad boy death walking. The kind of bad boy that Dice would torture, play with, and discard later. He met her eye and walked right past her to follow us.

"Lead the way."

"Behave yourself tonight, Sav." Grayson stared him down. "All right?"

"What is the point of behaving oneself on a night such as this? I intend to indulge to the fullest." Dice took his arm and he looked down at her. "Aren't we, my dear?"

"Where you go, I will follow." She stuck her tongue out at me.

I rolled my eyes. "Come on, enough with this drama."

I shoved the kitchen door open wide and hurried through. The staff was already bustling to clean everything up and shut down. They wiped down counters and mopped the floors and tossed any food that'd been sitting in the hot window. When the cops showed up, we all got out. I tugged Grayson along, past the dishwashers and right to the back door. The metal door groaned as I pushed it open. The smell of the dumpsters filled my nose, but I just kept walking out into the night, where the rain washed away the stench of the bar and gave way to a cool, clean scent.

"Where are you hurrying us off to, Beautiful Creature?"

I didn't know why, but I liked it when he called me Creature. It was like I was his own special entity he couldn't take his eyes off. "This place where all the local bar workers go. Tourists don't know about it, but it's fun."

"We could use a little fun. Couldn't we, Sav?" He shot his friend a look.

Sav glanced down at Dice and chuckled. "I fear our definitions of fun are two very different things, my friend."

"For the better of it, I'm sure," Grayson muttered in that thick sexy accent.

"We've got time to change yours. Not all of us can be correct all the time. Indeed, it takes years of mastery of oneself to truly know what a state of good *fun* entails. A state of which you have yet to be a part of." Sav threw his arm around Dice's shoulder and pulled her in close. "Am I not correct?"

"I have no idea what you just said." She sidled in closer to him. "But it sounded pretty."

I sighed and gave Grayson's hand a squeeze. "Love at first sight?"

Grayson shook his head. "I'm not sure Sav is capable of love like that. You should warn your friend."

A chuckle escaped my lips. "Well, don't tell anyone, but neither is Dice. You should warn your friend."

"In that case, it's a match made in a loveless hell." His lips spread in a wide smile, and I couldn't help but move in a little closer to him. We wound our way down the streets and around corners until we came to a nondescript door at the back of a tall brick building.

There were no people waiting outside. I slammed my hand on the door three times. It echoed with that hollow metallic sound. A large man opened it and stepped out. He was tall and imposing, with a round belly and muscles to match. The rays from the streetlight reflected off his bald head. He folded his arms in front of him. "What do you want?"

Dice and I shared a look then the three of us all fell into laughter. "Benny, these are my friends, Grayson and Sav."

"They cool?" He looked them up and down.

"Yeah. They're good." I waited for Benny to give us the go-ahead.

Grayson and Sav seemed completely at ease, like walking into a strange place with a strange bouncer was no big deal. Benny stepped to the side and held the door open. Dice went up on her toes and pressed a kiss to his cheek. "You're a good man."

He lowered his eyes to the ground and smiled. "Why you gotta roll me like that, Dice?"

"Oh, Benny, baby, you don't want me to roll you." She patted him on the shoulder and walked through the door and up the stairs.

Sav stopped by his side. "Many a man would fall to that woman."

Benny leaned in. "That woman could bring any man to his knees easily. Careful, friend."

"Consider me warned." Sav followed Dice.

I put my hands on my hips. "And what does that make me, Benny boy? The sweetest of the sweet?"

"Piper, you are the silent killer. The one no one sees coming. A lesson to all men." He offered me his hand. When I took it, he placed a small kiss on the back of my hand. "One they will never forget."

"I agree. You are a rather unforgettable, Little Creature."

Benny pointed to Grayson's face. "And that right there is why you are a lesson to all men."

"As no other could be." Grayson motioned for me to go through the door first.

Why did my heart have to flutter that way whenever he looked at me? We were fun. This was fun.

Nothing more. Yet, that connection was there. It sizzled between the two of us. It moved through my body and pooled low in my stomach. Where his skin brushed mine, pulsing excitement radiated from it. As we walked up the stairs, I sensed him behind me even though he didn't make a sound, not even on the squeaky stairs. Yet, I felt him like a warm shadow behind me. He was a tickle on the back of my neck. It was an awareness I'd never felt before.

When we reached the top of the stairs, the room opened to a huge area. The entire ceiling was made of glass, and lingering drops of rain clung to it. The moon shined down on us through purple clouds and gave the entire room a hazy, magical feel. Against the wall to my left stood a bar.

"Hey, Piper! Heard you got broken up by the cops," John the bartender called to me.

I pulled my jacket off and handed him my purse across the bar so he could hide it for me. "Yeah, it sucked. Dice and I were making a killing, too."

He took my stuff and stowed it. "At least you get an early night."

"This is my friend Grayson." I motioned to him.

John's eyes roamed over him. "Nice to meet you."

Grayson gave him a nod. "Likewise, mate."

I didn't know what it was or why I wanted to be

closer to him, but the Brit had caught my interest. More so than any guy had before. Was it his playful nature? The composed way he handled himself in a fight? Or was it simply the fire I felt between us?

"What'll it be for you two?"

Just then the music picked up and my hips started to sway of their own accord. There was something about the way the beat of the music and the fun feeling of the night made me want to move.

"Be right with you." Grayson turned from John and grabbed my hand. "Shall we?"

I glanced around the room, where there were couples dancing and spinning around. "You know how to salsa?"

"There isn't much I don't know how to do." He wagged his eyebrows at me. Then, to make his point, he spun me around and pulled me in tight to his body.

His hips swayed rhythmically to the music, and I followed. Suddenly, all there was, was him and me. His body pressed to mine, moving in a way I'd never seen a guy move before. He was sleek and cool yet full of passion. His hand splayed across my back, and he guided me around so effortlessly. I was helpless not to respond to him. When he met my eye, I felt hypnotized by the deep mahogany color in his. He spun me around and pulled me in, so my back was to his chest.

"Well matched, are we not?" His cheek brushed mine.

Breathless, I whispered, "I'd say so."

His lips brushed my ear and a jolt shot through me. He turned me once more and my chest pressed into his. He was so close his heady wine scent filled my senses. Like a rich Pinot Noir. He wrapped his hand around the side of my neck just under my jaw and his other hand around my back.

"Piper," he whispered just before taking my lips.

His mouth pressed into mine, warm and firm. Electricity shot through my body, and I found my hands wrapped in the lapels of his jacket pulling him in closer. His tongue tangled with mine for a sweet, teasing moment and then he pulled back. "Aren't you a surprising little creature?"

I wanted to know if he felt it, too. The fire? The sizzle? Did he want more of my lips? More of my touch? Dice catcalled me from a table off to the side and I glared at her.

"You want to get out of here?"

He nodded and pulled me toward a door leading toward a dark outdoor balcony. The second we were outside he pulled me into him, and his lips slammed into mine. We were walking but I didn't know where to. His hands were on my body pulling me with him, and my feet followed his just as they had when we were dancing. Tiny drops of rain hit my too-warm skin and I didn't care. We turned a corner and suddenly we were alone. We'd just met and yet I didn't mind being in a dark corner of the roof, hiding in the shadows with him.

Heat radiated across my body, and I wanted closer to him, more of him. His hands pressed into my lower back, and he was close, so close I could feel every inch of him surrounding me. If I wasn't careful, I could drown in a man like Grayson. He was all-consuming and so much more than I thought I was ready for.

I pulled back from our kiss. "Wait, just a sec."

Instantly, he stopped and took a small step back. He was breathless and licked at his bottom lip. "Too much?"

I sighed. "Yeah."

"I felt it, too." He leaned back from under the overhang of the roof, tipping his face back to the rain. It fell in small drops over his face and into his hair. When he shook it out, his hair fell in wild waves around his face.

"Bit too intense for just meeting." I tried to hold the regret from my voice.

"So, then we talk and meet each other all over again." He shrugged.

"Oh, good. Maybe my picker isn't so broken after all," I muttered under my breath and leaned against the brick wall behind me.

Grayson stepped from the rain and leaned against the wall next to me. "I'm sorry, your what is broken?"

I sighed and gave a light chuckle. "My picker."

His face fell into confusion. "I've not heard that one before. Is it an American thing?"

I snorted. "No, it's a Piper thing."

"Explain." He crossed his arms over his chest and looked like he was settling in.

"Are you sure you want to hear this?"

"Oh, I'd say my attention is fully piqued." He waved me on. "Explain about the picker and what it does, and how it works, and what exactly is wrong with it. I find myself intrigued."

Laughter bubbled from my lips. "It's a me and Dice thing. If there is a guy who is unreliable, disappointing, and most likely a narcissist of some sort, I will attract him like a fly to shit, and to top it all off, I will be attracted to him."

A smile played on his lips as he pressed his hand to his chest. "Should I be offended?"

"Only if you're unreliable, disappointing, and or a narcissist."

"I think I'm safe from all of the above." He licked

his lips. "You really do get stuck with the sorry sort, don't you?"

I nodded then shrugged. "It's life."

"Well, I'm not that sort."

"Oh, my darling Grayson, isn't that something one would say to try to outsmart the broken picker?" I teased and bumped him with my shoulder.

"One would." He winked. "Let us test the picker then."

Excitement ran through me. Was this a little game of get to know me we were playing? Or was this just more games. "Test away."

"What do most of the disappointing disappoint on?"

"Two things, actually: showing up and actually doing what they say they're going to do. Wait, no, three things." I held my fingers up.

He grabbed my hand and placed a small kiss on the tip of each of my three fingers. "What's the third?"

I was hypnotized by his mouth and the way his lips kissed and sucked at my skin. "Umm, what?"

"The third thing, Little Creature." His accent rubbed over me like silk.

I shook my head, clearing away the haze of want. "The third is when they hear about my sad, sad story and baggage, they run for the hills."

This was always a good way to get the dirt out in the open and see where my picker had taken me.

"All right, let's hear it then and see if you can get me running for the hills." He waved me on.

I squared my shoulders and arched my eyebrow at him. "Okay, I've been a foster kid all my life. When I aged out, I moved in with Dice and that's it. My sad little story, no family, no real connections. Just my one best friend who is like my sister."

He didn't move.

I waited.

He still didn't move.

I waited some more.

He said nothing.

"Well?" I didn't want to stand here and have a staring contest.

"Well, what?"

This was like pulling teeth. "Go ahead. Give me your thoughts."

"Oh, I was still waiting for the part where I'm supposed to run for the hills." He stepped in closer to me. "If you want me to run, which I never will, you'll have to come up with something much scarier."

I moved in closer, completely intrigued by his low voice and half-smile. "Like what?"

"Like demon wars, or cursed friends, or dark

warlords hellbent to kill you or possess you." He ran his finger down the side of my cheek. "Family isn't made of blood, love. It's made of the ones you choose to hold around you. From where I'm standing, you and your daring friend over there have got one already."

Why did his words have to melt me from the inside out? This was a bad sign I like him too much, too fast. "All right."

I wagged my eyebrows at him. "True test of running for the hills? Are you ready?"

"Hit me." He ran his hand through his hair and the tangled wet strands just fell back into place.

"Tuesday night I'm working at the pub in Salem."

"Salem? Not Boston?" His brow furrowed.

"I was helping out tonight. You come and have a proper date with me after my shift, and we'll see if the picker is fixed." It was ballsy on my part to challenge a guy so early on. But what was the point of wasting my own time if he wasn't worth it?

"Oh, I'll be there, Sassy Creature." He pressed a light kiss to my lips. "I am dependably boring."

I began to take a step back from him. "Somehow I doubt that, Sexy Brit."

"Where are you going?" He chuckled. "Are you leaving me like this?"

"A challenge has been issued and accepted. Until Tuesday then." I blew him a kiss and turned for the door. If I looked back at his delicious ass, I wouldn't be able to leave. And I had to go get Dice and leave before what was left of my damaged heart was given to him for one night of fun.

CHAPTER FOUR

GRAYSON

Tuesday

"No, I am not bloody well going there right now." I pressed my phone to my ear and held it there. High atop the Evermore Academy castle, in the middle of New York City, I fought for an ounce of patience to deal with this bullshit right now.

"Why?" Sav asked so simply, so calmly. He took a bite of something that sounded like a crisp apple.

"Because I don't want to." Piper was waiting for me, and here I was at the top corner of the school, in the only spot that got reception, arguing with Sav. The girl had laid out a challenge, and I'd be damned if I failed it on a first date. I still tasted her lips on mine whenever I thought about her.

"Why?"

"Because I have more important things to do." I ran my hands through my hair and gazed out over the busy city life. It would take me four hours to get to Salem from here. Two if I sped down the highway the way I planned.

"Such as?" I could almost picture Sav lying on his bed with apple in hand, lazily taking bites while staring at the ceiling.

Such as a date.

"None of your business."

"Such is the ways of a complicated two-hundred-year-old vampire. Whilst amid an ancient prophecy foretelling of a future that might not be as secure as The House of Shade would trust. Priorities."

"Shut up, Sav."

"One does not simply shut up, when one's best friend must continue on the path of that of a child. It's time to put away childish things."

"You do a bloody good job of reminding me of my age. You're not that far behind. But need I remind you, I am forging ties that will have a lasting affect through the vampire community?"

"Are you talking about in Salem with a certain

sassy bartender that has captured the attention of the reluctant heir, or are you talking about the Witches?"

"Piss off."

Atlas Savage had a bad habit of pinching nerves he shouldn't be touching. Was he right? Maybe. Did I care? Kind of. Was I going to return home to live out a destiny that wasn't my own? Hell, no.

"The truth is agony, my friend. To which you have little time to own up to it. In the scheme of life, each pays their dues to the gods, and the balance must be met."

"Do you listen to half the bullshit that comes out of your own mouth?"

He took another bite of apple. "Do you listen to half the bullshit that comes out of my mouth? Free wisdom is priceless."

I rolled my eyes. "I can't be doing this with you right now."

"Facts are facts, my friend. And the fact is, you've got to bring your arse home."

A ball of fire flew from within the halls of the darkened school and soared up toward the sky, lighting up the dark walls like it was midday.

"Fuck."

"What's happened?" Sav's voice changed from casual too serious in a moment.

"I think we're about to be attacked."

"I shall be there momentarily."

I shook my head. "We can't just have a random vampire moving about killing things."

"Like they would spot me. It's as though you've forgotten what my job is."

Silvery power flowed out in front of the halls like seeking vines. They bathed the hallways and courtyard in a silvery glow. The low hum of an alarm sounded, and I knew shit was about to go down.

"Right, got to go, mate."

"Grayso—"

I ended the call and glanced down at the courtyard. A huge phoenix flew from below and straight up toward the sky. Tuck, a fellow guardian of the witches, was also a phoenix shifter. If he was out this late and not in Zinnia's bed, something was really wrong. He flew high above us, balls of fire shooting from his dark feathery tail. Each one hit a torch on one of the four towers of the school, igniting them into huge warning lights. Fire traveled down the sides of the school, lighting the torches in the hallways and the dorm rooms. In seconds, the whole school would wake and be ready. Those who were trained would take up their positions. Those who weren't trained would go into a secure place. I hated that they were so young and faced with so much. But I would be damned if I let any of my crew get injured on this night.

Serrina, the Witch Queen of enchantments, sprinted out from one of the hallways across the courtyard. She looked like she hadn't slept at all, with dark bags under her bright blue eyes. Her blond-streaked hair was in wild tatters, and her clothes were wrinkled like she hadn't changed in days. This was not typical for the beauty but stress did funny things to people. "What's happening?"

I dropped down from my perch high above them all and kept to the shadows. No one saw or heard me, but I wanted all the info I could get.

"Warwick is attacking." Zinnia, The Siphon Queen and High Queen of all of Evermore, was in full control. Truth was, I liked her, had even helped her find love. Because if a Shade couldn't, then I'd make damn sure she would. She practically vibrated with power as her silvery magic clung to her dark hair and pale skin. She spun in a circle, looking to the top of the walls that surrounded the school like a fortress and toward the thick metal front gate.

"What? Why?" Serrina's eyes widened and streams of her red magic seeped from her fingers. It danced along the ground at her feet like pools of fabric.

I love this lot and their fantastic powers.

Zinnia pointed toward the main gate. "I have no idea. But I want them all coming from one direction. I don't want warlocks just invading from every wall. It's better if we contain the flow to one spot where we can focus our power and attack. Can you force them to the front gate?"

Smart girl.

"I can force them to go away if you want." Serrina pressed her lips into a thin line. "Or send them all straight to Hell."

Zinnia shook her head, and that midnight hair flew all around her face. "No, let them come. It's time they learned who they're messing with. We've been nice long enough. If power is what they respect, then power is what they will see. But it'll be on our terms."

Sometimes the only way to stop the violence is with strength. A hard lesson for one so young to learn.

Serrina gave a single nod to Zinnia then let her magic flow over three of the four walls of the school, bathing it in a dim red haze that I was sure our enemies wouldn't see. I pressed my hand to it and instantly I felt the need to go toward that front gate. The warlocks would be walking right into a kill zone and not even know it.

Tabi, another of the Witch Queens, sprinted across the second floor toward us. She planted one foot on the edge of the railing and launched herself up into the air. A gust of wind caught her, and she landed next to Zinnia. Yellow magic sparked in her wild curls and over her dark skin. Her bright orange sweatshirt stood out like a target in the dark night. I was going to have to watch her closely.

The scent of magic filled the air. It was dark and pungent, matching the kind of power most of the warlocks had. They would be here in a moment, and I would take up arms like I vowed to do.

"Incoming?" Tabi turned to Zinnia.

She nodded. "Warlocks on the rise."

As the Siphon Witch, Zinnia would feel their power a mile away. As a vampire, I, too, felt it crawl over my skin, like pins and needles. Vampires existed within the world of Evermore, but we didn't engage the witches. We lived our lives and they lived theirs. But over the years, the world had gotten smaller, and with that came the need to forge alliances. Others may not have understood it, but I knew this was the way. Zinnia and her court were the future, and I would work among them for as long as it took. They had my respect and my friendship. Tonight, not one would die on my watch.

Tabi wiggled her fingers and streams of yellow magic flew from her fingertips into the ground. Vines sprang from the earth like poles, and I leapt from the shadows of the wall and darted to the other side of the courtyard as the vines covered the walls, like reinforced steel beams.

Tucker landed right next to Zinnia in a tornado of flames. The heat brushed at my face and scorched the grass around him. His feathers melted away, and he stood there in nothing but jeans and boots. Steam rose off his body in the cold November air. His chest heaved and puffs of smoke came from his mouth. "I didn't see anything around the school."

"Doesn't mean they aren't there." She felt magic moving around the outside walls just like I did. "Kill the alarm."

My lips pulled into a tight smile. *Show time.*

Tuck gave one sharp whistle, and the low hum of the alarm died, leaving us standing in silence. Even the normal noise of the city around us stopped. I could hear their pulses racing in their veins, smell the nervousness on their skin. And yet, I knew they'd stand strong. It was one thing I admired about the Witches. Even in the face of fear they showed tenacity, and that to me was courage at its best.

A few feet away, the air shimmered and the smell of our allied Warlocks filled my nose. I chuckled to myself. *Oh, this was going to be a shit show. Of the best kind.*

An explosion struck the ground right beside Zinnia. Her body jerked back from the force of it. I sprinted into action. Rocks and dirt soared through the air with her. And I turned toward the hallway she'd been thrown down. At the last second, I used my speed to grab her before she cracked her head against the wall. I wrapped my hand in her shirt and let the momentum of her take us both. From the corner of my eye, I saw another explosion, and Tabi was thrown off the second-floor balcony. I slowed Zinnia down and let her slide across the floor just as I took off toward Tabi.

"Zinnia! Zinnia, where are you?" Tuck sprinted back toward her, and I knew she would be okay, even as she staggered to her feet and the smell of blood filled the air.

I ran around the students like they were cones in an obstacle course. I wove my way through them like a hot knife through butter. Golden streams of magic flew from her hand as she fell toward the ground. Her arms pinwheeled, and I launched myself off the ground. We collided midair and I wrapped my arms around her. We plummeted toward the ground, and I twisted in midair. My feet hit the ground and I skidded for a few feet. I placed Tabi on the ground next to me.

She gave me a wink. "Thanks, Gray."

I didn't wait. I just turned and ran into the fray, shoving people away from death. Magic exploded like grenades, one after the other. Bright colored magic filled the air and pooled on the ground at my feet. I leapt over them, avoiding whatever the hell it was they were trying to kill each other with. The scent of blood lingered on the wind. It sent my body into overdrive. The need to fight and move faster coursed through my veins. Zinnia marched out into the middle of it all. Silvery magic exploded from her fingertips, catching the power bombs before they hit.

She threw out her hands, tossing those balls back over the front wall. Flashes of light lit up the sky like bolts of lightning during a storm as each of those energy balls crashed on the other side. Three Warlocks floated on the other side of the wall, high enough to look over. Their bodies were hidden in shadows, and bright orange flames danced within their hands. Fire spewed from their palms, shooting like flame throwers over the top of the wall, torching Tabi's reinforcing vines. I threw my arm up, shielding my face from the heat. The vines caught fire, curling, and crumbling to dust.

A ball of fire flew through the shimmering air in the middle of the portal and those wicked Warlocks came charging through to take up arms with us. Ophelia, Queen of potions and the most deadly women I'd ever met, sprinted through with her daggers drawn. If Wednesday Addams had a twin, it would be O, with her long black hair and pale skin. Cross, her soulmate and crazed warrior Warlock, was hot on her heels. She froze only feet from Zinnia and her eyes widened. She pointed toward the blood on her sister's face.

"They did that to you?" Though she was tiny, she was terrifying, with her long straight hair braided into a fauxhawk, her body strapped with leather holsters full of daggers, and a leather potion pouch hanging from her hip.

She swiped at the cut on her head and more blood coated the back of her hand. "Yeah."

"Sons-a-bitches." Ophelia gritted her teeth and pointed one of her daggers toward the front wall. "Cross! Up and over!"

Without missing a step, he pumped his arms, sprinting ahead of her, then turned to face her and gave his back to the gated wall. He cupped his hands in front of him, and Ophelia sprinted straight at him. She pumped her arms, moving faster, and at the last second, she leapt toward him and placed her foot in his cupped hands. Cross threw up his arms, tossing Ophelia high into the air. She flipped and twisted like they'd practiced this move a hundred times. She disappeared behind the towering front gate.

I hurried toward Tabi and muttered, "I'd hate to be the one who faces that wrath."

"Are you insane!" Zinnia yelled toward him. "She'll be hurt."

Cross arched his eyebrow at her, giving her a "Yeah, right" kind of look. His gold eyes glinted like an animal's in the dark and a wide, predatory smile spread across his face. "No, *they* will be."

"Right you are, mate." But he didn't hear me.

As if on cue, screams sounded from the other side of that gate. Explosions of different colored power fired off like a rainbow, illuminating the building beyond. Cross chuckled. "See? Told ya."

He turned from them and darted toward the corner of the courtyard where the gate and wall met. Like a freaking spider, he leapt up and grabbed hold of the wall then bounced off it, grabbing a piece of the gate then back to the wall and to the gate again. Within seconds, he'd scaled the wall and was over onto the other side.

Now, this I have got to see.

I ran toward the wall and leapt on top of it. When I looked down at the mayhem on the street, I chuckled. An army of Warlocks was there outside the walls firing magic as high into the air as they could. Tiny Ophelia was making her way through the crowd like a tidal wave. She reached into the pouch hanging from hip and threw a vial at the girl in front of her. Hot pink magic exploded, and the girl fell to the ground.

I stepped off the wall and dropped down on to the other side. Still, no one saw me, and I liked it that way. I sprinted in the opposite direction. When I got to the last few rows of the army, I grabbed one of the Warlocks by the back of his shirt and threw him down the street toward Ophelia and Cross.

Ophelia threw a vial at the guy and a huge bubble wrapped around him. He banged against it with his fist and yet it did nothing. He simply floated away into the night. I threw another one up and they blasted them with magic, binding their power and forcing them to the ground. It was lucky for them. I'd seen Ophelia do far worse than trap a couple people.

I spun through the crowd, using my speed to strike out quickly. Dislocating a knee here, breaking an arm there, and causing complete havoc. Screams followed in my wake, but I didn't care. Screams came from within the walls, and I ran back toward the school. I had to be everywhere and nowhere all at once. I pumped my arms, feeling the adrenaline fly through my veins. Wind breezed through my hair and over my face. I hurled myself back over the wall and landed just next to the main gate.

The portal shimmered once more, and Maze sprinted past. Zinnia lashed her magic around him like a silvery, glittering whip. He froze for a moment with his hands trapped by his side. Neon green power seeped from his fingers. Tarot cards shot from the pocket of his black tactical pants. They swirled in a circle of madness above his head. She yanked on her power, dragging him back to her side. She dropped him to his feet and pulled her power away from his body.

He rolled his shoulders and narrowed his green eyes at her. "Don't. Do that again."

I flinched for a moment, ready to step in. Maze was the deadliest psychic known in the world. His magic was both volatile and damaging. He glanced in my direction and gave a quick head shake as though he knew I would leap between the two of them. I froze, waiting to see what he did next. My friends always trusted him, but he was questionable . . . at best.

Zinnia got in his face. "Why the hell are they attacking us?"

. . . I mean I was wondering . . . sort of.

"Our house got blown up." Maze shrugged. "They think it's you."

"What?" Her eyebrows shot up. The castle shook as a blast of magic struck the front gate.

"Vengeance is a way of life, and the council wanted its due."

The Warlock Council were the bastards who ruled all the Warlocks of Evermore. The evil sort that myself and my mates had been working to overthrow for weeks. In truth, the Vampires had been working for years on killing off the High Witch King, which Zinnia did, and now the Council. We had to unite them all for what was to come.

Maze's eyes went milky white for a split second. It sent shivers down my spine, and I waited for him to come out of whatever trance he was in. He grabbed Zinnia's arm and yanked her to the side just as a car hurled over the gate and smacked into the ground then tumbled end-over-end right toward where she'd been standing. The sound of crumpling metal filled the air, and pieces of the car flew off in different directions. Tuck landed behind the flipping car, and flames shot from his hand in two long streams. It slammed into the car, stopping its thunderous tumble. The car stood on its front bumper, teetering back and forth.

Flames caught on the engine, and the whole thing erupted in a ball of fire. Black smoke billowed from it like a mushroom touching the sky. The smell of burning rubber and gas filled the air.

It was going to tip back on them. I darted into the courtyard, running so fast I was a blur. I propelled his body forward and slammed my shoulder into the flaming wreck. The car launched up off the ground and soared through the air back over the other side of the gate. Screams sounded and a loud crash filled the night.

"What kind of wankers throw bloody cars into a school?" *I mean, really.*

"Who knew you could throw cars?" Zinnia arched her eyebrow at me.

"There's lots you lot don't know about me." So much they all didn't know. I wanted to tell them, but how could I? My life was never meant to be my own.

Another car came flying over the gate and I moved to the side, catching it easily. The metal crumbled and bent around my hands. Glass exploded out from the windows and rained down around me. I spun in a circle and threw the car back over the wall. A ball of fire exploded up from the street and smoke billowed up to the sky.

A huge ball of magic slammed into the front gates,

cracking them wide open. I rolled my eyes. "Bloody fantastic, that is."

Shards of metal flew in all different directions like arrows searching for a target. I let my speed carry me around the courtyard, catching piece after piece and stopping them from stabbing anyone. I dropped them to the ground then stomped down on them until the metal curled up into a harmless ball and not a lethal weapon. "If you can't play nice then you don't play at all."

A flood of Warlocks rushed over the beat-in gate, using it to climb inside. They moved like tiny ants, running in all different directions, leaving hell and magical bombs in their wake. Heavy smoke and dirt hung in the air, forcing me to cough with each gasping breath. Maze hesitated with me by his side, like he wanted to stay to fight beside me, but also wanted to face the line of Warlocks that had begun to overrun us.

I glanced down at my watch and back to the chaos that rained down on us all. I was not going to make it to see the girl I'd made a promise to. *Apologies, Piper.* And I ran headlong into the fray.

CHAPTER FIVE

PIPER

Salem, MA

My picker is good and damn broken. I am never trusting it again.

"You sure you want all of this?" Jimmy the cook behind the line arched his eyebrow at me.

"Don't ask questions with your judgy-judge face on. Just give me the food." My shift was over, and Grayson was a no-show.

Tuesday had come and gone. No sign of the Sexy Brit. Was I going to eat my feelings? Yes. Did I care? No. Because French fries were reliably delicious and so was cheesecake.

Jimmy chuckled and ducked his head to meet my eye through the metal shelves. He was younger than me, maybe twenty, and lived as hard of a life as I had. He was gaunt, with dark skin and a bright cooking cap. The night was nearly over, and they were wiping down the counters and flat top.

"Bad night?"

I sighed. "Bad guy."

He nodded. "I feel that. My girl is pretty bad, too."

"Jimmy." I lowered my voice. "You're dating the hostess. She's sweet enough."

"Yeah, and she bat-shit crazy, too." He winked. "It's always the sweet ones you gotta watch out for. But I love me a little crazy."

I gave a humorless chuckle. "Yeah, well, I love me some stability."

What was I expecting? Him to show up like some knight in shining leather to come and be with me? Shit like that didn't happen to people like me. Deep down, I thought he was going to show up. I took extra time with my hair and makeup. I even got new underwear for the occasion . . . just in case. Busted out my cutest work shirt and pants. But this was typical for me: they promised, and I believed. For someone who had walls like the Great Wall of China, I really was an ass for letting that sweet smile and accent behind mine. And it wasn't even difficult for him. I might as well have opened the doors and screamed, Please come and do your worst.

Jimmy nodded. "I got you." He opened a brown paper bag and dumped even more fries in it and a few chicken tenders. On top of the turkey burger I'd ordered, and cake.

"You're a good man, Jimmy."

He placed the bag of food on the shelf between us. "Feelings have to be eaten sometimes, Bo."

"Damn straight." I grabbed the bag of food and headed out of the kitchen. The last few people were mopping the floors and doing side work. I gave them a wave as I shoved my arms into the jacket.

"Bye, guys."

They all gave mumbled goodbyes. The kind of goodbyes that only exhausted servers said at the end of the night. I held my food closely, ready to dig in and let the deliciousness soothe my ghosted ass.

Disappointment. It was a way of life for me when it came to men . . . or family. When I opened the door, the cool air hit me, and I huddled into my jacket. Fog drifted from my lips with each breath I took. The heat from the bag seeped into my fingers, and I hurried my steps down Essex Street. It was after midnight and this time of year Salem shut down. The busy season was over, and it was dead. The stores that lined the street were dark and empty. I'd done this walk almost every night from the bar on Essex to the house Dice and I rented together.

I glanced over my shoulder for the third time. The hair on the back of my neck stood on edge, like someone was watching me. I wrapped the handle of the plastic bag around my hand again and gripped it tightly. If someone was coming after me, I would swing this bitch for their head, hoping the glass bottle and heavy food container would make an impact. Usually, it didn't bother me, but tonight there was something eerie in the air I couldn't put my finger on. Tonight, when all I had was the whipping wind to comfort me, I minded a whole hell of a lot.

I slid my phone from my pocket and hit the number for the one person I could always count on. One ring. "What's up?"

"Dice?" I lowered my voice to a whisper and looked over my shoulder again to the empty streets and dark storefronts.

"What's going on? Are you okay?" Her voice rose with alarm.

"I'm being followed." Even though I couldn't see anyone or anything, I felt it in the shadows and in the cold chill on my skin.

"Okay, where are you?" I heard her crashing

through our house, the scrape of the closet door where we kept our bat, and her heavy footsteps down the hall leading toward our front door.

"Essex. I'm on Essex. Almost to the ice cream shop." The street was wide enough that I could walk down the center of it and not be too close to the storefronts of any place I could get grabbed. Yet, when I looked around again . . . nothing.

"I'm coming. Stay on the phone with me. Just keep moving." The sound of our door creaking open and closed filled the line, and I knew she was already on the street heading toward me. We lived so close to town, we both walked to and from the pub for work. "Can you see them?"

"No." There was nothing but the sound of my own breathing. I knew I wasn't crazy. There was something here, something dangerous.

"How many?" Her breaths were coming in quick puffs now, and I got the feeling she was running.

"I can't see anyone. I just know." A low hiss came from a few feet away and I spun in a circle. "Shit! Who's there!"

"Stay with me, Piper. Keep moving. Run if you have to. I'm almost there!" Panic rose in her voice and my own strangling heartbeat matched it.

I didn't want to run, didn't want to seem crazy. But

something or someone was following me. I took a running step forward and was instantly yanked back. A vise-like grip crushed my wrist, sending shooting pain through my arm. Something stabbed through my jacket and dug into my skin . . . Knives?

A scream ripped from my throat, and I was shoved to the ground. My face slammed onto the cobblestones, and I felt my cheek split open. Warm liquid seeped down my face. Dice screamed into the phone, but it was too late. I was being dragged down an alley into thick darkness. I held that damn phone like a lifeline, like if she could just hear me, she could find me. "Dice! Help!"

The stone scraped across my skin where my shirt rode up. I pulled back, fighting for my arm, fighting the hold. I glanced up, trying to fight my assailant, yet my mind couldn't comprehend what I was seeing in the darkness. This figure, this shadow, couldn't have been more than five feet tall.

I pulled back on my arm hard, yanking it free. I scrambled to my feet and swung out the bag of food. It connected with the dark figure. The sound of shattering glass filled the air and the bagful of contents exploded wide open, littering the area with food and glass. The thing moved so fast I could barely see it. Cracking pressure smacked into my chest, and I went airborne. Another scream ripped up my throat. I slammed into the brick building behind me and my elbow went through the glass window, cutting my jacket to shreds.

I sucked in a gasping breath as I slouched to the ground in a balled-up heap. This was it. I was going to get raped and die here in an alley like some freaking statistic. My arm was yanked away from my body and then a set of sharp teeth sunk through my jacket into my skin. I groaned, my head spinning and swirling with black dots. Yet, that pain brought everything into sharp focus for a split second. My hand flexed and I dropped both the food and the phone.

"Dice," I whispered in a voice that didn't sound like my own.

My body slumped to the side and my gaze fixed onto two glowing points in the darkness. They moved closer and closer, yet I felt no fear, only comfort. A low feral growl filled the air and it sent tingles down my spine. I wanted to move, to get away, but I couldn't. I felt broken and bloody. Bruises were already forming, and I was sure my arm was broken. Yet, the assault had stopped.

Those glowing eyes came closer, and I drew in a sharp breath. This wasn't right. It couldn't be right. I'd cracked my head too hard. I was hallucinating. A lion, a freaking lion the size of a hippo emerged from the shadows. Its mane was so thick and full of deep browns, sandy blondes and striking black. Every muscle rolled and moved like the predator that it was. It rolled back its lip, exposing its long fangs. Whatever my attacker saw had it scrambling back against the brick wall at the very end of the alley, trapping it there.

I dragged myself a few feet away off to the side. The lion moved past me with not so much as a look. Its tail swished and flicked from side to side, and that continual low growl rumbled deep in its chest. When it got closer to the huddled ball that was my attacker, it froze, the growling going completely silent. I glanced from the lion to the shadows. *Please eat it and not me . . . please, please, please.* Just when I thought it would spring forward, a gust of wind came from just above me. Not the kind that came off the water. This was like I was being fanned.

My eyes snapped up to find a man with hulking black wings landing just beside the lion. "What are you waiting for? Kill it."

He was beautiful, more beautiful than anything I'd ever seen. Even more so than Grayson. I found myself wanting to get closer, like with him here nothing could or would touch me. His hair was a silvery color that seemed to catch the moonlight. His body was all long, lean muscle and there were long swords strapped to his back between his wings. Loose leather pants hung from his slender hips. He was shirtless and even in these freezing temperatures, he didn't look cold.

He held his hand out toward the lion. "Slow down. I can't understand you when you go that fast. No, my lion does not suck! Maybe you just speak to it like shit."

Then the lion's body seemed to melt into a ball, contorting and twisting into something else. Gone was the lion and in its place was a huge man. He was taller than the other, with bulkier muscles and even larger wings. His hair fell in a sandy mess over his eyes. He motioned to the ball against the wall. "Taliam, look!"

I'm going to die. In a puddle here while hallucinating a shape-shifting lion.

I followed his gaze and for the first time I really looked at my attacker. This wasn't some big man. This was a girl. A tiny girl, with wild blond ringlets falling around the sides of her angelic face. Small fangs bit into her bottom lip, and her eyes glowed an emerald green as she cowered away from them. She wore nothing but an oversized T-shirt and a thick black trench coat that was about five sizes too big. Mud covered her feet and up her legs.

The slim, silver-haired one, Taliam, eyed her closely for a second longer than I had. "Well, shit. Collias, what the hell are we going to do?"

The other one, Collias, ran his hand through his hair. "Shit."

"Just . . . really . . . shit." Taliam nodded.

A gust of wind filled the alley once more, and another angel landed beside the two of them. She was much smaller. She'd be almost delicate looking if it weren't for the swords strapped to her back, the knives on her hips and thighs . . . and boots. She wore a dark brown leather bustier that had crisscross straps down her back and across her stomach that matched her brown leather plants. She drew one of the swords from her back and spun it at her side. "What the hell are you two waiting for? We've got heirs to watch over. Kill the demon and be done with it."

Collias pointed to the small girl. "Shiiiitttt."

The woman's eyes widened, and she drew a phone from her pocket. With the flick of her thumb, the phone rang once, then a deep voice rumbled something. She cleared her throat. "Matteaus, we've got a problem."

I wanted to let the darkness take me, so I didn't

have to feel the numbing pain or cold of the ground. A moment of peace where there was only me and nothingness. Either long moments or short ones passed by, I didn't know. I reached up to my head and felt the warm blood sticking in my hair. When I pulled my hand away, I glanced at my crimson covered fingers.

"No, don't think about it." The women came to my side and wrapped her fingers around mine. "All will be well."

A groan escaped my lips, and I didn't know how I would survive this. Pain lashed through my body, and I wanted to let go. Not to fight anymore. I was so tired. The wind kicked up once more, and it cooled the blood coating my body, sending a deep chill into my bones.

"What the fuck is this?" a voice boomed, and heavy footsteps moved closer to me.

I didn't flinch away, instead I felt . . . safe. Like this man would protect me even through his voice was gruff and harsh. There was something ethereal and warm about it, like if I just followed him I would leave this world and move on to the next.

"We found her like this," the woman answered. "Because of that."

She pointed to the figure huddled in the corner. The man groaned. "What the hell did the damn Royals do now? Aidenuli, aren't you supposed to be watching them?"

"All of them?" a deeper voice sounded.

He leaned over Matteaus's shoulder, and his face came into view. He was hulking, with long, wild, black hair that fell from his head past his shoulders. His skin was tan, like he'd spent days on the beach. A thick scar ran through his eyebrow, and a dark goatee surrounded full lush lips. Black wings with purple-tipped feathers spread from his back and were nearly as big as Matteaus's.

He reminded me of Jason Momoa, but in a much hotter kind of way. "Matteaus, come on. Have you met them?"

Matteaus let go of a heavy sigh, and when I looked up at him, he stood over me with wild multi-colored hair that held blonds, browns, and even some red hues. Even in the dark of night, I wouldn't forget the intense sapphire color of his blue eyes. He was deadly harsh and beautiful. He leaned in closer to me.

"I've seen worse."

I chuckled and it was a horrible sound that hurt my ribs. "Everything hurts."

"I know, little one." Black wings spread out behind him, and they blocked out the light of the moon and

Aidenuli's face. I wanted to run my fingers over the thick oily feathers, but I just lay there, not moving.

"Am I dying?"

A smile spread over his lips, and he chuckled. "Not today."

"Oh, good." I wanted to sit up, but he placed his hand on my shoulder, holding me in place.

"Maybe not yet."

An ear-splitting scream broke the calm and I let my head fall to the side. I looked out toward the end of the alley and there was Dice with her phone in her hand and a bat on her shoulder.

"Aidenuli, now," Matteaus growled.

Aidenuli soared at Dice and grabbed her upper arms. She froze and her mouth dropped open into an O-shape. Her eyes went wide, and a small squeak came from her throat. The bat clattered to the ground at her feet. "I-I . . ."

"Shhhh." His voice was so low and lulling. "You didn't see this."

She shook her head, and her blond hair flew around her face. "I didn't see it."

"Your friend fell down the stairs . . . she'll be fine."

She nodded and said in that monotone, zombie-like voice, "She'll be fine."

"Wha- He's lying. Angels don't lie." Was this all

some kind of weird dream people had right before they died?

A round of chuckles sounded and Matteaus leaned in closer. "We're not those kinds of Angels."

Matteaus stepped back from me, and Aidenuli's face filled my vision. "Your turn."

A hazy, drunk feeling overcame me. It was like the moment when you've drunk enough to have fun, right before you drank a bit more and fell off the cliff to spiny town. Suddenly, my pain subsided, and I sucked in a deep breath. "My turn for what?"

He locked eyes with me, and I fell into the many flecks of amber in them. "To forget."

CHAPTER SIX

PIPER

The smell of disinfectant stung my nose, and a rhythmic beeping filled my ears. Pain, aching pain, surged over my body. I groaned, squeezing my eyes shut tighter. Cold air went into both my nostrils, and I shook my head, still refusing to open my eyes.

"Piper?"

I didn't want to wake up, wasn't ready. If I could just sleep a bit longer, I'd feel so much better.

"Piper, come on." Dice's urgent voice came from just beside me.

I felt like I was drowning and trying to pull myself from the depths. Why was it so hard to wake up? Why did I want to stay in this comatose-like sleep?

"Piper Camilla Santiago. You open your eyes right now," she snapped.

I forced my lids open, and everything was hazy. Her face was blurry, and the world seemed to be spinning. "Whoa. What the hell?"

She sagged against the side of my bed and sucked in a deep breath. "You scared me!"

"Why?" I glanced around at the curtain hanging beside my bed and the people rushing by. Monitors were stuck to my chest and finger. Clear fluid ran from a hanging bag to an IV running from the veins in my forearm. "Why am I in the hospital?"

"Because you're a complete and total clutz."

I tried to sit up, but pain exploded in my head. I fell back onto the pillows. "What happened?"

"Dude, you don't remember?" Her eyes went wide. She looked as bad as I felt. Her thick blonde hair was tied in a messy knot on top of her head. His sweatshirt looked like it was covered in dirt, and there were weird holes in the shoulders. She was paler than her usually milky pallor, with streaks of dirt on her cheeks and forehead.

I closed my eyes, trying to focus, to remember anything about tonight. "I remember being scared. I remember running. After that . . . not so much. Are you okay? What happened to you?"

"What happened to me? I freaking ran out the door to find you broken and bloody! My heart is still in my throat. Also, I might puke looking at you."

"That bad?"

"Oh, yeah, that bad." She nodded.

"So, um." I searched my mind for any memory of what happened. "What happened to me?"

She pulled the chair closer to the bed and leaned in. She lowered her voice. "Look, it's kind of embarrassing, but you fell down the stairs."

Flashes of black feathers, glowing eyes, and feeling so warm ran through my mind. None of that made sense. Confusion riddled my body, and I had to pull it together. I pressed my hand to my hair and froze. It was caked, knotted, and crunchy. I wrinkled my nose and pulled my hand away slowly.

Eww. "Is that blood in my hair? And what stairs? There's no stairs on the way to the apartment."

"Yeaaaaaa." She tucked her hair behind her ear. "The stairs by the ice cream shop."

I sighed and that movement hurt my side. "That's ridiculous. Those are barely steps. They're more like a slope."

"Tell me about it. It's like you threw yourself down them and kept on rolling." She paused as a nurse walked by. "It was pretty bad when I found you. There was a lot of blood."

"What's wrong with me?" I felt the pain, but I didn't know how bad it was. I fell? I didn't recall falling. I remembered being at the restaurant, getting my food, and starting to walk home.

"Well, the blood in your hair isn't as bad as it looks. There was a small cut, but it was deep enough to need two stitches. I've learned the head bleeds A LOT. And it is way more terrifying than I ever want to see again. And you got a little bump on the head with a slight . . ." She held her fingers up, making that small motion with her thumb and pointer. ". . . concussion."

"Concussion? Are you serious?" It felt like she was serious. I was exhausted and everything didn't feel in focus. Like I was looking at her from a distance.

"Only you would fall down those stairs and keep on rolling." She chuckled. "Like you didn't just stop at one stair, you decided to throw yourself down them all."

"That's stupid. They're so spread out." I pictured the stairs leading from Essex Street down to the ice cream shop and how spread out they were. They were huge, not steep at all, and like two feet long each. "What'd I do, just keep rolling, like one of those bad stunt men trying to keep on rolling down the hill, forward roll, push off to roll again?"

She threw her hands up. "That's what I'm saying."

My head pounded and when I sucked in a breath, my side hurt again. "It feels like my ribs are broken."

She shook her head. "Nah, you got lucky, it's just a bruise. Not even bruised ribs. Just a bruise over your ribs . . . it looks nasty, though."

"Greatttttt." I felt every bit as gross as I was. "I need a shower and my bed."

Something tingled at the back of my mind. Like I had some place to be or something to do. "I was scared. Like I was being followed."

"Were you?" Her face turned serious.

I hesitated, fighting with my own mind trying to recall anything. "I-I don't remember. I felt like I was, but I don't think I actually was."

"Yeah, you called me, and I went to meet you, and then I found you . . ." She motioned to me in the bed. ". . . like this."

"I must've tripped." Still, everything felt so hazy, like a dream. Like a memory that wasn't quite mine but was there just the same. I fought to try to remember more. There was nothing, except the thought of why I was going home at that hour and how I felt in that moment.

"Why are you making that face?" Her brow furrowed and she leaned back in the chair.

"What face?"

She pointed at me. "You know the face."

"No, I don't." I shook my head.

"You do." She pursed her lips. "Like you're forgetting to tell me something."

Then it all hit me at once. I'd been stood up, by Grayson. That Sexy Brit never showed up, and I waited for his ass. We had a connection. We had something I couldn't ever even describe. Something that felt older than the two of us. Like it'd been there the whole time, and when I found him, I found it. But obviously not, because he didn't show.

Eternally broken picker.

"Hey, I have a concussion. Who knows what I might have forgotten or what I'm thinking?"

"Right." She folded her hands and rested them on her stomach. "I totally believe you."

I groaned. "Grayson never showed."

"The Sexy Brit?" She sat forward. "I thought you two had something."

"So did I." For all the physical pain I had, getting ghosted stung worse. "My picker has failed me once more."

"I don't know. Even I thought there was something about that one. He seemed *different.* The way he looked at you, he was really into you. And leaving him with a challenge the way you did. That guy seemed like a hunter. The kind of hunter that doesn't let up . . . ever."

Maybe if Dice saw it, there really was something there. But even so, I was totally ghosted. "Yeah, but he didn't show up."

"Well, maybe something happened to him." Friends always do this. We make excuses for the guys we like thinking, Oh, maybe they didn't mean it, or Maybe they just forgot, or Maybe something horrible happened. When the truth of the matter is, if they liked us, wanted us, they'd show up.

I shook my head. "Nah, I'm not buying into that line of crap. When a guy wants you, he goes for you. End of story. No show means they really don't care."

"Oh, come on. Have some faith."

I rolled my eyes. "Faith in what exactly? My horrible track record or the realistic notion that facts are facts."

"What if he was at work and they made him stay late?" Her eyes went wide with excitement. "Or, he had to skydive from an airplane to save his hot friend from certain death."

A reluctant chuckle rumbled in my chest. "Tame a lion at the circus before it ate the ringmaster."

She hopped up on the foot of my bed. "Had to fly back to Sexy Brit land to make tea for his ill-mannered grandmother, who would despise the likes of us."

I leaned forward. "Got lost on a speeding train through the Rocky Mountains, never to be seen again."

"Got in a huge fight and was thrown through a wall and is on the fifth floor of this very hospital with his own concussion, except he's unconscious, stuck in a black hole of nothingness with only the memory of the girl he left behind." She folded her hands and pressed them to her chest. Then she batted her eyelashes and rubbed away a fake tear. "So sad."

"A truly tragic end to a beautiful beginning." I groaned and tried to run my hands through my hair, forgetting it was a caked, bloody mess.

Dice reached over and put her hand on my leg, giving it a little squeeze. "I'm sorry, Sis. Some guys just aren't what we expect them to be."

I nodded and forced a smile. "Maybe next time."

"There's always hope for a next time and your broken picker." She gave a light smile. "We never lost hope in the home, and we won't now."

"It was one date, one night. No big deal." If it was no big deal, why did it sting so much? "Right?"

"Right. Chuck it in the fuck it bucket." She hopped up. "Now, let's see if we can get you out of here soon. I don't like the smell, you look like hell, and my dinner got ruined."

"Yeah, I just wanna go home." *And lie in bed for a week or so.*

"I'm on it." She winked and headed out of the curtained area toward the nurses' station.

I closed my eyes, remembering his devastating smile, his wild chocolate hair, and the deep mahogany of his eyes. His voice ran through my head, *"Sassy Creature,"* and it warmed me down to my toes. I threw my arm over my face and huddled back into the pillows.

My damn picker is good and broken.

CHAPTER SEVEN

PIPER

Thanksgiving

*W*hy does the smell of apple pie always make me feel better? Oh, right, because I love to eat my feelings.

There wasn't anything pie or tater tots couldn't fix, in my book. Especially when it came to moving on and up. One night did not solidify a relationship. I knew it, Dice knew it, and clearly, Grayson knew it. The best thing I could do was put him right out of my mind and get over it. I was good at getting over things. When it came to the clean-up crew of my own heart, I was like a one-woman wrecking ball. Burning the bridges that hurt and dancing in the ashes was a talent of mine. Dice and I knew the drill.

We had a ritual for all things upsetting and it never failed. First, a buffet of all the deliciousness of our choosing, next sweatpants, then violent movie marathon.

I walked into the tiny kitchen of our tiny apartment. It was small but it was ours. The countertops were a cheap white laminate with matching white cabinets. The old hardwood floors ran through the whole house. They were uneven and creaked with each step we took, dipping in some places. It wasn't the most modern, but it was our home. The appliances were dated but clean, and they functioned just fine. We put our own little Salem style on everything, with flameless candles everywhere and dark burgundy walls that filled my dark little soul with joy. Everything about our place was dark, Gothic, and inviting.

I leaned against the counter and sucked in a breath. The smell of cinnamon and sugar drifted on the air, filling my senses. "I can't believe you made me *the* pie."

"Psh, I can't believe I made it either. Cooking usually boils down to a phone call for me. But since we are doing the *thing,* I figured why the hell not."

The thing being the bounce back from all the bullshit *thing*. Some days all a bestie needed was a little recharge time to remember who the hell we were and what the hell we were about. We were fantastic, and no mere mortal man would drag us down. At least in theory. Mostly.

"We are doing the thing." Just then the timer on the air frier dinged and I chuckled. "Tots?"

She pursed her lips and furrowed her brow, giving me a withering look. "Duh. Like I don't know you."

When I pulled the one drawer open, there was a mix of tots and fries. *Oh, the perfection of potato.* "What's on the other side?"

I yanked it open, and an involuntary squeal left my lips. "Chick-fil-A nuggets!"

"We both don't like turkey, and I'm not about to roast a chicken. I'll either kill the already-dead chicken, or us. Nuggets it is. Happy Thanksgiving." She reached up on the shelf and snagged a plate to hand to me.

I took it and began scooping food onto it. Another timer went off and I glanced at the oven. "Oh, you didn't."

"Variety is the spice of life, my friend." The door creaked as she opened it and pulled a pizza from inside. She placed it on the wooden cutting board on the counter then waved at it. "Ta da, a feast is served."

It wasn't a huge Thanksgiving dinner, but it was ours. We were our own family, always had been. Since we were ten years old and placed in the group home. We looked out for each other.

I got the pizza cutter and handed it to her. "It really is."

We left the kitchen and within two steps we were in the living room. We had two oversized chairs that took up the whole space and faced a flatscreen TV. Up the stairs were two bedrooms right across from each other and one bathroom that we shared. We'd taken the time to hang all kinds of Salem witchy shit on the walls and had black flameless candles spread around the room. Bright light was not our friend. If it was up to Dice and me, we would be creatures of the night and never go out during the day.

"Soooo, can you do it?" I dropped down into my plushy chair.

She froze. "Do what?"

"Come on, don't play dumb. You know what."

She groaned. "Piperrrr, you never like it when I do it."

"I do, I promise." I half-whined half-begged.

"You always get upset when I tell you the truth about things." She began to pull the blue velvet pouch she always carried from her pocket. She dropped it on the table then sat back in the chair and looked at me. "Promise you won't get upset."

"I promise." I nodded with excitement.

"Stop looking at me like that. It pulls your stitches weird." She wrinkled her nose and shook her head. "You know I'm squeamish."

"The doctor said I have to let some air get to it." I self-consciously cupped my hand over the small cut on the side of my forehead. "I can put a Band-Aid on it."

She settled back into the dark pillows and pulled the fluffy black sherpa blanket over her legs. "No, just don't make your happy psycho killer face."

"But I love my happy psycho killer face." I stuck my tongue out at her and pulled my own blanket around myself, making a little cocoon. "Now come on, roll 'em."

Back in the group home, Dice got her name rolling the dice in that pouch. They were a dark sapphire blue with ten different sides. Each side had a different symbol on it, and each represented something different to Dice. She'd learned the meanings of each one over the years, and now they were damn near infallible. Someone left them with her when she was abandoned as a baby. It was the only possession she had from her parents . . . maybe. She kept them her whole life, had even gotten in a fight or two over them. But mostly, she'd used them to do some fortune telling on the side for extra cash. People thought it was for fun, but I knew they were hella accurate. So accurate it hurt.

"Fineeeee. I'll roll. But get the bowl, because last time one went under the couch and I'm not about that life right now." She opened the bag and dumped the two matching dice into her hand.

I shot to my feet and ran to the shelf where we kept a cast iron bowl for just such an occasion. It always surprised me how rough and heavy the metal was in my hands. I made a fake throwing motion with it. "Catch."

She flinched. "Don't be an ass. That thing could kill someone. Which isn't funny considering you almost died . . . from a fall."

I walked over and handed it to her. "I didn't almost die. Like you said, a little bump on the head."

She took it from my hands and carefully placed it on the table in front of us. She made a fake gagging sound. "So. Much. Blood."

"Shut up." I plopped back down into my chair and grabbed my plate of goodies. I popped a tot in my mouth and then another. I spoke around the warm crispy goodness. "Go on, do it."

"Is there anything I'm looking for particularly? Anything you want to know about?" She began shaking the stones in her hands like she was standing at a craps table.

"Whatever the universe wants to tell me." *Tell me about love.* I didn't know why I was holding out hope for anything, but Grayson's beautiful face flashed through my mind.

She threw the stones into the bowl and we both leaned forward, watching them bounce around until they settled at the bottom with two different sides up.

I didn't dare take a breath. I knew she needed to concentrate on them. When her eyes went heavy-lidded, I knew she was locked in. Silence surrounded us and I found myself holding my breath.

"He's coming." Her voice was calm and matter of fact.

My heart leapt into my throat. "Who's coming?"

She narrowed her eyes at me. "Who do you think?"

I didn't dare say his name. In my mind I'd written him off and there was no going back now. *Kind of.* Maybe I was in that I like him, I hate him phase. The kind that went back and forth every other minute of the day. I pressed my lips together. "You're going to have to be more specific."

"Grayson. He's coming back for you."

Excitement filled my body. *Soooo, I'm in the I like him phase.*

She shook her head. "But not yet."

Instant deflation. *The I hate him phase took over.* "Why not?"

Her brows furrowed in confusion, and she leaned in closer to the dice. She pulled her blanket in tighter around her legs as she tilted her head from side to side, trying to study whatever it was she saw.

"Because he's in some kind of struggle or fight right now . . . oh, shit!" She jumped back from the dice.

"What? What happened?" I wanted to get closer to see what she saw but I knew it'd never work. Those symbols meant nothing to me.

I'd asked her what it was like to read them, and she told me it was like reading the strongest gut feeling in the world. There were signs, and she just read them. There were no sounds, but the symbols told her a story. No matter how many times I tried to roll the dice, I never learned, never even got an idea. For some reason, they just didn't stick with me the way they did with her.

Her eyes went wide, and she curled her hands in the blanket. "I-I can't be sure but it def looked like he was fighting again."

Fighting someone? "It wouldn't be the first time. Would it?"

"No."

Even that was worrying. Was he a brawler, always looking for the next fight? "Is he violent, Dice? Like, is he looking for it?"

"No." She grabbed the dice and cupped them in her hands. Her face paled, like something had seriously spooked her. "Piper, think twice about this one. Be ready when he comes back. Because he doesn't go looking for violence . . . but it always finds him."

"Wha—"

She grabbed my hand, squeezing it and cutting off my words. A chill went down my spine when she met my eye. "It finds him . . . always."

CHAPTER EIGHT

GRAYSON

*R*ight, *nothing like showing up late to a date . . . three weeks late.*

A lot had happened in such a short period of time. The simple truth was it was a shit show but sorted now. For the most part. I'd see in the fullness of time how things played out. But for now, I had time to myself, and I wanted to spend it with the Sassy Creature who'd captured my attention from the start. I stood outside the bar where she'd told me to meet her in Salem and sucked in a breath. The night was colder than when we'd met. Winter was upon us, and an icy chill pricked at my skin. The street was eerily quiet compared to those of Boston or New York City. It was like the town itself shut down, and now only the dredges of society scurried in the shadows. The pub where she worked was still open but there were barely any people there. Outside metal furniture sat vacant and even the portable heaters were covered up tight.

I pulled my jacket in closer around me and took a step toward the glass door. I didn't smell her warm honey scent lingering on the air like the first night, but it didn't mean she wasn't here. Fried food, burgers, and desserts also filled the air. This place was more a restaurant than a pub, with booths and tables scattered throughout and a large bar in the middle of the room. It was made of light hardwood with tall chairs all around it. TVs were stationed on the walls around the room. There was a big difference between Salem and Boston. I glanced around looking for her and caught the barest whiff of her scent.

Hope bloomed in my chest. Hope that she'd be here and hope that she'd forgive me for missing our one date. I wanted to prove that her picker wasn't broken regarding me. *Missing a date isn't the way to do that, jackass.*

Tonight wasn't as busy as when I met Piper. There was room to move and walk right through the tables straight to the bar. A guy stood behind the bar and leaned against the shelf behind him. He crossed his arms over his chest and blew a puff of air from his lips. When I approached the bar, he didn't move.

"What can I get you?"

I glanced around to no avail. "I'm looking for Piper. Is she here tonight?"

The door to the kitchen smacked open and hit the wall. Dice staggered through carrying a case of beer. She blew a stray strand of her blonde hair from her face. "No, she's not here."

Her tone was cold and dismissive with a hint of pissed-off. I'd been around enough women to know if you hurt the bestie, no amount of lava will thaw the chill the bestie would give. "Dice, lovely as ever to see you."

She slammed the box on the countertop and ripped the top open. "Wish I could say the same."

The guy moved to her side and glared at me. Like he was some kind of bodyguard. When I knew for sure that Dice didn't need one. He puffed his chest up. "We good here, Dice?"

"Nothing I can't handle." She pulled a bottle from the case and shoved it down into the ice. He gave her a single nod then walked over to the other side of the bar to chat up a waitress.

Oh, the death glare. I leaned against the bar. "Oh, come now, love. You can't honestly be that put out with me."

She froze with a bottle in hand and her head

snapped up. "Does talking that shit really work on people?"

"Usually." I shrugged.

"Leave." She rolled her eyes.

"I can't do that." Truth was I really couldn't. Piper captured my *interest*, and I wouldn't be swayed from it. She had a vitality about her that contradicted the way and style of Vampires. There was no cold demeanor with her. She was all fire, and I was here to get burned.

"So, try, lover boy." She turned away from me to toss the box into the corner.

"I find it difficult to get her out of my mind."

"Once again, try." She marched back over to the bar and mirrored my position. "You ghosted her for three weeks and then show up here like it's nothing. But it's something."

Bang. Right to the heart of the matter as a best friend should. The queens would've done so with knives and magic. This tiny human did so with words. Respectable. "Indeed, it is."

"And yet here you still stand." She motioned toward me.

"What if I told you, it was life or death?"

Dice pressed her hand to her chest and batted her eyes. "How very dramatic. And so very unbelievable."

A customer came up and I stepped to the side,

waiting while Dice took their order and poured the drink. The moment he left, I stepped back into place. "I'm being serious. One of my closest friends nearly died . . . I mean, he did die. But they got him back. But it was a . . . fight. Of epic proportions."

Technically, not a lie. Some of my closest friends had gotten trapped in unseelie and nearly died . . . some even died for real. But some shady deals were made, and they all came back. Mostly unscathed.

"Funny you should say that." She pursed her lips and narrowed her eyes. "Mine almost died, too. The night you were supposed to meet her."

My heart stopped in my chest. "What do you mean?"

"I mean if you bothered to show up, she would've been fine. Instead, I found her all bloody on the ground."

My stomach churned and I placed my hands on the bar top to steady myself. How could I react this way to meeting her one time? Yet, here I was three weeks later, following my infatuation back to Salem and to the ends of the earth if I had to. I would eviscerate any who hurt her. The realization was startling considering how short a time I'd known her. Her face haunted my dreams for weeks and my every waking moment.

I curled my hand into a fist. "Who hurt her?"

Dice stepped back and looked me up and down. "Protective. I approve."

"Who, Dice?" I ground my teeth together and felt my fangs sharpening in my mouth. Someone would die tonight if they weren't careful.

"Jeezzz, no one." She sighed. "It was an accident. She fell."

I sucked in a breath trying to let go of the violence that my blood called for. It was unusual for me to react in such a way. Normally, I didn't fret about things. *How intriguing.*

"Is she on the mend then?"

She paused, seeming to debate something within herself. She sagged and blew out a breath. "Yeah, she's okay."

"I have to see her." It wasn't a request.

"I'm sure you do." She shook her head. "Roll of the dice. Always right."

"Pardon?"

"Nothing."

"I've got all the time in the world." I was nearly two hundred years old. Time had different meanings. I could play young and impatient, or old with infinite time to give. I pulled up a chair and folded my hands.

She looked from my hands to my face and back again. "Seriously?"

"Every day, really, until I've spoken to her." I gave her a tight-lipped smile. "I could call Sav to join me."

She groaned. "Fine, hold on."

When she pulled out her phone, I smirked to myself. Her fingers flew over the screen as she typed up a text. "You know I don't like you."

"I know."

"Guys who ghost suck."

"I couldn't agree more."

She looked up from her phone. "But I like the protective action over Piper, so I'm willing to give you a second chance."

I gave her a single nod. "I appreciate that."

"You're shady." She leaned on the bar and pointed her finger in my face. "And I don't trust shady mother-fuckers. But she likes you despite her better judge-ment. And believe me, I don't think she should. I don't think you deserve her. And if you hurt her, I will hunt you down and make you regret it."

"Quite the impactful statement indeed."

She moved in even closer and crooked her finger to get me to move closer. I leaned in and she caught my eye. "There are bodies they still haven't found. Make no mistake: yours could be one of them, too."

"Understood." It wasn't the first time, or the last, I would be threatened by a woman of power. When Dice glared at me, I believed she was telling the truth. There would be a string of bodies all around her if need be.

She glanced down at her phone and sighed once more. "She'll see you. Her picker is definitely broken."

I hopped off the chair to my feet. "Not when it comes to me."

She rolled her eyes. "Right."

"I look forward to proving you wrong, love."

"I'm sure you won't." She glanced at her phone. "She'll meet you outside, lover boy. Don't let me down."

"I will endeavor not to." A thrill of excitement went through me as I turned away from her and headed to the door.

CHAPTER NINE

PIPER

hy am I doing this? I shouldn't be doing this. Damn it, Piper. Why do I always give second chances when they aren't deserved?

No, not this time. I wouldn't do it. I couldn't do it. I was going to meet up and tell him to his face that nothing would come of this. It would be satisfying. I practiced the words in my head. *Thanks for coming all this way but really, you're wasting your time. There's nothing between us. I need dependable not ghostable.* I paused, trying to find the sassiest reply I could. The zinger that would make him think twice about ghosting anyone ever again. Technically, he didn't ghost me, but he was damn late. Deep down, I wanted to be that strong woman who said no. The one who left him in the dust regretting his actions and always feeling like I was the one who got away. The one he would always think about and know that he messed up what could've been a good thing.

But the other half of me understood if something came up. It wasn't like I gave him my number to call or text me to cancel. Maybe something really had happened, maybe he wasn't a mistake, and maybe my picker really wasn't good and broken. Or maybe it was, and I was an idiot for even meeting up with Grayson. I was both excited and angry at myself. I always liked the things that weren't the best for me and yet, there was an attraction there. A chemistry that I couldn't explain or deny.

I shoved my hands into the pockets of my jacket. Fog puffed from my lips as I walked the dark streets of Salem. It wasn't super late, but it was late enough that people were tucked away home in the chilly night. It didn't take me long to get to Essex. But the moment my feet hit that brick road, my stomach flipped into knots. I was either going to shit or throw up. I didn't know which. I hated that all my nerves went straight to my stomach. Nervous? Right to the stomach. Excited? To the stomach. Angry? Also, right to the stomach. It was like the stupid thing was a barometer for emotions. Emotions I didn't want, didn't welcome, and damn well tried to stop having.

As I came closer to the pub, I saw a shadowy figure leaned up against the half brick wall. He made no move to straighten his stance. Instead, his lips pulled up into a half smile and he ran his hand through those messy chocolate waves.

I sucked in a breath and gave my best "I'm not pleased" face. Which included narrowing my eyes, pursing my lips and brief eye contact. "Hey."

"Oh, come now. Don't be sour with me, Little Creature." He ran his thumb over his bottom lip. "I can't be sour with you."

"I'm not sour." I was totally sour.

He rose to his feet and towered over me. "Ah, but do you really want me to piss off?"

"Yes." I groaned. "No." I tugged at the ends of my hair. "Yes."

"How very decisive of you." He gave a humorless chuckle.

I wanted to calmly tell him I didn't want to see him again and turn away with all the attitude I could muster. And yet, I didn't want to be unreasonable or unforgiving. Things happen, emergencies come up, people had lives. Tormented between pride and kindness was not an easy place to be. I wanted to be nice to him because aside from the not showing up he had it all. But then, he just wasn't there.

"Sooooo . . ."

"So." He arched the eyebrow.

Is this some kind of game to him? I didn't have time to waste with broken picker dudes. Yes, I was only twenty-three, but I'd wasted enough time with worthless people to last me a millennium.

"Right." I turned away from him and began walking up the street.

His hand snaked around my wrist, and he spun me back to face him, pulling me in close to his body. My hair fell from the knot on top of my head and went wild all around my face. His smile fell as his eyes bore into mine. My chest pressed to his ribs, and I tipped my head back to look up at him.

He brushed his fingers down my cheek and stopped just at the corner of my lips. When his eyes drifted down and locked on my lips, his tongue darted from his mouth, wetting his own. He lowered his voice. "Now, Piper, love. Are we going to be at loggerheads? Or are we going to enjoy each other the way I know we can?"

Heat radiated from his body into mine, and his forbidden red wine scent filled my senses. I licked my own lips, wanting to taste him. I fought the urge to go up on my toes and claim his mouth. Instead, I went up on my toes, just hovering an inch from his lips. I lowered my own voice to match his. "Nice. Try."

I dropped down from my toes and took a step back. "You want me?"

He swiped his hand down his face. "Eternally."

Smooth Brit. I shrugged. "Then earn me."

"Are we to play a game then?" He arched his eyebrow.

Excitement tickled my belly and my eyes widened. "Oh, I don't play games. Not my style."

He took a step toward me and bent low to whisper in my ear. His cheek brushed against mine, sending shivers over my body. "And here I was thinking you were toying with me from the beginning."

"And here I was thinking you should know better. If you caught me playing with you, then you've already lost." I blew him a kiss and snickered to myself.

"Sassy little creature, aren't we?" He crooked his finger at me to lean in closer. "Keep it up, I like it."

Without another word, he began to walk down Essex Street toward Crow Heaven Corner, the one store in Salem that might be open this late. "Are we shopping?"

"No, I fancy a nip tonight. Care to join me?" He glanced over his shoulder. "You won't regret it."

The way he played, the way he smiled, the way he

smelled, there was no doubt in my mind that I would regret it all. But if I was going down, it would be in flames. I moved to his side, and he offered me his arm. I placed my hand in the crook of his elbow.

"I didn't think people did this anymore."

"The lack of gentlemen these days astounds even me. To offer one's arm to a lady . . . well that's like offering an escort right through the gates."

I fell into step with him as he guided me down the streets. "The gates of heaven?"

A wicked smile spread across his face. "Whatever gates get you to where you want to be. I can't pretend to lead the way to either heaven or hell. But it will always be an adventure."

Snowflakes began to fall all around us, and I huddled into my coat as we stopped at a crosswalk at the corner of Essex and Washington Square West. The road was wide, accommodating multiple lanes of traffic and room for parking. Down the center was a divider with small trees and bushes. To one side was the first witch shop Salem had to offer and across the street was the Hawthorn Hotel.

"And where are we going to have a nip?"

He nodded toward the hotel. "I'm staying just there."

"You expect me to go to your room?" I tried to

sound appropriately appalled. But it was a failed effort. I was intrigued by this sizzling current I felt between the two of us and what it could lead to.

The light changed and he guided me across the street toward the hotel. "I said a nip, not a shag."

Warmth heated my cheeks, and I dropped my hand from his arm. "We're here for a drink and nothing more?"

"Piper, you are free to do whatever you'd like. You can go or *come* if you'd like. Either way, I will be here again tomorrow and will ask you out again tomorrow and the next day and the next day." He shoved his hands into his pockets. "I have all the time in the world."

I looked up at the red brick exterior and ornate double wooden doors. Each of the windows was surrounded by carved gray stone, with blue awnings hanging above each of the first-floor windows. The Hawthorne Hotel was tall and imposing, but it very much belonged in this town and matched the historical feel that came with all things New England. I didn't make it a habit to go into the Hawthorne. Eerie energy rolled off this place, and it sent goosebumps over my skin, so I tended to avoid it.

"You know they say this place is haunted."

"So, I've heard." He grabbed the door and held it

open for me. "One drink at the pub. We'll have a chat and see if we can get some things sorted."

"One drink." I stepped inside and instantly I was greeted with a heavy feeling. The hotel itself was beautifully preserved, with bright white woodwork, dark cushy carpeting, and sturdy antique-looking furniture. Recessed lighting gave the lobby a light warm color this time of night. It was so very quiet with only one person standing behind the front desk who didn't look up. Grayson didn't hesitate as he walked through the lobby and straight toward the tavern. He paused, letting me through the door first.

It was beautiful in an old study kind of way. Oak covered every inch of the room. From the floors to the ceiling. Even the posts in the middle of the room were covered in perfectly carved oak. Low tables were spread throughout with leather wingback chairs residing at each. There were no TVs or loud music. This place was elegant and quiet. With gold trim and polished glasses.

He moved to my side and pressed his hand to my lower back. I was all too aware of the tips of his fingers, the way his body turned protectively toward mine, and how gentle but firm he was. A fire crackled in the fireplace, and he led us to the table right in front of it. There was only one other couple, and they sat at the other end of the room in matching dark wingback chairs.

I slid my hands from my jacket and laid it on the back of my chair. Grayson froze, staring at me. I tugged at the sleeves of my black sweater dress. "What?"

"Lovely as ever." He motioned for me to sit across from him. Another shiver went over my body, and I tried to ignore it. He tilted his head to the side studying me. "Are you too cold?"

"No, there's just something about this place that gives me the creeps. Ghosts and all that."

"There are far worse, far scarier things in this world than ghosts." He sat in the chair and leaned back. When he steepled his fingers and pressed them to his lips, he looked like the villain in a movie. The firelight flickering over his face made his features all warm and shadowy.

A waiter dressed in a white button-down shirt, black vest, and black pants approached our table. He carried a silver serving tray. It was a far cry from the outfits I wore when working in a bar. "May I take your order?"

"Ladies first." He motioned to me. "What do you desire, Piper?"

I raised my eyebrows at him. *Loaded question.* I turned to the waiter. "I'll have a Pinot Noir."

The man gave me a single nod then hesitated. "I'm sorry, miss, but can I see some ID?"

"Absolutely." I was a bartender myself and I wouldn't begrudge a fellow service worker from doing their job. I rummaged through my purse and handed it over to him.

He chuckled and looked me over. "You don't look twenty-three."

"Oh, I look twenty-three and feel like I'm going on two hundred." I sighed and took it back. It was true. Life hadn't been easy for Dice and me. We moved around a lot and barely survived a lot of things. Mentally, it aged a person.

Grayson chuckled. "Me, too."

"You're twenty-three?" He didn't look twenty-three to me. He had an aged look around his eyes. Like he'd been around and seen some shit. It was the same look that Dice and I had after living the way we did.

"Going on two hundred." He glanced at the waiter. "Bourbon, neat."

When he walked away, we sat in silence for a moment staring at each other. There was a current between the two of us. He wanted me—that much was clear. And I wanted him. At least that was what my broken picker was telling me.

"So, what's scarier than ghosts?" I leaned back in the chair and crossed my legs. Two could play the coy cool game.

"Witches, warlocks, monsters, demons." His lips pulled up in a half smile. "Even vampires."

"And you believe all these things exist?" I folded my hands in my lap, squeezing them tight enough to pinch myself to maintain focus. *Don't look at his lips, don't look at his lips.*

He motioned around him. "This is Salem. The place where magic exists. Don't you believe?"

It was a city heavy with a dark history, magic, and legend. Did I believe? How could I not? Dice and I chose this place for a reason. It felt like home. It had an energy so strong, on most days it hung in the atmosphere, surrounding me like a blanket of protection.

"Yeah, I guess I do."

The waiter came back with our drinks. He placed little cocktail napkins on the table in front of us then our drinks. We remained silent through the whole process, just simply staring at each other. When the waiter walked away, Grayson grabbed up his glass and swirled it in his hand. Dark liquid clung to the sides of the glass as it ran down back into place. He raised the glass to his lips, never breaking eye contact with me.

"Here's to impossible things." He took a sip.

I raised my glass and took a sip as well. I placed the glass back on the table and sucked in a breath. We could dance around words all night long, or we could get to the heart of the matter. "What are you doing here, Grayson?"

"Earning you."

An involuntary smile spread on my lips. He was so smooth with me. I didn't know how to react or what to say. "You flatter me."

"It's quite easy with one such as yourself." He rested his glass on the arm of his chair and spread his fingers over the top of it, holding it in place.

I rolled my eyes. "Breaking out the charm on my behalf."

"Is it working?"

Completely. My picker was starting not to care that it was broken. "Yet to be determined."

"Good thing I like a challenge." The firelight danced in his hair and streamed over his body. His button-down shirt was open at the collar, exposing more of that pale creamy skin. Grayson sat with an easy confidence I didn't feel but could mimic with the best of them. He rested his ankle over his knee.

"And yet you failed your first one." Oh, the thrill of making a good point in the middle of a conversation. It was like scoring the winning point in a game that could last a lifetime.

He winced. "Indeed, I did. But one loss will only set me up to gain in the end."

"How do you figure?" I took another sip, and the alcohol warmed me from the inside out.

He leaned forward. "There are many ways to win a war. Our first night was sublime. Our second a loss. Perhaps we are in the even column, which brings me leeway to take the gold cup, so to speak."

I chucked. "Well, you'd win the gold cup on creativity hands-down. Now, dependability, I think you'd lose. Just so happens I'd take dependable over creative any day of the week."

"One can't make such determinations based on such a small sampling."

He had a point. "And yet all my warning bells are going off about you."

"Ah, the notorious broken picker?" He smiled over his glass before taking a sip.

"Without fail."

"This time I would say you picked right."

"And yet . . . you were a no-show." Facts were facts. I waited. I'd ended up in the hospital and obsessing over him for weeks. Weeks of wondering if I'd done something wrong. If he thought about me, too. If he didn't feel the way I did. And if he had felt the way I had, then why didn't he come? In my mind, the truth was a very black and white, simple thing. He didn't want me the way I wanted him. Guys show up when they want a woman. Simply put, that was the reality of things. And no amount of flirting would change that.

He groaned. "Indeed, I did not. However, in my defense, the reason I did not show up was in the service of a friend. He fell ill and nearly died. I couldn't very well leave him like that. The recovery has been long and difficult. I am a loyal person. And I can be loyal to you, too. But you should know, you must know, I was going to come for you that night."

"How would I know that?" A rush of butterflies hit my stomach and I had to look away from his intense gaze.

"Because you can feel this thing between us just as I can."

That unspoken sizzle that shot through my veins and went straight to my stomach. It was magnetic, and wild, and free, and I wanted more of it. I hated the war in my head. Hated it more than anything. Because doing this and still knowing all it was going to do was end up hurting me later sucked. Yet that silly hope of mine whispered through my mind. *Maybe he is the one. Maybe it was a fluke. Maybe it is finally your turn for a happily ever after. No one was perfect, least of all me. Why should I expect perfect from him?*

"Piper, look at me," he purred in that sexy accent, drawing my gaze back to him. "This isn't a mistake. I am not a mistake. And your picker isn't broken."

I took a sip of my wine and sighed. Because in that moment, Grayson got me hook, line, and sinker. I tried to steel my heart against him and kill the hope that would inevitably be there for my own happily ever after that wouldn't come. And yet I knew what the next move was going to be. I knew when I walked through the door to the hotel.

"So, how are the rooms here?"

A wide smile spread across his face. "Full of pleasures to be had."

I knew my own personal hell was coming. But if I was going down this road, it might as well be while riding him. I chugged down the rest of my wine. "Care to show me?"

He rose to his feet, leaving his drink behind, and offered me his hand. "Anything you desire."

I am so screwed.

*M*y pulse raced in my veins and excitement filled my body. My hand fit perfectly with his, like our fingers were meant to be wrapped around each other. My skin tingled where we touched. He was so calm, so smooth as he walked us out of the tavern and toward the elevators, like he had every confidence in what was about to happen. When we got to the doors, he dropped my hand and pressed the button. I stood there on the edge of wanting to leap on him and wanting to run. Everything in me desired Grayson, and the only reason I wanted to run was to guard my heart from falling for him. He was too everything: too perfect, too hot, too suave, too sexy.

But I wasn't about to miss the chance of a lifetime

because I was afraid of the future heartbreak. He might not even break my heart. We stood in silence with the tension sizzling between us. I turned toward him, and he didn't face me.

"Wait."

That one word sent a thrill down my body. "For what?"

"Everything, Little Creature. Everything." The elevators dinged and the doors slid open. Grayson motioned for me to go first, and I sauntered by him.

When I spun around to face him, he stepped into the elevator and pressed the button. Yet he never took his eyes off me as the door slid shut. The moment they did, he prowled toward me, backing me up against the wall. His body pressed into mine and he placed his knee between my legs. He placed his hands against the wall behind me, caging me in. Adrenaline pumped through my veins. He was so close yet so controlled. Heat rolled off his body into mine and he pressed in closer.

"Are you sure about this, Piper?"

I nodded up at him. "I'm sure."

"And the broken picker?"

I threw my arms around his neck. "What picker?"

His lips crashed into mine, and my whole body went on fire. The burning flavor of bourbon filled my mouth as his tongue danced with mine. His hands wound around my body and pressed into my skin. I felt every bit of him as he pulled me closer to him. I needed him closer, wanted him closer, like I never wanted anyone before.

The elevator bell dinged and we came to a stop. He pulled away so quickly I wasn't ready to stop. I had to have him . . . all of him. The door slid open, and he grabbed my hand, pulling me from the elevator and down the hall. He walked with such casual swagger, like he had all the time in the world, and I was burning from the inside out. How was it possible to want someone so much and yet know they'd be the end of me? But if I was going down, it'd be with flaming multiple orgasms that only a guy like Grayson could do.

He pulled the key from his pocket and unlocked the door. He threw it wide open, and I was tired of waiting. There was a point between black and white when you didn't want to walk in shades of gray anymore. And my decision was made. I pulled him to face me, and without hesitation, I jumped up and wrapped my legs around his hips. I wrapped my hands in his hair and yanked him to me. Our mouths came together, and I groaned in pleasure. His lips were firm yet soft against mine, and his tongue was warm, wet perfection. When his fingers splayed over my ass, I tightened my legs around him.

He staggered back toward the bed, and we fell onto it, cushioned by the mattress and a mountain of pillows. When he pulled away from my lips just to kiss down my neck, I threw my head back, giving him more room. His lips left a wet trail over my skin. Suddenly, my boots were on the floor and his hand snaked up my thigh, covering every inch of my skin. He looped his finger to the band of my panties and tugged them down ever so slowly. I wriggled against them, wanting them off now, but he didn't speed up, just kept the controlled, leisurely pace. A warm chuckle rumbled in his chest.

"I'm going to enjoy making you wait."

I couldn't think, couldn't respond, all I knew was him and this moment. With quick fingers, I unbuttoned each button on his shirt. It fell open and I paused for a moment. He was perfection. Pale skin covered perfectly sculpted muscles. He was slim and sleek like an athlete, with a dusty trail of hair leading right below his belt. When I pressed my fingers to his stomach, his muscles tightened and jumped to my touch. A low growl escaped from his lips, and I needed to feel every inch of his skin. The lower I ran my hand, the higher on my thigh his went. Soon his hand was between my legs and I let my knees fall to the side.

"Exquisite." He glided his fingers over me.

My breath caught in my throat. Everything came into focus on that one point. "Inside, go inside."

"Like this?"

My hips rolled of their own accord, and I felt each of his leisurely strokes. Electricity pulsed through my body and sizzled over my skin. I wrapped my hands in his open shirt and pulled his face toward mine. I thrust my tongue into his mouth, letting our flavors dance together. *Holy shit, is that his thumb on my . . .?* I'd never known a man who could do something like this. Pleasure shot through my body, and I wanted more, wanted hard, and faster.

"More." I breathed against his lips as I fumbled with the buckle on his belt.

"Yes, love, more." With one hand, he pulled my dress up over my head and tossed it to the side. "Off with that then."

I couldn't focus, couldn't concentrate on his words. All I felt was the perfection of his fingers and a rhythm that was driving me toward the perfect release. The small whisp of fabric between the cups of my bra snapped and it fell wide open. Cool air drifted over my breasts, and Grayson hissed in a breath. He leaned down toward them and took one in his mouth, tickling the peak with the tip of his tongue. I nearly levitated off the bed. My back arched and I cried out.

How was he everywhere and nowhere all at the same time? His belt fell free and I made quick work of the fly on his pants. I delved my hand below his waist and wrapped my hand around him. With the first stroke, he hissed in a breath and his hips bucked toward me.

I smiled to myself. "Good to see I have an effect."

He glanced down between our bodies. "Always."

It was all so delicious, so perfect. Pleasure wracked my body as I hurled toward ecstasy. Tingles pulsed low in my belly, and I was so close. *More, like that. More.*

He backed off, slowing his pace, and I was frantic for more. "Don't stop."

"Patience."

"What?" My head thrashed on the bed. "So close."

"Not yet." He pulled his hand away and I wanted to put it right back where it was to finish what he started.

I nearly protested the loss, but then he climbed over me, resting between my legs. When he looked down at me with those hypnotic mahogany eyes, I couldn't look away. "You ready for me, Piper?"

I couldn't answer, only stare at the perfection of his

body and the length between his legs. I nodded at him and wrapped my leg around his hip, urging him forward. Urging him to take me. Grayson leaned forward and ran himself up and down the most intimate part of my body, coating himself in me. I wanted to urge him forward, to be frantic and hard, but there was something about the way he took his time. The way he controlled himself. The way he controlled me and my body. I found myself surrendering to the moment and letting my knees fall wide. I rocked my hips, inviting him into me.

Grayson pressed his hips forward and my body parted around him. He hissed in a breath and froze. Sweat beaded his body and he pulled back then pressed in again going even farther. I rolled my body, wanting all of him deeper and harder, but he kept up that slow, torturous speed, going just a bit further each time. When his hips ground into mine, he arched his back and groaned.

"Mine."

Tingles covered my body from head to toe and my hands landed on his hip. I pulled him closer, begging him with my body to move. He rolled his hips, sliding in and out. It was a dance between the two of us. Slow and sensual. I felt every inch of him moving against me, heard every breath he took, tasted his skin on my lips. Grayson was overwhelming yet perfection. He leaned down closer, and his chest pressed to mine, forcing our skin to touch in all places. Sweat and friction built between us in a tango of limbs and movement.

Connection sizzled between us like the moment was so right and there was nothing else in the world, just the two of us at this one perfect point in time. He kissed down the side of my neck, running his tongue over my skin. His hand drifted up my arm and he twined his fingers with mine. When he met my eyes, he didn't let go. His rhythm turned faster as he ground against me. There was no control, just us moving as one toward something greater than the both of us.

It was too much. Overwhelming. "Gray?"

He didn't look away. "Right here. I've got you."

He did have me, totally and completely. In this moment I was his and only his. I squeezed his hand and moved my hips to his pace, letting him take me exactly where we both needed to go. The muscle in his jaw ticked as he ground his teeth together and drove into me harder. My body quickened and I felt myself starting to fly higher, soaring toward pleasure. Ecstasy exploded through me and every muscle in my body let go at the same time. I dug my nails into his hips, pulling him closer to me.

"Fuck, Piper." He drove into me harder, finding his own release.

His back arched and I couldn't get enough of him. My body wanted more of him always. I cried out, holding him tighter until the wracking waves of pleasure subsided. My chest heaved as I fought to catch my breath. Grayson leaned down and pressed his forehead to mine. "See? I got you."

Breathless, I smiled and felt the last strings of my resistance to him go right out the door. "Yeah, yeah, you got me."

CHAPTER ELEVEN

GRAYSON

*T*he sun had already begun to set, and it was barely late afternoon. Light gray sky began to give way to pink as snowflakes fell from the sky, twisting around each other in a slow, peaceful dance. It wasn't a turbulent blizzard. This was the kind of snow movie makers prayed for. Yet, I didn't dare move off the bed for fear of waking Piper. Her long, wild hair drifted over my chest, and her deep even breaths told me she was still asleep. Her warm honey scent lingered on my skin and filled the room. I ran my fingers through the ends of the strands, letting them twirl around my fingers and fall back on my chest.

The bed was a mess, with only a single pillow and a sheet remaining. It was tangled around both our bodies, binding us together with her legs thrown over mine. It was a comfortable, possessive way of lying, and it didn't bother me in the least. Piper was perfection, with her attitude and completely vivacious nature. Life with the Witch Court had given me a reprieve from the monotony that I'd been living in, with adventures of killing the evil king and reuniting the magic of the witches and warlocks. But now that the strife was handled, it left me in a place of indecision. To go back to a fate that I didn't feel was my own wasn't an option. But Piper, she was a choice. A choice to live, to feel, to be.

So, I watched the slow snow fall and listened to her easy breaths, relishing the moment of peace. She thought her picker was broken, but I would do for her what no other had done. I would be there. I'd fucked up the first date, but I wouldn't after this. There was a beautiful, complicated simplicity in the way Piper thought. It was all taking responsibility for oneself rather than blaming the bastards who treated her that way in the first place. Which made her both strong and delicate at the same time, with a touch of eternally intriguing in a world of predictability.

Her breathing abruptly changed yet she didn't move. The muscles in her body tensed against my side but I continued to play with the ends of her hair. A normal human wouldn't notice these little changes, but I noticed everything about her. Her eyelashes fluttered against my skin for the barest second before she slowly began to disentangle herself from me.

"Good morning."

She jumped and rolled off me, pulling part of the sheet with her. She glanced at me from under her thick eyelashes. "Morning."

She kicked her legs over the side of the bed and sat there with her back toward me. I curled myself around her and pressed a kiss to her shoulder, tasting the sweet saltiness of she skin. "Would you like some breakfast . . . or should I say lunch?"

"Lunch? What time is it?" She looked to the window like the gray sky would give her any indication of the time.

"It's about two in the afternoon."

Her body tensed and she leapt to her feet and pulled the sheet with her, leaving me naked on the bed. "Oh, my God. Dice is going to kill me!"

"Have you committed some kind of offense?" I chuckled and watched her race around the room collecting her clothing, trying not to look at my body.

"Yes." She spun in a circle. "Well, no."

She froze with the sheet wrapped around her body like a toga. Her hair was a wild mess all around her face, and her lips were just a touch swollen from my kiss. The only thing missing was my bite mark on her neck. A forbidden thing for the lover of a Shade. Yet, she was so tempting my fangs ached to sink into her.

"Which is it, Little Creature. Yes, or no?" I leaned back on the bed and put one leg up, letting her look her fill. Her body was burned into every inch of my memory. Might as well let mine be burned into some of hers. She stared at me for a long moment, those emerald eyes raking over me. I could almost feel it, like she was touching me herself.

She shook her head. "I have to find my phone."

I'd heard it vibrating across the room only a few moments before she woke. I pointed by the door. "I believe you dropped your purse there last night."

She hurried toward the door and grabbed her purse off the floor. When she dove for the phone, it was already ringing. She didn't hesitate to answer. "Hey! Proof of life!"

I didn't want to make out like I could hear the other side of the conversation, but it was so easy with my supernatural abilities. Dice groaned on the other line. "This is not how we roll. I get that you're on some kind of devil dick . . ."

Devil dick? I fought not to laugh and kept my face impassive.

". . . but proof of life is necessary."

Piper tilted her head back and blew out a deep breath. "Yeaaaah, I got distracted by the thing you just said."

So, I do have a devil dick? This was deeply pleasing.

"I was tracking your location with the Find My app. Sexy Brit is lucky you answered. Otherwise, I was going to kick in the door, SWAT-team style, and kick some ass." The worried tension left her voice though I could tell she was still annoyed for Piper making her worry.

Piper tucked her hair behind her ear and glanced at me, giving me a half smile. "That won't be necessary."

"Wouldn't be the first time."

She stepped into her underwear and pulled them up under the sheet. *Shame, that is.* Piper struggled to keep the sheet in place as she stood up straight and pulled her panties the rest of the way up her thighs. She let go of a chuckle. "No, it wouldn't. Remember that?"

"Oh, I remember."

A light smile played on Piper's lips. "He was never the same."

"May his balls rest in pieces." She chuckled. "So, are you gonna ride that devil dick to work or what?"

"It's not that late. I'll be there." She spun around

and snagged her bra off the corner of the chair where it'd been thrown last night.

"Girl, your shift starts in like, half an hour."

Piper held the phone away from her face and squinted at the time. "Shit!"

Dice sighed. "I'll meet you there. I got your uniform."

"Life saver."

"So, you gonna ride that D all the way to work or what?"

"Byeeeeee." She hung up on Dice and turned her back to me then threw the sheet behind her and right at the bed. It fell across my legs, and I took the hint and pulled it up to my hips.

"Leaving?"

She pulled her bra on then realized I'd cut the middle of it. "Well, that's not holding shit together."

"Beauty such as those should not be trapped." I watched as she threw the scraps of what was left of her bra to the floor and pulled her sweater dress over her head.

She turned back toward me and gave me a half smile. "Sooooo."

"So?" Was she going to do that awkward morning-after thing? Where we had a perfect night together only to be thwarted by unspoken questions.

"I have to go to work." She slid her boots over those flawless legs she'd had wrapped around me only a few hours ago.

I rose off the bed and stood in front of her with the sheet draped around my hips. I wrapped my hand around the back of her neck and pulled her into me. She staggered forward and fell into me. I tipped her head back and pressed my lips to hers. The tension instantly left her body as she sagged against me. I loved the way she felt against my body and tasted on my tongue. I pulled back and smiled.

"Tonight?"

She squinted her eyes. "What about it?"

"I think we should have a proper date."

"A proper date?" She stepped away from me and slid her arms into her jacket. "Look, this was . . . this was . . . well, it was nice. But I have work and stuff. I don't have time to —"

"Time to test me against your very fallible picker?"

She groaned and ran her hand through her thick hair. "I don't. I don't want to."

But everything in her eyes told me she did want to. There was a glint of hope behind those bright green eyes. She shifted from one foot to the other, and I grabbed her hand and ran little circles on it with my thumb. "You don't have to do anything you don't want to. But you're a lovely Little Creature and I'd like to see you again."

"Look, I'm not looking for pretty words. I need—"

"Dependable."

She sighed. "You're like, perfect. But a girl could forget herself in perfect."

"Would that be so bad?" For all the strength and attitude the woman had, she was soft inside where it counted. The world and circumstances could've made Piper hard and bitter. Instead, they made her cautious and picky. Which was admirable given the life she'd led.

"It could be." She shrugged.

"Or it could be something *more*." We both didn't know where this would go. But why kill it before it even started?

She let go of a heavy sigh. "Fine, one date."

"I'll be there."

She sighed. "Sure, you will."

"Have faith, Little Creature. I'll be there tonight when you get off work." I cupped her cheeks and placed a light kiss on the tip of her nose. When I pulled back, she looked up at me with those wide eyes of hers and I couldn't help but smile. It was like she didn't know what to make of me.

"If you say so." She backed away from me and

headed right toward the door. When she got to it, she bumped right into the handle and winced. "I had a really nice time."

"For me as well. Wait you don't have my number."

I pointed to my phone resting on the dresser. "I've already got it."

"But how... you know what. Never mind. Later." She fumbled for the handle, jiggling it a few times before she yanked it open.

"Until then." I held still, waiting for that deer-in-headlights look to leave her face. Yet, it never did as she darted for the door and let it close quickly behind her. Her footsteps hurried away, and I smiled to myself. Piper was completely intriguing in a contradictory sort of way: strong yet delicate, complicated yet simple, sweet yet sassy.

I shook my head and headed for the bathroom, letting the sheet fall to the floor. Every muscle in my body felt at ease. There was no tension or worry. My night was set, and the plan was simple: spend it with Piper. Nothing more, nothing less. I turned on the shower and let the water run. In only a few moments, steam billowed from behind the white shower curtain.

I didn't want to wash her lush scent from my body, but if I was going to make tonight memorable, I had to bring my A-game. I stepped into the hot stream and let it run over me for long moments. I felt the shift in the air first, the movement of something magical that didn't fit here with me. I groaned and grabbed the bar of soap.

"You're not meant to be here."

"Neither are you, mate," Sav called from the other side of the curtain.

I scrubbed over my skin. "Mirror travel is not an open invitation."

"I think your memory does fail you. Perhaps it's been too long for you." I could see his shadow moving behind the curtain.

"And yet I don't remember extending the invitation." I tossed the bar of soap onto the shelf. Atlas Savage was my oldest friend. He knew all my deep dark secrets, as I knew his. But he was here for one reason and one reason only.

"And yet I don't recall ever needing one."

I switched the water off and ran my hands over my soaking hair. I yanked the curtain to the side and a towel hit my face. I caught it and dried my chest and arms. "I'm busy."

"With the human?" He scoffed. "Your taste as of late has been interesting to say the least."

"Piper, her name is Piper." I wrapped the towel around my hips and stepped out of the shower.

Atlas stood in the doorway with his arms crossed over his chest. His white hair fell over his eyes and blocked half his face. Poe, his crow, was perched on his shoulder. He arched his eyebrows at me. "Indeed, her fragrance lingers on the air. Joyous night?"

"Do the rules of gentlemen no longer apply?" I pushed past him as I walked back into the room.

Sav turned in the same doorway and leaned against the door jamb. "Do you not see the logistical problems of this situation?"

Annoyance flared in my chest. I yanked the dresser drawer open and pulled my sweater out. "No, I fail to see the logistical problems."

"You are endeared to this one."

Shrug. "So?"

"I have never seen you so." He walked into the room and dropped down on the couch. He spread his arms wide across the back and slouched into the cushions, making himself comfortable.

"Don't tell me you're jealous someone is taking my time." I knew what he was getting at, but it didn't have to be a concern. I pulled a pair of jeans from the dresser drawer and threw them on the bed along with the sweater.

He caught my eye. "Shades are not permitted to love."

"Who said anything about love?" It was a ridiculous notion. "Hasn't happened in two hundred years. Won't happen now."

"But the curse"

"Has nothing to do with me. I will not fall to it, and no one will be hurt in the process. I find her intriguing." The curse of The House of Shade had lingered in my family for centuries. My father fell to it before I was born, and yet I'd vowed never to get that close. And I'd stuck to that vow.

"And what of the girl?" His face was so placid, bored even.

"What of her? We are only exploring each other. A companion doesn't interfere with the curse."

"Are you only offering companionship?" He sat forward.

"Can a person not date and just see where things go?" Piper and I were just getting to know each other. She was intoxicating and exciting. I wanted to offer her a different opinion of her picker. Show her there was more to life and that she could trust someone even if they messed up. We didn't have to end poorly, or end at all. We could know each other. I could give her all the things she craved and she . . . she gave me life.

"Where they go? Have you forgotten? This is the

year of the prophecy. The curse lingers over you like a shadow at midday, and you want to see where things go. Change her, keep her for a while, then be done with it. For both your sakes."

"Change her? Now who's the mad one? I would not extinguish a light such as hers and relegate her to that of Night Spawn." I shook my head and shoved my legs into my jeans. Night Spawn were vampires that weren't born but made. They suffered all the weaknesses of vampires. Those legends existed for a reason. I would not take the sun away from Piper, or the taste of food, or even life. Because those Night Spawn were dead. It wasn't like being a born vamp like myself or Sav. We were a whole different ballgame.

"A vampire and human can only end in two ways. It would be naïve to think otherwise. And we, my friend, are not naïve."

"And what would those be?"

He rose to his feet to head back to the bathroom. He climbed up on the sink and stood in front of the mirror. He placed his hand on the mirror, and it rippled under his touch. He pushed his hand forward and the mirror gave way to him.

He looked at me through the doorway with a sorrow-filled face. "Heartbreak or Death. And for you my friend, something much worse."

CHAPTER TWELVE

PIPER

"It's weird, right? Like so weird." I pulled bottles from the rack in front of me and started placing them in the cabinet behind the bar. It was the same closing-down routine each night: lock away the liquor and clean up all our shit. It wasn't a super busy night, but it was enough that the bar was sticky and trashed. The garbage was full of bottles and napkins from the night. All I wanted was to get out of here. But at the same time, I was moving at a glacial pace because I didn't know if I actually wanted to see Grayson or not.

He was magnetic and overwhelming. Last night was an out-of-body experience. He did things and said things to me that no other guy ever did or said to me. His deep voice rumbled in my ear, saying all the filthy things with all the confidence in the world. My body responded to exactly what he wanted. I was helpless not to.

"Not really." Dice walked around the outside of the bar, wiping down the counter with a beat-up white rag.

I grabbed two more sticky bottles and shoved them back into the cabinet. The glass bottles clanked together, and I stood up straight. "But he's all, I'll be there, and I'm all, No, you won't. And I am trying to not get my hopes up. I mean, can you imagine a second time? Because I really can't. I mean last night was . . ."

"A night of screaming multiple orgasms that you'd like to repeat on a daily basis from now until forever?" She paused and stared at me with that very direct I-know-what-you-did-last-night kind of face.

I held my hand up, stopping her. "Dice."

"What?"

I grabbed more bottles, shaking them around as I spoke. "What if he wants more?"

She shrugged. "Do you want more?"

"No." I paused. It would be nice to have someone to call my own, or depend on, or sleep next to and say good morning to every day. The idea of that made me want it. "I mean, yes."

I shook my head. "No, definitely no."

Sure, there were pretty pictures of what life could be with the perfect partner. But perfect wasn't something that happened to someone like me. I lived in the real world and stuck with the things I knew were dependable. Work, Dice, and some fun nights out.

"No?" She sighed and moved farther down the bar, running the rag in small circles over the wooden counter.

I shook my head. "No."

She finished off the counter and threw the rag across the room to the bag of rags on the floor then put her hands on her hips. "Brutal honesty right now?"

I nodded. I could always rely on Dice to give it to me straight. Even if I didn't want to hear it. "We all want that. We say we don't, but the truth is, we all do. There's a basic driving need to have a deep love life. Which we all want, even me. But for now, we're making the best of what we've got."

"You're not wrong." I chuckled. "Does this mean you'd toss me aside for a good guy?"

"Psh, we are lifers." She pointed from me to her and back again. "Sorry to disappoint. But you're stuck with me."

"I like the sound of lifers." Truth was, we'd always

been from the day we met. I sighed and locked the cabinet. "But I like the idea of having someone, too."

"It's the best of all worlds. Besides, it's not like we're going to go to an inn in Vermont, find a small town where Christmas is a days-long festival and there are hot cocoa carts every few feet. This isn't a Hallmark movie. This is real life."

Salem was a beautiful town surrounded by old homes with character for days. In the fall, the leaves turned a rainbow of colors. In the winter, the snow was white and fluffy. Even in the spring, when things were still cold, the fresh buds gave way to new life. Truth be told, if ever there was going to be a picturesque happily-ever-after, it would happen here, in the place of magic and old New England beauty.

"Oh, I don't know. Salem is pretty idealistic for made-for-TV movies about finding your perfect soul-mate." This place could be that ideal. It was one of the reasons Dice and I called it home.

Dice sighed and shook her head. "Yeah, well it looks like it actually might be."

"What?"

She pointed toward the window over my shoulder. "So much for your broken picker. Prince Charming awaits."

I glanced over my shoulder and there he was,

standing outside in the cold, waiting for me. He was devastating in his long wool peacoat, dark jeans, and boots. Snow had been falling all day long, yet it hadn't stuck, not really. It barely coated the ground, only clinging to the long dead foliage on the streets. It clung to his hair, giving his waves a messy, damp look. When he met my gaze, he didn't wave or move to come inside. Instead, he just gave a half-smile and a nod to come out.

"That man is sly." Dice shook her head and gave a wistful smile. "And trouble."

"Don't I know it." I forced myself to drag my eyes away from him and turn back to her. "Dice?"

"Yeah?" She walked to my side.

"That guy scares me. Not in a violent kind of way. In the this-one-could-really-hurt kind of way." I lowered my voice. "Not sure I want to do that."

"Since when has fear held us back from anything we've wanted to do?" She threw her arm around my shoulder and gave a squeeze. "Better get going."

"I gotta finish up here."

Dice rolled her eyes and dropped her arm. "I got this. But don't forget: I require proof of life."

"I'll try not to let the devil dick distract me." I grabbed my jacket and purse from under the counter and shoved my arms in. I pulled my phone from my purse and peeked at it. "I'm still sharing locations with you. And I owe you for finishing up tonight."

"I'll settle for Sav's number. See if Sexy Brit has it, will ya?" She winked. "Talk about trouble."

I pulled my hair from the collar of my jacket and threw it over my shoulder. "It *is* our dream to marry besties."

"I could do with a Sexy Brit of my own." She pushed me toward the door. "So go, get us one."

I let her push me and I made my feet carry me the rest of the way. When I opened the door, the cold hit me in a refreshing-happy-to-be-out-of-the-stuffy bar kind of way. The air hit my lungs and a thrill of excitement ran over my body. It pooled low in my belly and gave me goosebumps. He was here, like he said he would be. I felt myself melting for him. The no-show was nearly forgotten, erased in one night of passion and a perfectly beautiful man waiting for me.

"Hey." I bit my bottom lip, not knowing how to greet him. Did I go for a casual hug? Or a kiss, after the night we shared? Was I meant to be close and comfortable with him, or more formal?

"Good evening, Little Creature." He stepped in close to me and wrapped his arm around my shoulders, pulling me into him.

His lips came down on mine. Not the intense play

he gave me last night. This was warm and tender with a touch of heat. His fingers pressed into me, and I felt myself melt against him. My toes curled in my boots, and I lay my hands on his chest. A current of heat ran between us, and I felt my fingers curl into the lapels of his jacket of their own accord. It was like, anytime I got even remotely close to Grayson, I lost control of my own body. When he pulled back, he smiled down at me.

"So much life about you." He turned and began walking while keeping me tucked under his shoulder.

I leaned into his body and his heady red wine scent drifted over me. "Is that a good thing?"

"For someone like me, eternally." His arm slid from my shoulder down to the small of my back.

"Where are we off to tonight?" I held my breath, hoping this was going to be a real date, not just a trip back to his room. I wanted Grayson, but whatever happened tonight would tell me exactly where we stood.

"Right there." He pointed to the hotel across the street from the pub.

My excitement dampened. I liked Grayson. He was smooth and exciting. Best of all, he showed up. Sex with him was mind-blowing, but was he going to make this all about sex? Or was it going to be more?

Either way, I had to know. We walked across the brick road and straight into the lobby. The furnishings were modern and sleek-looking. They were a far cry from the hotel from last night. One wall was made entirely of brick, while the others were painted a lighter color. Geometric art covered the walls and complemented the bright colored modern furniture.

Grayson kept his hand pressed to my back and he guided me straight toward the elevators. He didn't stop to check in, just pressed the button to take us up. The door opened right away, and we stepped in. *How very efficient.* I was trying not to be annoyed. I had, after all, gone to his hotel room with him last night and spent the entire night with my hands on his body whispering his name. I wanted it again, wanted him again. But it would be nice to have an actual date, where we sat and talked, perhaps got to know each other more. Unless this was all he wanted, in which case, cool. I just needed to know where I stood.

When the doors opened, I froze. "What are we doing?"

He frowned and cocked his head to the side, staring at me. "I thought dinner might be a lovely idea. Unless you'd prefer something else?"

I stood there on the rooftop of the hotel. There wasn't a person in sight. It was totally empty. All but for the twinkle lights hanging overhead and the heaters surrounding one seating area. It wasn't a normal table but more like a lounge area, with thick cushions and a warm fuzzy blanket waiting. A warm fire flickered in the center of the table in front of the low seating.

"No, this . . ." I swallowed. ". . . this is nice."

"I thought it might be." He motioned for me to choose whichever seat I wanted near the fire. Everything was smooth about Grayson. He was calm, never in a rush, and always in control. There wasn't anything I didn't like about him.

I smiled and dropped down onto the comfortable cushions. Warmth surrounded me from the outdoor heaters and the flickering fire. He grabbed the blanket and threw it over my legs then joined me. "Wine?"

"Yes, thank you." I was suddenly self-conscious about still wearing my uniform. Well, a black T-shirt and jeans. I felt underdressed with just my coat on. Like I should be in some kind of nice outfit, like what I wore last night.

He took the bottle from the ice bucket and poured it into the waiting glasses. "You look lovely tonight."

I ran my hand over my wild hair. "Are you reading my mind?"

"Oh, you think you're lovely, too, then?" He handed me the glass.

"Smooth, very smooth." I took a sip, hoping it'd steady my excited nerves. I glanced around at the nearly empty roof top, noting only a single server off to the side playing on her phone. "Umm, did you rent this whole place out?"

There was that casual shrug that he did so easily. As though he'd rehearsed it a thousand times to become the perfect amount of sexy and nonchalant. "It wasn't that busy to begin with."

"Why?" I would've sat with everyone around us. It didn't matter to me."

"I figured a little one on one attention would be nice after a busy night of work." He slid in closer to me, resting his arm across the back of the bench. His fingers brushed over the edge of my hair, the way he'd done this afternoon when I'd woken against his chest.

"We both know what I do. So, tell me, what is it that you do?" The chic clothing, the hints of being well-monied all intrigued me. .

He hummed to himself and ran his thumb over his bottom lip. "Private security."

"You must do well." Renting out an entire rooftop just for me? Perhaps he wasn't just a hot Brit off the street.

"What can I say? It pays the bills." He ran his hand through his hair then took a sip of his wine.

I motioned around to the empty rooftop. "Clearly."

"I'll go a long way to get what I want." He met my eye and for one intense moment it felt like his gaze was focused on what he wanted . . . me.

"And what is it that you want?"

He still didn't look away. "Nothing less than the world."

The waitress came over with two plates of food. She placed them on the table in front of us and couldn't stop staring at Grayson. She was cute in a plain sort of way, with mousy blond hair and big brown eyes. She was small with dimples in her cheeks. "Can I get you anything else?"

"We're good." He didn't take his eyes off me.

Good man.

I forced myself to keep looking at her. "Thank you."

She turned and left with a flounce in her step. I glanced down at the plate and grabbed a chip covered in cheese. "No less than the world, huh? Ambitious endeavors."

"Depends on what your definition of the world is." He, too, took a chip and popped it into his mouth.

"What's yours?"

"I'm not as interesting as you. What is it that you want?"

I chuckled to myself. "No less than the world."

"And your definition of the world is?"

His playful smile, the way his body leaned toward me, and the glint of mischief made me want to go along with this little dance we were doing. He sparked my interest like no one else. In my mind, I heard the challenging rhythm of a tango that the two of us were about to do.

"Now, would it be fair for me to share and for you not to? Where's the fun in that?" I turned to face him fully. My legs brushed his knees, and I threw the other half of the blanket over him to share in the warmth.

"Are we to play then?"

A small thrill went through me at the thought of him playing with me. "And the terms of this?"

He took a sip of wine. "If I'm to answer then you must as well."

"Deal."

A wicked smile played on his lips. "Deal."

"Why does this feel like a deal with the devil?" I popped another chip in my mouth and let the spicy warmth melt on my tongue.

"Oh, I'm harmless, really." Even in that sexy British accent, I didn't believe he was harmless. I'd seen him throw a man over a bar and fight off the rest. Harmless was not a word I would use to describe Grayson.

"If we both believed that then neither of us would be sitting here. Because I don't do harmless, and you don't seem the type to be capable of it."

He held his glass up to me in a slight salute. "Indeed."

"And yet, I've clearly caught your attention."

The fire light brushed over his features, leaving most of them in shadow. "Undivided, in fact."

"Care to share why?" I knew I was cute and sassy in the ways that counted, but to me, it seemed kind of unreal. Grayson was rich, handsome, and confident. So, the question was why a girl with no family, with no connections, and with trust issues would appeal to him?

He placed his glass on the table and sat back against the booth. "Simply put, I find you fascinating."

A burst of laughter escaped my lips, and I nearly spilled my drink. "I'm not all that interesting. I work, I go home. I hang out with my friends."

"And yet so alive."

"And alive is a good thing?" Wasn't everyone alive and going?

He nodded. "Very."

His intense gaze made me want to squirm, and yet,

I didn't. I raised my eyebrow, facing him head-on. If there was one thing I learned about Grayson between the sheets, it was that I had to match him, challenge him, even. He liked when my fire met with his own fire. "Well, I'll try to stay alive for you."

"Yes, do."

"What about your family?" I took another bite. I was barely hungry, but I needed to do something with my hands . . . and mouth.

He groaned and let his head fall back. "Shall we do this quickly?"

"The quicker the better." I didn't want to linger on family, or the lack thereof, in my case. But I knew with people, a lot of who they are came down to family. Even my limited one had an impact on me.

"Right, my father died before I was born. My mother, a gentle wise woman, raised me. God love her, she was patient even with my antics. I'm a bit devilish, you see . . ." A smirk played on his lips. ". . . my uncle stepped in as a sort of father figure. He wants me to come home more often."

"Why don't you?"

It was the first time I'd seen him slightly uncomfortable. "Stalling that visit, I suppose. Your turn."

I sat up straight and brushed the crumbs from my hands. I was used to this question. I'd practiced it to make minimum impact and maximum exit strategy. "My parents died in a car accident when I was two. I barely have any memory of them. And for a while, I was moved from one foster home to the next. Until they placed me in a group home when I got older."

"And that's where you met Dice?"

"Yep. There was a time when we both thought we might get adopted to separate families, but it never worked out. By the time you hit fifteen, you kind of start to lose hope. So, we made our own family. That's it."

"You're very resourceful."

That wasn't the usual reaction I got. Usually, they held my hand, pulled me closer, or tried to show sympathy with a serious sad face. But Grayson didn't do any of that. There was no pity party. "I like to think so."

"I admire that."

"Why?" *Intriguing.*

He pushed his plate away. "If there's anything I've learned over the years, it's that it's not always blood who is family. I've built my own family, and I find it gratifying."

Why did that make me feel so much calmer? Like he understood what it was like to have people who were important. People I needed. "I like that."

"Me, too."

"So, I've caught your attention." I leaned in closer to him and rested my hand on his leg.

He glanced down at my fingers then back up to my lips. "It would seem so."

My picker might've been broken, but when it came to reading the people around me, I was dead on. I might've turned a blind eye to my gut feelings for a pretty face, but when it came to lying, I was a human lie detector. I met his gaze and held it. "I just want to tell you something."

He waved me on. "Oh, please, do tell."

"I have no interest in playing games." I'd been through enough guys, enough relationships, and enough drama. Could I play games? With the best of them. Did I win? Often. But even the best games eventually lost my interest.

"You, my Little Creature, could never be a game." He moved in closer. Our bodies were nearly on top of each other.

"Oh, no?" I whispered. "Then what am I?"

A deep chuckle rumbled in his chest. "The best kind of playmate."

CHAPTER THIRTEEN

PIPER

*H*e *didn't even try to come in with me.* He walked me home, kissed me good-night, and left me at the door. Left me wanting him after a night of being wined and dined, topped off with great conversation. He was the perfect amount of delicious. I flipped over in my bed, kicking the blankets off then pulling them back on. I'd gotten only a few hours of sleep, and I couldn't quite figure out why. My mind was a whirl, analyzing every little touch or thing he said. Even more so, thinking about the night before. I flopped over onto my stomach and shoved my face into the pillows trying to find an ounce of sleep.

I counted to one hundred and focused on the little flickers of light dancing behind my eyes. *Deep breath in, deep breath out.* It wasn't exactly the early morning hours, but for a bartender, it was. I flipped over again and shoved my pillow into the right position and lay down with a sigh. I kicked my leg out like it was a temperature gauge to cool my too-hot skin. The man was addictive, completely and totally addictive. I didn't know up from down. But deep down, I liked the excitement of it all. It was a different kind of high, knowing he was going to be around for the foreseeable future. I should've been able to sleep in, to rest easy with the feel-good excitement. But I was too worked up to sleep. Deep down, I wanted to see him again. I almost craved it. Being around Grayson was intoxicating in a way I couldn't explain. My phone vibrated on the bedside table, and I scrambled for it. My pillow fell off the side of the bad as I sat up and kicked some of the blankets off. I slid open my phone and went to the text messages.

One hour. Be ready. -G

I jumped from the bed and hurried to my dresser. *Be Ready.* Two little words sent shivers down my spine and excitement through my body.

An hour later, I was showered, shaved, and dressed to the nines in my black boots, leather skirt, and black V-neck sweater. I let my hair fall wild down my back and around my face. I took extra time putting dark liner around my eyes just to make them pop. One last finger-comb through my hair and I was ready. I darted from the bathroom and slammed into Dice. Her hair was a tangled mess of knots, and her eyes were barely open.

She glared at me. "What the fuckkkkkkk?"

"Gotta go. I'll text you later." I waved to her as I hurried down the stairs.

"No devil dick is worth being up this early!" she called after me, but I was already in the living room.

I didn't know if I should sit and wait, or if I should put on my coat and go outside. I paced back and forth for a whole two minutes that felt like an eternity before the doorbell rang. I forced myself to take a breath. *Calm down, Piper, calm the hell down.*

When I opened the door, he stood there in the late morning sun, caressing his hair, with that half-smile on his face. "Hello, Little Creature."

"Hey." I tried to play it cool but couldn't stop the butterflies dancing in my stomach.

"Shall we go?" He offered me his arm in the gentlemanly way I wasn't used to.

I stepped down onto the steps and took it. "Where are we going?"

"I thought we might have a bit of an adventure today." His accent was light and playful, like at any moment he was going to be like, Psych, you suck and I'm out. Even being around him for two minutes made his mood infectious.

"Oh, adventures are the best form of entertainment."

He turned and motioned to a dark, sleek-looking BMW 840i sitting on the curb. The windows were tinted nearly black, and I could tell the car was a driving machine. "Then let us have one for the day."

"Are you after my days?" We walked down the stairs and stopped at the car, and he opened the door for me. I dropped into the deep seats that seemed to hug my every curve. They were already warm, and a steady stream of heat blew on my feet. The dash was lit up like a rocket ship. Even the gear shift glowed.

"Nights, too." He winked and closed the door as soon as I was seated.

I chuckled. "Greedy."

He was in the driver's seat within seconds, pulling his seatbelt on. "Greed is just another word for allowed to have some fun."

I raised my eyebrows at him. "I didn't think one of the seven deadly sins should be a guideline for fun?"

He threw his head back and laughed as he pulled away from the curb. "Eh, they're more like suggestions, if you ask me."

"Kind of like the yellow light you're about to go through?" I pointed to the traffic light hanging in front of us.

"It's not red, is it?" He didn't take his eyes off me.

I dared to glanced away from him. "No."

He pushed the accelerator and the car surged forward, and I sank into the seats. Dark slush splashed up around the tires, and he didn't even blink. He motioned to the open street before us. "See, just a suggestion."

"Do you always live like this?" I motioned to the car and the world around us. Grayson treated it all like a playground. Like every day was made for fun. Yet, deep down, there was something behind his eyes. Something serious lingered behind those mahogany depths.

Shrug. "Sometimes I work."

"Work hard, play harder?" I barely observed that world speeding by us. I didn't pay attention to how fast we drove or where we were going. It was just me and him in this tiny space together with all the time in the world ahead of us. And I wanted to know him, to know everything he could ever want to tell me.

"Any time you want it harder all you have to do is ask." He gave me a sideways glance that was half-playful, half-serious. He turned the wheel, guiding the car down another street.

I chuckled. "Oh, you don't have to worry. I'll tell you exactly what I want when I want it."

"Direct." He pulled onto a highway. "I like that."

"What else do you like?" I wanted to know more about him. It was all part of the game, wasn't it? Prying knowledge from each other to decide if we actually liked one another or not. While at the same time appearing to not pry too much while remaining interested. That was dating in a nutshell. But with Grayson there was something different. I felt . . . freer.

"In London, there are nights when it gets so cold, all you can do is hunker in and listen to the rain next to the fire. Perhaps with a good book. But also, it falls like a blanket of silence. Not very different from the snowfall in the winter here. That I like. I prefer nights to days. I prefer to do rather than to do not."

How intriguing. "So, take a chance?"

"Indeed. On everything. At least once." He curved off an exit ramp and guided the car easily to a restricted area.

I glanced around and didn't recognize a single thing. "Where are we?"

"Do you trust me?"

For the first time in forever, I could answer this question honestly. "Yes, I do."

How odd it felt to say that I well and truly trusted someone. It wasn't a feeling I was used to, but for some reason it came so easily with Grayson. Like, he didn't go through my walls—he just danced right around them. When, in reality, I wanted him to get beyond my walls. I wanted to trust someone, to have them near and know they were mine and I was theirs. It was a simple way of thinking, and it wasn't real life, but it'd be beautiful if it could be.

He waved to the guard and the gate slid to the side. We pulled through a thick fence. The car glided forward until we reached a tarmac. A lone private jet stood waiting with the door open and the stairs lowered for passengers. I sat forward, looking around at the hangar and the bright lights of the airport. "Are we flying somewhere?"

"Would that bother you?" He put the car in park and unbuckled his seatbelt.

I shook my head as threads of excitement nearly had me bouncing in my chair. "So long as we could be back for my shift tomorrow."

"Do we have a curfew then?" He opened his door and started to get out.

"Not on your life." I heard his light chuckle as he closed the door behind himself.

I watched his easy swagger as he strolled around the front of the car and to my side. He opened the door and offered me his hand. "Shall we?"

I took it. I didn't know where we were going or what we were doing, but my heart was hammering in my chest with delight. No one had treated me like this before. I was lucky to get a slice of pizza and a drink out of most guys. But Grayson clearly took the time to plan this. To do something special just for me. When I rose to my feet, he didn't let go of my hand. We walked to where a man in a pilot's uniform stood at the foot of the steps.

"Mr. Shade, a pleasure to see you again." He was an older man with gray hair fanning back from his temples and deep smile lines around his face.

"Gerald, always good to see you. Allow me to introduce my date, Ms. Santiago." He motioned to me.

I offered the pilot my hand. "Nice to meet you."

"Lovely to meet you, Ms. Santiago." He quickly shook my hand then smiled at the both of us. "Flight time is only an hour, so please make yourselves comfortable."

Grayson stepped to the side and let me go up the stairs first. When I entered the plane, I sucked in a breath. It was like something out of a movie, with plush carpeting, beige leather seating and dark wooden accents. It was masculine but classic. Dots of sunlight streamed in through the little round windows that lined each side of the plane. To my left was a long couch with two lounge chairs, all surrounding a low table. I walked farther into the plane, feeling over-whelmed. "Nice wings you got here."

They both chuckled behind me, and I turned around to face them. The pilot gave me a small nod. "My co-pilot is getting things all set. If you need anything, just pick up that phone." He pointed to it, on the wall near the front. "Otherwise, we'll have the door locked up tight."

"Thank you, Gerald." Grayson gave him a clap on the shoulder, and they went in opposite directions. The pilot found his way to the cockpit, and Grayson strolled past me to the back of the plane.

He opened a cabinet and grabbed two bottles of water. "Drink?"

"Please." I dropped into one of the chairs as Grayson fell onto the center of the couch. He spread his arms across the back of it.

The stairs rose and the door slammed shut, sealing us into the cabin alone. I opened the water and took a sip, trying to calm my nerves. "Do you always travel like this?"

"No."

"So, this is new for you, too?" I glanced out the window as the engines started.

He met my gaze. "No."

"How very cryptic of you." I crossed my legs and his eyes landed on my thighs. I felt them on me, and it heated my skin.

The plane turned to the side and started moving down the runway. "Are you going to tell me where we are going?"

"No."

"A man of few words tonight." I ran my hand over the leather seats and then down my legs. He tracked my every move.

He crooked his finger at me and gave me that half-cocky smile. I rose to my feet and sauntered over to him. But I didn't sit beside him. I waited there, standing with my legs touching his. The warmth from his legs seeped through his pants and into my legs. Grayson tilted his head back and peeked up at me, then he sat forward and ran his hand over the back of my knee. His fingers drifted up my thigh and I widened my stance, giving him more space to move. A tremble ran over my body, and I couldn't hide the anticipation I felt for his touch. When the tip of his finger toyed with the edge of my panties, I gave a little sigh.

"Don't tease me."

"A tease would imply I'm not going to do anything, and I plan on doing many, many things." He slid them to the side and ran his finger over me. Back and forth at a slow, tantalizing speed. My stomach tightened and I wanted more, needed more.

The pilot came over the intercom. "Passengers, please remain seated. Prepare for takeoff."

"Best sit down, love." But he didn't stop teasing my body with his finger.

I dropped one knee next to his hip then threw my other leg over to the other side, straddling him. I rested my hands on the back of the couch just as his finger slid inside me. A moan eased from the back of my throat and my hips bucked of their own accord.

"You're sweet, Little Creature." He moved his hand perfectly to edge me toward that perfect moment, and yet, it wasn't nearly enough.

"Need you." I reached between us and unfastened his belt.

The plane accelerated down the runway and lifted off just as I freed him from his pants. He was ready for me, and I was needy of him. I rose up over him and lowered myself down.

"Aw, fuck, Piper." His hands dug into my thighs as I slid down farther, stretching myself around him.

It was almost too much. So delicious, yet so tantalizing. I moved over him, finding that perfect rhythm for us both. His hand slid up my body and he cupped my cheeks and brought my face down to his. Our lips smashed together as he wrapped his arm around my body, dragging me closer. His tongue tangled with mine, and I dug my fingers into his shoulders, holding on for dear life. I felt every inch of his muscles through his shirt. It was almost our little secret: fully clothed but so connected in the most intimate way.

I threw my head back, arching into him for more. His fingers tangled into my hair, and he ran his tongue over the side of my neck. A deep growl rumbled in his chest, and he slammed his arms across the back of the couch. Sweat beaded his brow as he met my eye. I placed my arms behind me, grabbing onto his knees and slamming my hips down on him. My body tightened around his and I reveled in the feel of him. I needed him hard, fast.

"That's it." He reached down between us and ran his fingers over that little point that would drive me higher.

My breaths came in quick pants. Every muscle went rigid, and my body tightened around him. His hips bucked up into mine, and he didn't take his eyes off me. I couldn't hold back anymore. It was all too frantic to stop now. My body took over and all I could see was him. The muscle in his jaw ticked. "Come on, Little Creature."

With so few words and I edged even closer. He increased his speed, and I was done for. Pleasure shot through my body and a moan escaped my lips. This high in the clouds and I was higher than the plane itself. Grayson wrapped his arm around my hips, flipped me onto the couch, and drove into me. His body slammed into mine and I spread my legs wider for him. A groan rumbled in his chest and he shuddered against me, his breath heavy in my ear. His lips found mine for a perfectly gentle kiss. He pressed his forehead to mine and cupped my cheek. Our excited breaths mingled together, and his lips pulled up in a full smile that mirrored my own.

He ran his hand over my hair, brushing the strands from my face. "Piper, love. You are everything."

CHAPTER FOURTEEN

GRAYSON

"I've never been here before." Piper looked up at the opulent building with a wide grin. The stairs leading up to the Metropolitan Museum of Art were iconic and even now people lounged on them, enjoying their lunch and the atmosphere of the city. Though it was chilly, and our breaths fogged the air, nothing ever seemed to stop on Eighty-second Street. The air was crisp and cooled my skin from the heated moments we'd shared earlier. Her honey scent drifted toward me, and I found myself wanting to be closer.

I stood beside her, looking up at the building and the three huge archways that rose from the stairs up to the roof. Glass windows were stretched between each entrance, and glass doors lined each of the archways.

They reflected the scene across the street back at us as people walked in and out of the Met like it was Grand Central Station.

"New experience. For you, Little Creature." Everything about Piper was new and full of awe. She looked at the world with interest and excitement mixed with a healthy dose of skepticism. She was nobody's fool and yet the most alive woman I'd ever met. A thing that I had long since lost. But with her, I found it again —that zest for life that left a vampire.

She rolled her eyes. "I've had plenty of experiences. More so than most."

"Yes, but not with me, and I plan on adding to your list." When we reached the door, I pulled it open for her.

"You already have. I'm an official member of the mile high club now. Thanks to you." She ran her hand over my chest as she walked by, then dropped it and kept going.

I chuckled and shook my head. I followed her into the Great Hall, where she stood frozen, staring up at the high, vaulted ceilings. The Met was beautiful in a bright marble white sort of way. People wandered in all different directions, and a low hum of chatter filled the air. It wasn't like being at a stadium but more like that moment before a show started and people were whispering to each other excitedly. There were stairs leading in all different directions and to the many exhibits. I could wander through the collections for an eternity and not lose interest. Except tonight, there was only one thing I was interested in.

"Where shall we go?"

She pointed to the left. "How about Greek and Roman Art?"

"Oh, the Greeks, people never cease to find them fascinating." I turned and the two of us moved together. I found myself reaching for her hand and taking her fingers within mine. It was so tiny yet warm to the touch and fit perfectly.

"Don't you?" She motioned to the first statue we came upon. "The myths are pretty cool. All that power and stuff. Can you imagine having superpowers? Like strength or speed?"

A thread of guilt assailed me. I had all these things —strength, speed. I could hear the conversation two rooms over if I so choose. Not to mention the blood magic that came with my family line. The kind of blood magic I didn't speak of or even dare tamper with. "Hard to fathom, isn't it?"

"What do you suppose it'd be like?" She took a step back and looked up at the statue of Zeus. It was carved from a huge slab of marble and the lights overhead gleamed off its shining surface.

"Exciting and exhausting." I sighed and smiled at the completely inaccurate statue. He was always depicted as an older man with a big white beard and flowing white hair along with flowing robes. In reality, he was an old-as-time swinger having parties day and night.

Piper wrinkled her nose and giggled. "Why exhausting? Seems like it would be fun to me."

"Well, can you imagine the responsibility that comes with power like that?" We turned and headed toward another statue.

She gave my hand a little squeeze. "Do you feel like you have a lot of responsibilities?"

Observant little creature. "Ah, well, interesting you should ask. Sometimes, yes, I do."

"What kind of responsibilities?" She stopped at another statue of a woman. This one was beautifully done, with long flowing hair and full lips. Her eyes were sculpted into a wide round look that gave her a hint of seduction. "Has to be Aphrodite. She's too beautiful not to be."

Aphrodite is beautiful but vapid as the day is long.

"The kind that weighs heavily on the mind and the kind that a woman like you can make me forget." Like forgetting an impending prophecy and forgetting to guard the only witches who could save the world, not to mention a curse that plagued the family name for centuries. I found myself wanting both to return home and to completely avoid it. With Piper in tow, how could I leave, if even for a moment? She breathed life into the mundane.

She began to back away from me with a smile, pulling me along with both hands. "Ohhhh, what a compliment. But also, what a good sidestep of my question. I'll have to be smarter next time and see if I get an answer."

"You, my dear, are bloody brilliant."

She leaned in and gave me a quick little peck on the lips and turned away. "I am, aren't I?"

"Eternally impressive. So, tell me . . ."

"No, no." She wagged her finger at me. "If you aren't going to answer my questions, why would I answer yours?"

"I'll make you a deal." I wrapped my arm around her shoulder and pulled her close to my side. I ducked my head and let my lips brush against her ear.

"More deals with the devil," she whispered as she toyed with the button on my coat.

"More like devilish." I gave her ear a little nip, and she let go of a tiny squeal. "So, no deals?"

"Oh, even the devilish intrigues me. So, tell me your deal and I'll see if my soul is worth it." She spun out from under my arm and pointed to another statue. "Do you think Hades is as dark as they say?"

"Incredibly so, twisted and obsessed with Persephone. Their kid is even more twisted."

She spun out of my hold and walked around a pillar. I held still, waiting to see what the little creature would do next. She peeked at me from behind a pillar on the side of the room and tilted her head to the side like she was thinking. "I haven't read about a kid?"

"I was just, you know, wondering what a kid of theirs would be like." The lie tasted sour on my tongue, and I instantly regretted it. I wanted to tell her the truth about everything. I found myself wanting to tell her the secrets of the world that humans just didn't see or know existed. The Greeks were real and still roamed the earth, using their powers for all sorts of things. Hades and Persephone did have a kid, and he was a shit. But I said nothing.

"So much so you've forgotten your devilish proposal?" She turned and leaned her back against the pillar.

I walked around the pillar and stepped in closer to her, taking in that sweet honey scent that made my fangs ache like a newly-made vampire. It made me wonder what she tasted like. "How could one forget proposals when it comes to you?"

She chuckled and shook her head, sending those wild waves all around her face. "Smooth, so smooth. Now, what's the deal?"

I met her bright green eyes. "You give. I give."

She tilted her head to the side. "And what does that mean exactly?"

"You give some info and I'll give you some in return." Truth was, I wanted to tell her everything, or at least as much as I could without bringing down Vampire royalty and the Fallen on myself.

Our world was a secret one, and it had to stay that way. The Fallen, a group of deadly fallen angels, ruled our world with an iron fist. Any information being leaked to the humans would set any of them off, and it would mean my head. But for Piper, I would push that line and more.

She licked her lips and her eyes danced with excitement. "Deal."

Oh, the games she liked to play. I so enjoyed them. "And your first question is?"

"Responsibilities? What are they and why avoid them?" She twisted away from me and sauntered out of the room toward another filled with brightly colored African art. The pieces were each eloquently sculpted and covered in bright reds, yellows, and greens—all vibrant, natural colors that spoke of nature.

I trailed closely behind her as she walked in a small circle around a mask set on a display stand. She gave me a coy smile then looked away, making me want to get her attention even more. "I'll wait."

She waved a dismissive hand and turned away from me to look at another piece, almost like she knew I would follow. I strolled close to her side. "My uncle would like me to return home and . . . take over the family business. I would prefer otherwise."

Her lips twitched like she was fighting a smile. "What does your uncle do?"

"No, no. I gave. Your turn to give." If this was the game, I was going to play to win. And the win would be knowing Piper inside and out. The fascinating creature that she was.

Her face fell and her eyes narrowed in that guarded way she had about her. Like talking about herself made her uncomfortable. "Tell me your fondest memory from childhood?"

She pressed her fingers to her lips thinking. "Hmm, that's a good one."

I waited as she let another piece of art capture her attention. She stood there for long moments just taking it all in, while all I did was stand there and take her in. I studied her every expression, the way her body glided, and the way her hair flowed with each of her movements. She was captivating.

"Once, when I was younger, they took us all to this woman's house. She donated her time to the kids. She was an artist and gave us lessons. We got to paint and make little sculptures. I was horrible at it. I'm not much of an artist."

"Why did you like it?"

"Because it was perfect and fun. She had us at her house and it was all eclectic art everywhere. My own personal Met. I loved every minute of it."

"It does sound fun." I'd never experienced something like that. Just kid stuff. But two hundred years ago, they didn't have art lessons for children. "But you're not an artist?"

"God, no." She snort-laughed. "You should see the stuff I made. It's unrecognizable."

"I'd love to see it." I wanted to see everything.

"Not on your life," she teased and walked away from me.

I enjoyed this, being wrapped around her little finger. It was a new experience for me. Apparently, Piper was full of things I hadn't had in my long, long time here on this earth. "Next question?"

"Ohhh, aren't we in a giving mood?"

"I tend to be generous, yes." I waved her on as we strolled into a room full of contemporary art. It wasn't my favorite, but I appreciated it for what it was. "Ask me."

"When was your last relationship?"

I chuckled. "Define relationship."

"Play on, player." She gave me a bump with her elbow but the muscles around her mouth tensed ever so slightly. Like she was putting on a playful bravado, but her guard went up just a bit more at the thought of me being a player.

"Nothing like that, Little Creature. I just haven't had my interest caught in a while. My last relationship was many years ago. She was lovely. But in the end, we were better off as friends."

She gave me a skeptical look. "Does she think that?"

I pulled out my cell phone and handed it to her. "Call her if you like. I'm sure you'll both get on quite well."

Piper scoffed. "Ballsy. I like it. Kind of like that weird painting over there."

"You know I rather like you." Truer words were never spoken.

A breathtaking smile spread across her face. "Mutual adoration it is, then."

She is eternally charming. "And what is it that you want today?"

She wrapped her arms around my waist and pulled me in closer, hugging me to her. My arms fell around her shoulders, and she looked up at me with those hypnotic eyes of hers. "Nothing less than the world."

CHAPTER FIFTEEN

PIPER

*E*xhaustion overwhelmed my body. I felt it in my bones and in the tenderness of my muscles. Even my eyes were dry and heavy. I stumbled into my bedroom and nearly fell over as I ripped off my work shirt. After spending the entire day yesterday walking around the city with Grayson and working my insane shift tonight, I was beat. All I wanted was my bed and to let the oblivion of sleep take me. It was busier than I'd seen it in weeks. I threw my shirt into a pile on the floor and quickly peeled my jeans down my legs and kicked those to the ever-growing pile of laundry as well.

I dragged myself to the closet and picked up the sweatpants I'd worn the day before and yanked them onto my legs. They were warm, fuzzy, and comfortable. I spun around in a circle and grabbed my favorite sweatshirt off the foot of the bed and shoved my arms in. It was dark gray and fell off one of my shoulders but also baggy enough for it to do exactly what I needed. I was looking for my full comfort mode, complete with warm fuzzy blanket, pillow, and sweats. All I needed was the perfect messy bun and my night was made. Dice was already passed out down the hall, and I was left to my own devices. I hadn't seen or heard from Grayson all night, but I'd gotten a "Good morning, beautiful. Have a nice day." via text and it was more than enough for me.

Something was moving differently between us. It was like even when he wasn't there, I carried him with me like a second skin. I could almost feel his moods and intentions from a distance. He occupied my thoughts daily and I couldn't say I was sorry about it. There was a point, and I didn't know when it happened, that he turned into the person I wanted to say good morning to first and good night to at the end of the day. It'd happened so fast and so naturally, like we were always meant to be. I didn't know how I felt about that. Part of me wanted to rebel against losing my heart to a guy like Grayson. The other part of me . . . well, for the other part of me, it was too late.

As if summoned by my thoughts, my phone buzzed

with a text from him. *Hello, Little Creature. How was your night?*

Crazy busy. I sighed and fought the urge to climb into bed. If I lay down now, I would be out cold, and I just wasn't ready to say goodnight to him yet.

My phone vibrated again with another message. *You must be knackered.*

Exhausted. I wasn't lying. Even my eyelids were trying to force me to sleep.

Those three little dots popped up, then his message came through. *Best get you to bed.*

I chuckled. *Cheeky Brit. Always trying to get me into bed.*

I consider it my life's work.

Laughter burst from my lips. *My, my, aren't we ambitious. And here I am with a goal of finding my favorite fuzzy socks.*

Open the door and I'll help you look.

I froze. He couldn't be here. Not now. Not when I looked like . . . this. This ensemble wasn't a dating stage outfit. And though I was falling for him and felt totally connected to him, this was a 'we're entirely too comfortable with each other but it was still all the love' kind of outfit. One that someone wore when they'd been together for longer than six months. Not in the new stages. I stared down at my phone for a moment trying to decide if I needed to change or just go for it.

Chuck it in the fuck it bucket. I sighed and walked out of my room and down the stairs past the kitchen and living room then straight to the front door. I hesitated for a moment, still debating with myself if I should change into my "cute" loungewear, and decided nope, he was going to get the real me. This is what I was. I grabbed the doorknob and turned the handle. When I yanked the door open, there he was. In all his hotness glory.

He leaned against the doorjamb. "Hello, Little Creature."

"Hey." I rested my head against the door.

I expected him to be dressed in his dark jeans and one of his even darker sweaters that were clearly expensive and looked like they were made just for him. Instead, he stood there in his gray sweatpants and a long sleeved black thermal shirt that clung to his sleek, muscular body. His peacoat hung open, and a dark scarf lay smooth around his neck. He looked good even in lounge clothes. *So damn good.*

I stepped back and opened the door wider for him. Without a word, he strolled through the door like he owned everything in sight. He spun around and looked at me. "I love the place. It's very well done."

I glanced around at out little slice of Salem heaven and gave him a smile. "It is, isn't it?"

Uncertainty riddled my body. I didn't know what to do next. Exhaustion ate at me, and I found it difficult to muster the excitement I actually felt about seeing Grayson. He stepped in closer to me and ran his hand over my cheek. "You look right knackered, love."

"Is that a nicer way of saying I look like shit?"

His lips parted in a smile. His eyes softened as he looked me over, and something in my chest fluttered. His thumb brushed over my skin. "You could never appear so."

Charmer.

"Not even like this?" I motioned to my baggy sweatshirt and pants.

"A good friend of mine told me never to trust a girl who didn't wear sweatpants when she was alone." He let his hand run all the way down my arm to my wrist. Then he reached for my hand and twined his fingers with mine.

"Words to live by." I swayed on my feet and gave him a slow blink.

"I think bed is in order for you." He turned for the stairs and tugged me behind him. He didn't rush up the stairs or pull me too hard. There was nothing ever hurried about Grayson. It was a slow calm pace, like he knew I couldn't move any faster. When he reached the second floor, there were only four doors to choose from: mine, Dice's, the bathroom, and a closet. He didn't even look at me, just turned and headed straight for my door.

"How'd you know which one is mine?"

He glanced at me over his shoulder. "Lucky guess?"

I rolled my eyes. "Like I'm going to believe that. Are you stalking me?"

"If you must know . . ." He opened the door and pulled me inside. "It smells like you."

I fought the urge to lift my arm and take a whiff. "And what exactly do I smell like?"

"Honey and sunshine. The loveliest thing in the world." He pulled me farther into the room and then turned to close the door behind me.

Heat rushed my face. "Do I?"

He drew me in closer and leaned in. My heart skyrocketed as he came nearer. At the last second, he tilted his head to the side and pressed his lips to my neck in a light kiss. His lips were soft and warm on my skin. My toes curled at his slightest touch. Connection bloomed between us. Except this time, it was more and deeper than I could've imagined.

"If only you could see what I see."

I tried to look at my room and see it through his eyes. The walls were a light gray that I found soothing. I had a queen-size bed with a messy burgundy comforter balled on top of it. The pillows were strewn in all different directions. In the far corner stood a single dresser that I repainted a bright white myself after getting it from a garage sale last summer. Clothes were spread over the floor and spilling out of the closet. A single TV was mounted on the wall opposite the bed.

"Guess I should've cleaned up."

"I wasn't talking about your room, love." He chuckled.

I sighed. "I'm too tired to talk about me."

"Indeed." He guided me toward the bed and motioned for me to lie down.

When I climbed onto the smooth, crisp sheet, all the tension left me. I leaned back on the pillows, letting them cushion my head perfectly. It was like lying in my own personal bubble of comfort. I sighed and wriggled in, making myself comfortable. Grayson slid his coat from his shoulder and threw it over the corner of the bed along with his scarf. Then he walked around the bed and snagged the remote off the side table. He flicked the TV on and found an old movie I didn't recognize, but at this point, I didn't care. All I wanted was him curled up next to me for the night.

He kicked off his shoes and climbed in beside me. When I made no move, he grabbed the blanket and fanned it out over the two of us, making sure I was completely covered. He threw his arm over my head and slid it in behind my shoulder. With the lightest touch, he pulled me in closer to him. I tucked into his side and rested my head on his chest. He was so warm, so soft. The position felt so natural to me, and yet we'd never lain like this before. It was so . . . familiar.

"You don't have to clean up for me. Everything is perfect just the way you are. It's human, no?"

A yawn overtook me for a moment. "I suppose so."

He moved his leg in between mine and I tucked mine over his. We fit together like two perfect pieces. It was so comfortable, so warm. I slipped my hand under his shirt and rested it on his stomach. Grayson flinched ever so slightly.

"Bloody hell, woman. Have you been keeping those in the icebox?" Yet, he didn't move away, didn't try to shove my hand back. He simply held there, letting me torture him with my cold fingers. They started to warm against him, and I felt myself melting into his side.

"I'm sorry if I pass out on you. I'm sure this isn't what you had in mind."

He ran his fingers through the little strands of hair hanging from my bun. "As a matter of fact, this is exactly what I had in mind." His words rumbled in my ears. "I just wanted to spend time with you."

If I hadn't fallen for Grayson Shade by now, that might've thawed my frigid heart and made me his. I glanced up at him. "I'm glad you decided to."

"Most brilliant decision I've ever made." He pulled me tighter, and warmth spread over the two of us.

It wasn't the frantic, electric pulse I felt when we were intimate. This was different. It was like the entire world faded away and there was nothing else but the two of us curled up to each other so close we were nearly one. Connection bloomed between us. I felt it deep in my soul. It was like finding someone I'd known all my life. Familiar. It wasn't an I-finally-found-you moment. No, this was like an oh-there-you-are-I've-missed-you kind of a moment. How was it possible to miss someone you'd never met but at the same time feel the complete relief that came along with finally finding them? Lying next to him, I felt whole. Grayson sighed and rested his head against mine. He held me tight to his side like I was his most cherished thing. This was perfect. This was us. This was what I'd been searching for and didn't even know it.

When the realization hit me, I nearly jolted out of my skin, but I held still. There was no way I was going to ruin this moment between the two of us, but all I could think was, *must be love.*

CHAPTER SIXTEEN

PIPER

*A*n hour had passed since the bar closed and still no sign of him. Worry ate at my insides, but I also didn't want to come off as some kind of crazy girlfriend. But at the same time he'd never not shown up when he said he'd be there. Well since the first time. This morning, he slid out of my bed with a light kiss and a promise he'd be here, and yet . . . nothing. I pulled my phone from my purse for the third time. No messages. I didn't want to be *that girl*. The girl who chased the guy who didn't actually want to be caught. If he didn't want to be around me, then fuck him. Maybe last night was too much for him? It was the most intimate night of my life, and all we did was sleep.

Last night, something was different between us. We weren't playing or dancing around each other. It was easy and pure. Just the two of us wrapped up in each other. I'd fallen asleep against his chest with his fingers in my hair. I still remembered the exact rhythm of his heartbeat and the steady way his breath brushed through my hair. The warmth of his arms around me and how safe I felt was burned into my mind. So why after a normal, nice night like that would he just not show up?

"I'm going to text him." I sat in my big comfy chair and yet couldn't find a comfortable position. I sat forward then leaned back, then forward again.

"If you don't text him, I'm going to take your phone and do it for you." Dice sat in her own chair, playing on her phone. She didn't look up from the screen, just kept playing the game.

"I'm gonna do it." I typed across the screen a perfectly tailored text. "How does this sound? Hey, just wanted to make sure we are still on for tonight?"

She paused and looked up from her phone. "Add the eggplant and splashing emoji and I think you've got true poetry."

"Dice, come on. This is serious. He's going to stand me up, and this time I really have no idea why." Just the thought of that made my heart sink. I more than liked Grayson. There was so much fire between us, I didn't understand why he wouldn't show up. I hit send and waited for it to say delivered. Once it did, I flopped back onto the chair.

We'd spent some mind-blowing nights together and yet last night was so simple, so benign. Just falling asleep in each other's arms. Flashes of the two of us wrapped up in my blanket ran through my head—even the way we curled together, so perfectly, like two imperfect pieces coming together. It wasn't passionate or frantic, it was just *nice,* connected to him in a way I'd never been connected before. I looked down at my phone. No three little dots telling me he was going to respond, just the delivered message.

I jumped to my feet. "I can't just sit here and wait. If he wants to be done, then he needs to say it to my face."

"I think you have to give him more than thirty seconds to respond."

I shook my head. "No, I know something is wrong."

"Orrrrr, you're letting your past experiences color this one. He's probably just running late. You've got to relax." She pulled the blanket from the back of the chair and wrapped it around her legs.

There was something off. I knew it deep in the pit

of my stomach. He wasn't coming. I knew he wouldn't. But I had to know why. We were perfection together. None of it made sense. Not unless he didn't like me the way he said he did. *Rules to live by, Piper. When a guy acts like he doesn't want you. . . believe him.*

"I'm just gonna go ask. Calmly and rationally." I walked over to the coat rack and pulled my jacket off the hook and shoved my arms into the sleeves.

"Right, because the way you're beating up your coat says calm and rational." Dice waved to the door. "Go forth and collectith a new set of balls for our mantel."

I shoved my feet into my boots and yanked open the door. "I'm not collecting his balls."

Yet.

"Sure. Text me later." Dice waved to me and slouched back into the chair, burying her nose in her phone.

"I will." I walked out the door with my head up and shoulders back. I curled my hands into fists, giving myself the bravado I didn't feel. Maybe I would get to his hotel room, and he'd just overslept, or perhaps some work came up for him.

Right, and he just forgot to send a text that'd take two seconds.

No, don't be like that. He's a good guy. He'll show up. He said he would.

And being late and not saying a damn word about it isn't a sign.

I was both disappointed in him and myself. So disappointed I didn't feel the cold or the icy sleet that fell around me. My boots slipped on the sidewalk, but I still wasn't going to stop. I was only a few blocks from the hotel. I took a smaller back road toward Salem Commons. It wasn't the direct street, but it would get me there fast enough. The streets were dark and empty, but this was my hometown, and I was used to it. This would be simple. I would just go to the hotel and ask him what's up. I didn't want a guy who didn't want me or got scared after one perfect night. Of that, I was sure. And I was damn good at walking away from that situation. It hurt, but I was good at it.

Any act that said they didn't want me, and I was gone. One of the rules to live bye. *Don't stay where you're not wanted.*

And if Grayson didn't want me, then I needed to hear it and move on. Was I being irrational? Probably. Emotional? Absolutely. But I was in too far now. I'd given a piece of myself to Grayson without even meaning to. This wasn't normal for me, and I wanted, no, I needed some stability to make me feel comfortable with that. And him not showing up wasn't helping with how vulnerable I'd made myself to him. I steadied myself for it. How could I have been so wrong? How could I have let my guard so far down in so little time? I was angry at myself and him at the same time. I fell for it so fast. It was so normal between us, natural, like breathing.

A lump formed in my throat. *NO. This is stupid.* I was not going to get upset just yet.

Maybe something did happen.

Who was I kidding? When it came to being abandoned, I knew, women knew when a man wasn't going to show up. It was intuition at its best, or were they just that predictable? Either way, we knew. But Grayson wasn't predictable, and yet in my heart I knew this was it. I just had to hear it for myself and know I wasn't crazy.

Why?

I opened my phone once more and stared down at the screen. I stepped off the curb and into the street. My boot slid on the ice. My arms pinwheeled and my phone slipped from my fingers and went flying into the gutter. I tilted forward then back. My body twisted and I suddenly stopped, catching myself before I face-planted in the street. I shook my head. *Great, just great.* That's all I needed, busting my ass in the middle of the street. I finally got my balance enough to take another step toward the curb.

Tires screeched and a horn blared. My head snapped up and all I saw were blinding headlights . . .

CHAPTER SEVENTEEN

GRAYSON

"*I*t's my bloody hour of need and where are you?" My voice rose with aggression as I pressed my cell phone harder to the side of my head.

Sav yawned on the other end of the line. "Where are any of us really? It's a question I ponder often."

"Are you taking the piss right now?" I paced back and forth from one end of my hotel room to the other. Even though it was a king suite, with my speed it only took a matter of seconds.

"I'm not taking the bloody piss. However, I do recall forewarning you that this would be a problem. I've not got psychic written next to my name and even I could see this coming." The sound of a crackling fire filled the background and light classical music drifted along with it.

Anger flared through my body. "Are we having a night to ourselves? Am I interrupting with my issues?"

"No need to get yourself in a strop."

I froze in the middle of the room trying not to crumble the phone in my hand. "I'm not in a strop."

"And one would perceive that this anger and attitude would indeed classify a strop."

"You're a wanker, do you know that?" I turned and headed for the bathroom. Every one of my muscles was rigid with tension.

He gave a dark chuckle. "Yet, you're the only one with the bollocks to say it to my face."

"Oh, I'll say it to your face." I stopped in front of the mirror and stared at myself for a moment. My hair was a disheveled mess. I looked more rested than I'd ever been, but my clothes were rumpled up and I'd never been more worried.

I'd woken up this morning with the lightest, most pleasant feeling in the world. Like everything was right and all I wanted was more of her. There wasn't a single thing I could think of that was more important or pressing. And therein lay the problem. Piper was slowly consuming me with her witty, sassy vivaciousness, and her sweet gentle side. The scary part was, I wanted to let her. I needed to talk to Sav, to get my head on straight. How could one little creature have me so backwards?

I hung up on him. This wasn't the type of conversation that needed to happen over the phone. I hopped up on the sink and pressed my hand to the mirror. I didn't make it a habit of mirror travel. Truth be told, it was kept secret among the vampire society, and before I went to work with the witches, I'd been told to keep it as such. The folklore was that vampires couldn't see their own reflection. The truth was the natural born Vampires could travel by mirror, but we kept our talent close to the vest. So, we didn't readily go near them in public even if we could see ourselves. But now I was alone, and it was my hour of need.

I closed my eyes for a moment thinking about exactly where I wanted to go and who I wanted to see. I pressed my fingertips to the cool surface of the mirror and let my blood come to life. It wasn't the same kind of power of a witch or warlock, but it was deeper. Vampires felt it in our blood. We were never more aware of our bodies than when we called upon our blood magic. It was a warmth that spread from our chest and out toward our limbs.

The surface gave way to my intentions and rippled under my touch. I opened my eyes and pushed my hand forward. It felt like slowly dipping my fingers into icy water. It drifted up over my skin, chilling me to the bone. The blood in my veins slowed, and my body cooled. I moved forward and stepped into the mirror and walked forward. This was different than magical portals. It was like walking into a long dark hallway with a light at the end. I strolled through there, listening to only the echo of my own footsteps.

My heart raced as I neared the end of the hall. The light was another shimmering mirror, and I pressed my hand to it and shoved my way through. On the other side, warmth touched my fingertips, chasing away the cold of the mirror travel. I shoved even more and stepped into Sav's room. It was the middle of the night in London, and he was already comfortable in his bed. He lay there shirtless, with a red velvet blanket draped low over his hips. Tattoos covered his upper body and laced around his shoulders. Across the room, a huge fireplace flickered with a warm burning light. It popped and fizzled, giving the room a warm glow. Shadows danced between the carved wood paneling that covered the walls. The floors were a dark wood that matched the walls and ceiling. A bevy of shelves lined the wall across from his bed and were full of old books that Sav had collected over the last hundred years or so.

He dropped his book on his chest and glanced up at me with those multicolored eyes of his. "Oh, you've arrived. Shall I call Titus?"

"You'll do no such thing." I curled my hand into a fist and began pacing at the end of his bed.

He rolled his eyes. "Very well. Tell me, reluctant Prince, what brings you home?"

"Don't call me that, and I'm not home." Annoyance ran through my body. I'd never been more so.

"Then what would you suggest I call you? You are the crown Prince, and this is your home."

Don't hit him. Don't hit him. I paused and put my hands on my hips. "Don't be a prat."

He sat up and rested his arm across his knee, giving me a withered look. "Something vexes you?"

"Do you bloody well think?" I began pacing again. The castle had me on edge. Being home was not something I planned on, but something was more important. "That woman. That woman vexes me."

"And this surprises you? Did you not see your own face when you saw her? Like a moth to the flame. Besotted." He shook his head. "Horrible to watch, really."

"Besotted is right." I ran my hands through my hair. "I can't think straight. It's like the woman is under my skin."

I pulled at my shirt, trying to get it away from my skin. She was everywhere, and I wanted it so damn bad I could almost feel her. Sav kicked his legs over the side of the bed and threw his blankets off. He rose to his feet and snatched a shirt off the end of the bed. He glared at me as he shoved his arms into it.

"Did I not warn you of the things to come? Do you wish to suffer the same fate as your father? Because I do not wish it." He slashed his hand through the air. "I do not want to see you fall to the curse, not now, not ever. No woman is worth that. People depend on you. A kingdom is yours to reign, and you are faffing about with some *human*."

He shook his head and glared at me. "I've never seen such selfishness from you."

"Selfish? Me? Really?" I spent months disguised as a much younger vampire to rid the world of evil and protect the future.

"Oh, yes, bloody selfish you are. You'll fall to the curse and then what? For what?" He turned away from me and grabbed the book off the bed and threw it against the wall. It slammed into the wood, splintering it as it wedged into the wood. "A *woman*."

He spat the word as if it was a curse. In this house, love was a curse. A woman could be the end of a good man and there was no going back. Once it was done, there wasn't anything anyone could do to be saved. Love was pain, quite literally, in The House of Shade.

"You're right." I sank down on the edge of the bed. Piper was everything, and that was the problem.

"I am. I don't want to see you descend into madness never to return. You know what must happen to feral Vampires." He sank down beside me.

Feral Vampires, if they couldn't be saved, were either executed or locked away in the dungeons until they eventually died of the madness. The kicker was it usually only affected made vampires, the kind that had to die to become a vampire. The transition was so hard that their fragile minds couldn't handle it. Even so, most made Vampires didn't rise. It took twenty-four hours and if they didn't wake, they were gone forever. It was a gamble that some Vampires took. But when The House of Shade was cursed, none of us believed a born royal vampire would fall to it. Until my father, and cousins, and other distant family did. As the head of the royal family, my uncle would never take a wife and I . . . I would be the same. Because to love was madness and death for any who shared the blood of The House of Shade.

"I'm well versed."

His hair fell over his face and his shoulders sagged.

"I've been the last sight for many of the fallen feral. I don't want to be your executioner. Just not you."

"Then it's decided." I rose to my feet and already felt myself hurting at the thought of not seeing Piper tomorrow or the next day. Sav stood up beside me.

"Where are you going?" My voice sounded deflated and hollow. I didn't want it to be this way between the two of us. I thought we could enjoy each other, be friends and lovers without falling. So many other people lived in relationships like that. But she was too spectacular, and I felt myself growing more attached daily.

"You've got to be daft if you think I'm going to leave you alone to do this. I've seen the way you look at her. Nah, mate, I'm here for the duration."

"You're a Shade man through and through." Atlas Savage was the dangerous right hand of the crown, and he would make sure it was done. Even if deep down I didn't want to, this was the right thing to do for us all.

"More than that, I'm your best mate. So let us go." He walked around me to the full-length mirror that I'd come in from. He pressed his fingers to it, and the mirror gave way under his hand as he pushed through. He glanced at me over his shoulder. "Are you coming?"

"Yes, I am." Trudging through the mirror and back

toward the hotel felt like a death walk. I'd never hesitated more in my life. This had to end. If I fell fully for her, there would be no turning back, and I could kill Piper in the process if I went feral. Humans were so frail, and Piper was no different.

When we stepped through into my bathroom at the hotel, I stood there for a long moment trying to think of every way I could to get out of this. To save us from the chaos that my family curse would bring. I pulled my phone from my pocket to see if she'd messaged me. I was supposed to be there. I'd told her I'd meet her. But I hadn't shown up. I'd done the one thing she hated most. My heart sank to see her one text and to have not answered it.

Maybe that'd make it easier for us both. If she hated me, it might make it easier. When all the while I just wanted to prove to her that she could rely on someone, and it would work out and be okay. But nothing about this was okay.

I tapped my phone in my hand and glanced at Sav. "I have to do it to her face."

Piper deserved at least that much. Deep down it was tearing me up to leave her, but it would be worse knowing she wasn't in this world because of me, all because I was so desperately close to falling for her.

He pressed his lips into a thin line and nodded. "I'll be here."

I headed for the door and walked out, leaving him there to clean up the pieces of myself when I came back. It was easier to focus on the patterns of the green carpet as I walked to the elevator rather than on what I was about to do. The elevator ride was a blur of thoughts and potential faces she'd make when I told her I had to leave. Dread filled me and I didn't want to see the disappointment in her eyes or the hurt that would befall her face. When I got to the lobby, my stomach sank. I knew it would only take me a minute to get to her house from here. It was too fast, too soon. If I waited just a minute longer then we were still together, if only for another moment in time. But why prolong this for either of us?

I was out the door and into the cold air. Icy sleet rained down on me, prickling my cheeks and turning my nose cold. I glanced up at the sky, looking for a hint of the moon and the peace it usually brought me. But there was no peace for me here under the dark cloudy night sky. A subtle hint of honey drifted on the breeze and my whole body ignited. She was here, she was close. Excitement flooded my body at the thought of seeing her. Then came the sharp pain of knowing we had to break up and this would be the last time. My head snapped to the side and there she was, sliding her way across the road with her hands out. Like she was trying to navigate the thick layer of sleet on the road.

The sound of screeching tires filled the air and my heart stopped. "NO!"

I ran toward her using every ounce of my speed. The headlights shined over her body lighting her up. She didn't have time to move or react. A bellow ripped from my throat when I realized I wasn't going to get there in time, either. The car careened around the corner and slammed into her. She flew up over the hood, her legs twisted at weird angles. Her head smacked into the windshield and snapped back. She flew off to the side and the car kept on going, but I couldn't go for them. I only saw her. Only wanted to get to her. I skidded to Piper's side and fell to the ground beside her.

"No! God. Piper." My voice hitched in my throat. Her little body was broken and bloody. A deep gash ran from her hair line all the way down her cheek. Each of her legs was bent at awful angles. My hands fluttered over all her wounds. *What the hell do I do?* The smell of blood filled the air and began to seep from her body. "No, Little Creature, no."

Her eyes fluttered open and closed not seeing anything. "Gray . . ."

Her voice was so thready, so weak. Her breaths were shallow and barely moving her chest. My heart tore from my chest. This couldn't be happening. Not to her. Not tonight. There was no time for an ambulance. They'd never get here in this weather. I ripped my coat off, covering her little body trying to keep it warm. *Where was a bloody witch when I needed one*!

A rattling cough quaked her body and she groaned in pain. Blood sprayed from her lips and coated her face. A lump formed in my throat. "Shh, don't say anything. I've got you."

I pulled her into my arms and held her closer to me. But I felt my jeans soak through with her blood. I threw my head back, screaming, "SOMEBODY HELP ME!"

But there was no one. It was too late, and Salem was a ghost town. Her body quaked in my arms. "Wh-where were you?"

"I'm here, love. I'm here." I brushed the hair back from her face, but when I pulled my hand away it was soaked with her blood.

Every sound was amplified and all I could focus on was the slow shuttered beats of her heart. They were slow and far between. Even her body began to cool. I rocked her back and forth, holding her tighter, trying to protect her from ice and cold.

"Gray, what happened?" Sav was at my side, pulling at my shoulder. "Gray, are you there?"

I couldn't speak through the ball in my throat and could barely see past the tears in my eyes. "Car. She . . . she was coming for me."

Her head fell back, and her eyes slid shut. I felt her body go limp in my arms, and I had to save her. Had to do something. I couldn't let something so exquisite and alive die on the street like this. I forced my fangs out and bit down hard on my wrist.

"What are you doing? No, Gray you can't." Sav yanked at my shoulder trying to pull me away from her.

I shoved him back with my one arm. "No! I have to save her!"

I held my wrist over her mouth and let my blood drip between her lips. I let it fill her whole mouth, but she didn't move, didn't swallow. It'd been too long since I'd heard a heartbeat. I lay her on the ground and pressed her lips together, massaging her throat trying to get her to swallow one last time.

"Please, love. Just drink. Just drink." Shudders wracked me from head to toe. "Oh, God! Let her drink!"

Pain like I'd never known seared my chest and ran up my throat. It was like lava burning me from the inside out. This wasn't us. This wasn't the end of her story. NO! I'd be damned if I let it be. She was everything right with the world, and I'd see her in it.

Sav pulled at my arm. "This is madness. You can't."

"I will save her!" I glared at him. "She will not die this day."

Her heart. I need to get her heart beating. I folded my hands over her chest and started pushing down, forcing her heart to beat. "Beat, just beat. Live! Damn it!"

"She's gone, Gray." Sav dropped down on his knees on the other side of her body. "Piper is gone."

"Don't say that! She's here! She's with me." I pressed down harder, willing her heart to beat and her blood to move. I called upon the blood magic I never use, the kind that controlled things it wasn't supposed to. *LIVE, LIVE, LIVE!* I forced everything I had into her ever-cooling body.

He shook his head and placed his hand over mine. "No, she's not here anymore."

I pumped her heart more and looked down at her beautiful face. I couldn't give up and just leave her here. She was *everything.* "She has to be good. Do you hear me! Stay, Piper, stay."

Sav grabbed my hands harder, forcing me to stop.

"It's too far gone. There's nothing more you can do. Newborns don't survive this amount of devastation."

He wasn't wrong. I knew he wasn't. The transition was hard even for those who were healthy. But I didn't want to believe it. I couldn't believe that no one would see her fiery eyes and playful smile.

"She was waiting for me . . ." My throat tightened "And I wasn't here for her."

"Death comes for us all." He met my eye. "And it has for her on this night."

How? How could he be so calm when the most magnificent thing in the world had left it so suddenly? *I can't just let this light leave.* I reached up, checking between her lips for my own blood. I sucked in a sharp breath. It was gone. There was a chance. She might come back, if only as a newly made vampire. My hands shook as I pulled her broken little body back into my arms.

"She drank it." I pressed a kiss to her forehead. "Good girl, you can do this."

"Gray, it's too far gone. She will not rise." Sav's shoulders sagged. "I'm sorry."

"You don't know that!" All my anger roared at him.

I would have Piper back. This wasn't the end of the story. I refused to believe that it was. She was so strong, so fierce, nothing could stop my Little Creature. I'd seen others come back and she would, too. I had to believe that. I just had to. If I didn't believe it, I might break and fall into a madness that would rival the curse.

"And when she doesn't rise in twenty-four hours?" He motioned to her lying so still in my arms.

I ground my teeth together. "She will. Now, either help me, or you can fuck right off."

Sav sighed then rose to his feet looking down on me. "Fine. Where do you want to bury her?"

CHAPTER EIGHTEEN

GRAYSON

"Are you sure you want to do it here?" Sav dug his hands into the ground, pulling up chunks of frozen earth and tossing them into a pile on the side.

No, of course, I didn't want to do this. But I was out of time and options. I had to save her. I needed to believe that my blood was in her veins, and she would come back. I held Piper in my arms rocking her and praying to whatever deity would listen. Tears leaked from my eyes and my throat had gone raw.

"Just keep digging."

He didn't look up at me just slammed his hands deeper into the ground. "I bloody well know how deep it needs to be."

"Then keep going." I'd picked this place intentionally. There were trees for cover, and it wasn't as visited as the other more famous cemeteries in Salem. I could stay, I could watch, I could wait for her. I had to wait for her. A large brick building with a rounded old bell tower stood beside it and would cast a shadow over a freshly dug grave. I swallowed around the word grave. This wasn't supposed to happen, and it was my fault. Piper wouldn't be cold and dead in my arms if I had been the man she'd hoped I would be.

"I should've been there."

If it wasn't for the bloody curse, I would've been tucked into bed next to her keeping her warm. I was meant to be there, not running away from the purest thing in my life.

"Fate claims what it must."

Sav kept digging, using his vampire strength to get to the right depth. Dirt covered him from head to toe, but I didn't care. I needed Piper to come back to me. There was no other option. Because a world without Piper wasn't a world worth having. I looked down at her and my heart ripped from my chest. She was too pale, her lips too blue, her wild hair too still. My body shook around hers, and all I could do was hold her and protect her in death. I didn't want the cold to touch her. I should've been there for her. I could've stopped the car with one hand. But my delicate Little

Creature wasn't made that way. But she should be. Damn it, she would be.

"Dig faster."

Sav paused and swiped his hand over his forehead. His chest heaved with deep breaths that fogged the cold air. He was soaked through with the sleet, yet he didn't care. He shoved his hair out of his face and threw his head back. "We're there."

I looked down into the dark hole and couldn't imagine laying her there. How did anyone lay a loved one so deep and away? It felt like once I placed her there, she'd be gone from my sight forever. Dead was a way of life, but this couldn't be it. Not for Piper. I held her tighter, fighting the urge to take her away and hold her forever.

Sav reached for her. "Let me lay her down."

"No." I shook my head.

"She will not rise, if she rises, until she is buried properly." Sav held his arms out to me. "Give her to me. I will do this for you."

"Out with you. I'll do it." I couldn't just hand her over. Let her go? No. My stomach turned, and my body repelled at the thought.

With one bounce he hopped out of the hole. He stood over me waiting, not saying a word. I couldn't move. My body was frozen in the moment in time where I just had to hold her for only a minute longer.

Sav placed his hand on my shoulder. "If you're going to do it, it must be now."

He was right. We only had so much time between when my blood was taken and when she could be buried. I reluctantly rose to my feet and stood at the edge of the hole. I couldn't imagine putting her there, and yet I would. I would say goodbye and pray that I would see her again in her next life. There was no light, only darkness, and she deserved all the light in the world. I hopped down and laid her on the cold packed dirt. This wasn't right. None of this was supposed to be. She was so pale against the dark dirt, her hair a matted mess and cuts riddling her body. My stomach rolled and I fought back the waves of nausea that wanted to take me.

I folded her hands over her stomach and straightened her hair. As gently as I could, I forced her legs back into place to lay straight and flat. The sound of her precious bones snapping forced a sob to escape my lips. Tears ran down my face and fell onto her as I brushed my finger on her cheek one last time. *This has to work. Please, God, let it work.*

"Grayson, we must." Sav urged me up out of the grave.

With one last glance at her, I jumped out and landed next to him. I bent and grabbed a hand full of dirt and sprinkled it over her body. I couldn't bear to see her like this. The life had left her face, and it was all my fault. I turned away and hunched over. My stomach rolled, and I fell to my knees trying to catch my breath. I grabbed two more handfuls of dirt and dropped them in. My vision blurred, but I had to keep going, had to cover her.

"Let me do this for you." Sav stepped in front of me and grabbed the dirt.

"No." I reached for more and kept on going.

Sav didn't listen. He moved to the other side of the pile and began helping me, and I didn't have the words to stop him. We worked in silence until I couldn't see her anymore, until the hole was completely full. I dug both my hands into the fresh packed dirt and hunched over.

Let her come back. Please, just let her come back

CHAPTER NINETEEN

DICE

*W*hat the hell does proof of life actually *mean?* I ground my teeth together and slammed the bus bucket down on the end of the bar. The bottles within rattled and shook. I mean, how hard was it to just send a five-minute text. No Devil Dick was *THAT* distracting that she couldn't take five minutes to be like "Hey, I'm not going to be home." or "Hey can you cover my shift? I'm not going to show up." But there was nothing from Piper. Not even a thumbs-up emoji after I sent her . . . I pulled out my phone to check it . . . twelve texts.

"Still no word?" The manager, Andrew, walked up next to me.

I shook my head. "No."

"It's really not like her not to show up. But I'm glad

you could come in to cover the noon shift for her." Andrew was a cute, simple guy. He was about our age but looked younger with short blond hair, light brown eyes, and a clean-shaven baby face.

Don't remind me. I was worried enough as it was. "I know. I have to admit I'm kind of worried."

It wasn't like Piper to not text me or call. We were attached at the hip. More than two hours without communication, and we both would send the other a "You dead?" gif just to check in. But I hadn't gotten anything. And the sinking feeling in my stomach wouldn't stop until I heard from her.

Andrew gave me a solemn nod. "Do you know where she might be?"

I glanced out the window and down the street. "I think so."

He glanced over his shoulder at the empty restaurant. "It's pretty slow right now. Why don't you just go at least check to see if she's okay?"

"Really? Are you sure?" I was already behind the bar reaching into the cabinet for my coat. "I don't want to make it difficult for you."

He waved toward the door. "Dice, go. You two are the most reliable employees we have. Just go check and come back if it's all good."

I threw the strap of my purse over my head,

making it a cross body bag. I ran around the bar and out the door. The only reason I said yes to covering her shift in the first place was because I thought she was okay, and I didn't want either of us to get fired. We had rent to pay, after all. But the later it got, the more that heavy ball in my stomach turned to nervous knots. My mind whirled with thoughts of all the things that could possibly happen, and I instantly regretted my addiction to all things criminal. Serial killer documentaries were not my friend at the moment. Visions of dead bodies in ditches came to mind and I shook them away.

She was probably all curled up in a king size bed with her Sexy Brit while I was over here worrying like a mother hen. And I was no mother hen . . . but a shitty worrier. My mind went to all the things wrong: dead, in an accident, in a coma in the hospital with no one to identify her, kidnapped. Any number of things could've been wrong. Even the weather was bad last night. What if she slipped and cracked her head open just walking? I'd seen her walk . . . it could totally happen.

I hurried to the doors of the Hawthorne Hotel and yanked them open. I marched through straight to the elevators. When Piper hadn't texted me the first night, I made her give me his room number just in case.

When the doors opened, I felt myself getting angrier. She had to be here and when I found her, I was going to kill her then hug her. Then kill her all over again. I stabbed my thumb into the button on the wall several times then crossed my arms over my chest, waiting for the doors to close. When they didn't close fast enough, I hit them again.

"Come on, come on."

The doors slid shut and I hopped from one foot to the other. When I got to his floor, I hurried out the door, the feeling of dread increasing as I got closer. I paused in front of his room for one second before I started banging on the door.

"Piper!" I called through it and banged three more times. "Piper, you suck. Proof of life now, or I will get a fire extinguisher and break the door down."

Nothing. No answer. I pressed my ear to the door. Silence.

I banged even harder and gave the door a kick for good measure. "Piper! Not cool."

"Hey, hon."

I jumped out of my skin and pressed my hand to my heart trying to force it back into my chest. When I turned to the voice, I spotted the maid staring at me from down the hall. "Holy crap, you scared me."

She chewed her gum like a cow while folding a

hand towel next to her cart. "Just thought you might want to know. That hot guy, he's gone."

I stepped back from the door. "What do you mean, gone?"

"Yeah, I haven't seen him. Then the girl at the front desk told me some other hot guy checked him out." She laid the towel on the cart and shrugged. "Thought you might want to know so you could stop all the banging."

I pulled my jacket around me tighter. The sinking feeling got worse. Where were they? What could she possibly be doing? I knew he had a private jet, but things weren't adding up. Time to pull out the big guns. I yanked my phone from my pocket and clicked on her name then to find her location. It wasn't something I used often but I would now. The little blue dot told me she was right down the street at the corner by Salem Commons. What the fuck? If she was having a winter picnic with that hottie, I was going to kill her again and hug her after.

I ran for the elevator and took it back down to the lobby and ran out the door. My boots slid on the sidewalk and my body tilted sideways. Suddenly, I was flat on my back looking up at the sky. Icy slush seeped into my jeans, and I lay there for a minute, just breathing.

I'm definitely going to have words with her.

I pressed my hands to the ground and the little salt pellets they used to melt the ice, which clearly weren't working, pressed into the palms of my hands. I staggered to my feet and dusted my hands off. A growl escaped my lips as I marched down the street. The sound of cracking ice filled my ears with each step I took. I pulled my phone back out of my pocket to make sure it wasn't cracked, and I followed that little blue dot on my screen all the way down the street to her. I stopped when it said I was where she was. I looked up and spun in a circle. No sign of her anywhere.

"What the hell?" I ran my hand through my hair, tugging at the strands.

I brought up her number again. This time I hit the call button. Her ring tone blared to life, and I spun around again searching for her. Nothing. I held my phone away from my ear and tried to find it. I took a step closer to the street and looked down. There it was. Beat up and in the gutter. If she wasn't so clumsy and had to get a heavy-duty case, it would've been toast.

When I snagged it, I held it up. Tiny crimson spots that looked like blood clung to the corner of the case.

Oh.

My.

God.

"Piper!" I looked around once more and there was no sign of her.

My hands shook as I dialed 911 on my own cell. *Breathe, Dice, Breathe.* But I couldn't. I knew something was wrong. It was like a sharp pain in my stomach that wouldn't go away. Like a tingling on the back of my neck that sent chills down my spine.

"911, what's your emergency?"

My voice quaked. "H-hello. Something happened to my friend."

"What's happened, ma'am?"

I looked around once more and suddenly everything felt too bright, too loud, too out of control. "I-I don't know. She's just gone."

"Ma'am, can you tell me where you are?"

"North Washington Square over by Brown Street." My voice quivered. "I just think, I just think something horrible happened."

"Police are on their way. If you'll just stay on the line until they ar—"

I hung up. What happened to her? She'd never leave her phone or me. We were like sisters. I couldn't explain it, but we just knew stuff about each other. Moods, feelings, desires, it was all just known between us. We didn't have to voice it or say anything —we just knew. And right now, I knew she was not okay. I felt it in my bones. Sirens wailed in the distance, and I held still. I didn't know what else to do or who else to call. I had to find Piper. Something was very wrong.

A police car screeched to a halt right next to me and two officers ran out of their car and approached me. The one on the right got to me first. He was taller with dark hair and pale skin. "Ma'am, did you call 911?"

I nodded. "Yeah."

He looked me up and down then looked around the park. "What's your name?"

"Dice, my name is Dice." I held her phone close to my chest. "My friend is missing. Something happened to her."

He held his hand out to me. "Do you know where your friend is now?"

"No." I shook my head. Was he kidding? Anger flared in my chest. They were supposed to help. "That's why I called you."

"Calm down." The other cop, the shorter one, strolled up in front of me. "How do you know she's missing?"

"She didn't come home last night, and I just found

her phone on the street." I held it out to them. "I found it here."

The taller one glanced down at it. "What's your friend's name?"

"Piper Santiago."

"How old is she?"

"Twenty-three." I watched them both just stand there. "Are you going to do anything? Write this down? File a report?"

They shared a look, and I grew impatient. "What? Someone say something!"

The shorter one sighed. "We can't file a report. For at least three days."

"Three days!" She was gone now. "It's already been like twelve hours. Three days is too long. We need to start looking now."

"Ma'am, there is nothing we can do right now. But you can come down to the station and fill out a missing persons report in two more days. That's how long we have to wait by law."

I had to find her now! Not three days from now! Anyone could be anywhere in the world in three days. "She could be dead in three days. Please help me. I'm begging you. She's not like this. She doesn't just leave. I swear it."

"I hear you. I really do. But there isn't anything we

can do. Come to the station in a few days and bring a picture, then we can get the report done." He handed me his card and without thinking I took it.

Was he for real? "B-but she needs help now."

"Frankly, you don't know that. She could just be out with another friend and lost her phone."

I shook my head. "She doesn't have other friends. I am it."

The taller one waved it away. "I bet she turns up at some point."

"Probably dead, no thanks to you!"

They didn't say anything just started backing away and heading to their car. I took a step toward them then froze. They really weren't going to do anything to help us. To help her. My panic turned into anger and determination. If they weren't going to help me look then I would do it my damn self. And I knew exactly where to start. With the last person who saw her, that sexy Brit . . . Grayson Shade.

CHAPTER TWENTY

GRAYSON

"We can stay no longer." Sav stood over me with his arms crossed over his chest.

"Then leave me." I'd been sitting here for two days. Two days of waiting for Piper to rise was one day too many, but I had to wait. Something in me just couldn't leave her here. The thought was abhorrent to me. Leaving her . . . no.

"You cannot remain. If she hasn't risen in twenty-four hours she's not going to." Sav squatted down beside me. "You've been in the elements for days, without food, water, or blood. You cannot carry on as such."

I bared my fangs at him and hissed. "Piss off."

He sighed. "It is time for you to accept this."

Deep down, I knew he was right. Piper was broken before we even started the transition. I wanted to believe that she was strong enough. But I felt she was gone. I placed my hand over the cold dirt and tried to remember her the way she'd always been to me: alive. Yet, flashes of her sightless eyes looking up at the sky filled my memory. "Where were you?" The question hit me like a ton of bricks. Where was I? I was scurrying about trying to avoid a curse that I didn't even bring down on my family. If only I had been there as I should have been. Piper and I, we belonged together. There was no doubt in my mind. Had it been even a day longer, I would've fallen head over heels in love. As it stood now, I was deeply attached, and it was my own damn fault I would never see her again.

I couldn't even explain to Dice what happened. I tried to save her, and I couldn't. That failure would haunt me for the rest of my life. It was such a human way to die, and I'd seen some messed up things in the supernatural world of Evermore. But this, in the real world, was the worst waste of life a person could possibly bear.

My eyes were dry of tears. Too many of them had fallen to the ground where she lay. The constant ache in my chest wouldn't ever leave me. I knew the pain of grief and would hold it close always as a reminder of what I had done and what I had lost. The world would be a little more gray. There would be no joy in art without her, and I could only pray that each time I got a smell of honey, it would remind me of her in this infinite life I had to spend alone.

I rose to my feet, and black dots swarmed my vision. I'd spent two days on my knees praying for a miracle I knew wouldn't come. "She needs a gravestone."

"I'll see to it for you."

"You'll show it to me before we place it here." I couldn't take my eyes off the dirt. "And you'll make it so her friend has closure. I don't want Dice to spend her life searching."

Sav nodded. "I'll see you home, then I'll return and ensure all is well."

"You're a good friend, Sav." I turned and met his eye. "Now take me home."

Maybe everyone was right. Maybe we were all damned to be cursed. And I was no exception. But I would return to where the cursed belonged. My life was never meant to be my own, and losing Piper like this proved that. I was cursed. I was damned. I had nothing else, and now it was my time to return to The House of Shade.

CHAPTER TWENTY-ONE

GRAYSON

High on top of a hill overlooking dreary London stood The House of Shade. It was the home I'd grown up in and at one time loved. I'd always known I had a duty to my people and to the crown. Lately, it seemed to weigh just a little bit heavier. I stood in my room staring out over the countryside and London in the distance. The grass had long since turned brown with the incoming cold and had only sporadic patches of green. The houses that lined the countryside were all decorated with twinkle lights in preparation for Christmas. In London, it was all motion and bright lights. It reminded me of New York City.

December in London was enchanting. December

in the castle was more so. It may have felt confining to me, but to others it held all the interest in the world. From the outside, it was dark and imposing with opaque windows. The castle itself was made of thick dark stones that carried from the outside to the inside. The front wall stood tall, with an iron gate that rattled each time they raised or lowered it. Multiple towers rose from the main building, each of them with cone-shaped roofs that stood stark against the sky.

A single winding road led up to the castle, and The House of Shade emblem sat at the entrance to the gate and in a stained-glass window on the front of the castle. On the inside, candlelight illuminated the dark halls in huge chandeliers and sconces that gave every room a warm glow. On the outside, twinkling lights hung from the roof and around the doors. It was a simple, elegant look that remained timeless at Christmas. Not overdone but just nice. It was a sight I would've loved to show Piper. I could almost picture her smiling up at the lights and the huge castle I called home.

A flash of her broken body in my arms ruined the vision of her smile. I flinched, shaking my head, trying to clear the thoughts. Dirt on her face. Blood everywhere.

"Grayson!"

I spun around. "What? Why are you yelling?"

Sav walked into my room and closed the door behind him. He was dressed in burgundy dress pants, black leather shoes and a black button-down shirt that was open at the collar, showing his raven tattoo. Even his hair was somewhat combed.

"Because I've been saying your name for five minutes."

I turned from the windows extending the length of my wall toward the mirror on the other side of the room. My room had been the same for decades, with a mahogany four-poster bed and a plush crimson carpet that shielded my feet from the stone floor. The walls were also made of stone but had thick wooden beams running over them and up to the vaulted ceiling. The sun had already set, and court would be in session soon enough.

Thoughts of Piper and nothing else occupied my mind. I was going through the motions in the hopes that if I repeated things enough times, I would start to breathe again. "No need to shout. I'm here."

"And the look on your face tells me otherwise. Do try not to be a sad sack when before Titus." Sav grabbed my suit coat off the back of a chair next to the closet and threw it my way.

I caught it and slid my arms into the sleeves and

pulled them at the cuff and straightened my collar. Black, on black, on black. Like I was going to a funeral . . . all over again. I gave myself one more glance in the mirror then headed straight for the door.

"Let's get this bloody sideshow over with." I was home, but really all I wanted was to fall back into my bed and lie there until forever was over.

Sav opened my door and let me pass by him. I held my head up and kept my shoulders straight. If there was one thing a vampire knew how to do, it was bravado and right now, I needed all I could muster. It'd been months since I returned to this home and even longer still since I wanted to. Yet, now I had no place else to go, and I returned home to find the comfort I once had years ago. Comfort that was taken away from me by a chance night with a hit-and-run driver.

It was all so . . . *human.*

The halls were similar to my room, with dark stone flooring and walls. Wooden beams arched from the ground up the ceiling where they met in intricate carvings that ran over the ceiling. Warm candlelight lit the way to the throne room, and I felt that knot in my stomach tighten ever so slightly. I hadn't seen Titus since I left, and it wasn't on the best of terms.

Two double doors at the end of the hall were

manned by two other Vampires. As we approached, they grabbed the handles and pulled them back in a simultaneous move that looked choreographed. A mere human couldn't open those doors. When they opened, I felt all eyes swing toward me. I ran my hand through my hair and forced that half-smile I was known for.

The throne room was the centerpiece of the castle, with thirty-foot ceilings, wide open space, and warm wooden beams going in all different directions. A single throne sat on top of a dais at the head of the room. Two flags hung on the wall behind it, both bearing the symbol for The House of Shade. It was a single silver sword with deep red roses winding around it, and it sat on a black shield. The same symbol was made of stained-glass, and when the sunlight shined through, it would project the crest onto the middle of the floor.

Courtiers milled about on the expensive furniture spread around the room. Some kings of the past wanted to make their subjects uncomfortable. Not Titus. He preferred them all to feel at home, to know they always had a place here. Even the newly made Night Spawn Vampires, some of whom held tradition like a talisman against the tide of change.

They were all adorned in modern chic clothing,

mostly black and mostly leather, the women with their heavy eye makeup and slicked-back hair and the men in their tailored pressed suits. Blood fountains were spread throughout the room with crystal Waterford glasses standing next to them. Even the staff blended in with their black attire and discreet silver trays. I strolled into the room with Savage by my side.

"Say the word and I can clear the lot of them," he murmured low enough for only me to hear.

I shook my head. "That won't be necessary."

"Grayson, darling." My mother swept into the room like a breath of fresh air. That was the thing about Moira Shade. As a Vampire, she never fit the mold. My mother was lovely, and gentle. She was soft, with light words and an easy hand.

"Mother." She brought a true smile to my face. I couldn't say I was the easiest of children, but my mother had the patience of a saint.

She kissed both my cheeks and pulled me in for a quick embrace. The smell of fresh soap surrounded me for a moment. She was dressed in a light brown dress with gold overlays that looked more like shining lace. It covered her arms all the way up to her neck and complemented her pale skin. Her hair fell in loose curls down to her elbows. A golden band held the stray wild pieces back from her face while pieces of ribbon threaded through her curls. Her eyes were a deep chocolate brown, and she didn't look a day over thirty.

"Have you kept your hands clean, my dear?" Her accent was far more regal than mine—which spoke of the years she spent in court. Each word was clear, clipped, and pronounced.

Visions of my hands covered in graveyard dirt filled my mind. When I didn't answer, Sav cleared his throat. "But of course, Lady Moira. We are ever the epitome for decorum within Vampire society."

We both paused, staring at him for a moment. I didn't know whether to burst out laughing or shake my head. In all the years we'd been friends, decorum was not on our list of things to do. My mother sighed and rolled her eyes. "You know, you are quite long-winded, if you don't mind my saying so."

"I have been made aware." Sav returned her smile. "But I always enjoyed my attempt to maintain my innocence with you."

Though my mother was not queen of the Vampires, she was revered as such. She married my father and was with him until the day he died. Even then, she still remained my uncle's closest advisor and friend. They'd grown into the comfort of ruling. Since my uncle vowed never to take a mate, I was the only living heir to the throne.

"Your innocence was never in fear of existing." She patted Sav on the cheek like a mother indulging her child. Not one other person in the room would dare attempt such a move. But there she was, smiling and patting him like he was her son. In truth, he might as well have been. "Lies do not become us, Atlas Savage."

"Indeed, they do not." His lips pulled up into a smirk and he kissed her cheek.

In truth, my mother was the only person Atlas would cow to. He adored her like a son would a mother, and she was all too happy to take him under her wing. She turned toward me. "Have you seen him yet?"

Him was always my uncle. "Not yet."

"This ought to be interesting."

"Ah, life with me is always interesting." I escorted her closer to the throne. One of the staff members walked by and offered her a glass filled halfway with blood. She delicately took it from him and held the blood to her lips, sipping it like a fine wine.

"Always has been, darling. Try as I may to bring you into line, you're always off . . . killing things."

"Ah, but I make the world a better place for all." She

wasn't wrong. I'd done my fair share of killing in a multitude of ways. But it was all justified . . . mostly.

"Indeed, dearest." That was my mother: always supportive, always gentle. She'd never killed a thing in the world, not even a fly. And yet, she was surrounded by death and political intrigue.

The sound of the doors groaning forced silence to fall over the room. We all turned, and there stood Titus in all his glory. Power rolled off him and through the room. Blood magic was a strength that all born vampires possessed. But it manifested in different ways. For my mother, it was the ability to heal. For Savage, it was his hunting and killing abilities. For Titus, it was total and utter control . . . and we shared that very same ability.

The ability to control people through their blood was a kind of power I never wanted to tap into. Luckily, that power only manifested within the House of Shade and only with the King and his heir . . . me. Everyone in the room gave him a gracious bow. Even my mother grabbed a handful of her dress and curtsied. Sav gave a low bow in honor of King Titus. Yet, I didn't budge. I stood straight and tall.

Titus stepped into the room, and all remained in their positions. He was regal yet modern, with long, sandy blond hair that flowed down to his shoulders and a matching goatee. His clothing spoke of modern wealth, with a tailored Armani pinstriped suit, white shirt, and black tie. His shoes were polished to a perfect shine. When he smiled, his fangs poked from his mouth. There was no fanfare about Titus. In fact, he was the calmest King I'd ever met. It was why he had a far-reaching friendships that extended across species and time.

His stroll was confident and strong, with the air of someone who knew who they were, what they were, and where they were going. When he reached us, he paused before me. His lips pulled up into a full smile and he gave a heavy contented sigh. "Finally, you have returned home."

"I have."

He clapped me on the shoulder. "You've been missed."

"It pleases me to know my welcome is always warm here." The court turned to look at us, taking in every detail of our interaction. Like there would be some scandal to speak of between us, when the only scandal was my reluctance to embrace what was to come.

He turned toward the rest of the court. "Leave us."

For a moment, no one moved. My uncle had never done such a thing before—ended court well before it even started. I glanced to Sav, hoping he would give me a clue as to what was happening, but all I got was a shrug as he turned for the door.

"Not you." I grabbed the collar of Sav's shirt and pulled him back to stand next to me. My mother didn't move, either. "Leave us" never applied to her, either.

When they began to move slowly toward the door, Titus waved his hand and a red mist drifted from his fingertips over the entire crowd. They all went with vampire speed out the door, leaving us within seconds. My eyes widened. I'd never seen him use such an easy display of power.

"So, I see things have changed."

Titus turned and strolled across the room. He picked up a glass and filled it in the blood fountain. "They grow restless and are waiting for a moment of weakness. Which we will not give them."

When he turned and met my eye, the message was clear. *Which we will not give them . . . GRAYSON.* "Why have they grown restless?"

He shared a glanced with Sav then took a deep sip. Blood dotted his lip as he spoke. "The prophecy is upon us, and it brings uncertainty."

"Perhaps they should try and see what it feels like to live it?"

"They are living it." He strolled back toward us. "What happens to The House of Shade affects them all. We must endeavor to remember that."

"How could I forget?" Everyone has reminded me day and night I was to return home, and was needed here. But I was out protecting my people from an immediate threat, not some prophecy lingering for hundreds of years.

He took a step toward me and spoke the words that'd haunted my dreams.

"Born in blood of the human vein,

Bound in death she'll rise to reign.

By the crown, an heir will mark,

For in the sun, she'll bring the dark.

Lost in thirst, she'll kill for sport,

Seek the prince who guards the court.

Mind the curse, yet hear her call,

For in her hands, we rise or fall."

"I know what the prophecy says. I have eaten, slept, and bled it. *She* is coming. Whoever *she* is. The question is what are we to do about it?"

"There is only one who is named." He held his finger up then pointed it at me. "You."

I gave a soft groan. "And yet I do not wish to be named."

"Wish it you may not. But live it you shall. I love

you, my boy. And your adventures with the Witch court are now legendary among our people. I thank you for them. You have done wonderful things." He took another step toward me and wrapped his hand around the back of my neck and forced his gaze to meet mine. "Play time is over, Reluctant Prince. Now the work begins."

CHAPTER TWENTY-TWO

DICE

"So, what you're telling me is that I've been waiting to file this missing persons' report it's now Saturday. Two days . . ." I held up two fingers. "Two days since she's been missing, and all you're going to do is issue a missing persons report and kind of spread her picture around?"

"Ma'am, try to stay calm. We don't just kind of spread their picture around." The sergeant sat behind his desk filling out the paperwork I needed to report Piper missing. I'd brought pictures, all of her physical description information, medical records, and even her cell phone, which I'd gone through a million times looking for a hint of where she might've gone, and yet there was . . . nothing.

I slammed my hand on his desk, and the precinct

went silent for a half a second before everyone started buzzing about again. The phones kept on ringing and people walked all around the aged desks. Officers milled about in their navy-blue uniforms with steaming cups of coffee in their hands. Sergeant Larceny cleared his throat. "We are going to do everything we can to find your friend."

"No, you are not!" I rose to my feet. "I want bomb-sniffing dogs, teams of people scouring the entire town looking, fliers on every window and every telephone pole. And I definitely do not see agents from Interpol standing here ready to follow that Brit to the ends of the earth to find her and bring her back, damn it!"

He leaned back in his chair and folded his hands over his stomach. "Yeah, I made a few phone calls. No one has ever heard of a Grayson Shade anywhere."

A growl rumbled in my chest. "Try harder."

"I'll do all that I can." But all that he could didn't seem like nearly enough. "Well, while you're doing that, my best friend is somewhere alone and afraid. You think about that over your next coffee break. Oh, and Sergeant Larceny . . . Larceny is a crime. Fix your damn name for your profession. That's like a stripper named Edith and not Destiny."

"Now, just you wait a minute." He began to wag his finger at me, and I turned for the door.

No amount of finger-wagging was going to intimidate me or get me to budge. If no one was going to leap into action, I would. Piper was my best friend, the only person I had in the world, and I would find her. We were a duo. I shoved the glass doors aside and marched out into the cold air. I didn't know where I was going or what I was going to do, but I had to think and walk off my anger to keep myself rational and moving. I needed a plan of action, and I needed one now.

I crossed my arms over my chest and pulled my coat tight around my body. Where was I going to go? Back to the empty house I shared with my missing bestie? Or to work, where all I would be able to think about was her, and everyone would just keep asking me if I'd heard from her yet. No. Action was needed. I couldn't eat or sleep knowing she just vanished. I had to know what happened to her, and I had to know now.

So, I walked and plotted and walked some more until I found myself wandering back toward home. The sun hung low in the sky, telling me it would soon set, but I couldn't seem to stop. My mind was a whirl of worry, and I just felt sick in the pit of my stomach. I drifted down a wide alley way that led back toward Essex. I'd always loved it down here on Artists' Row, but now it seems crowded with tents and too many people. Even the restaurant seemed too much. I used to enjoy all the little huts with their sculptures and paints and artists selling their pieces. Now, I just wanted to go home and get ready for my next step.

"Hey, psst," a deep sultry female voice called to me.

I paused and turned toward her without saying a word. She was tiny, with wavy blond hair that fell past her shoulders. Her lips were a bright red, and she had warm chocolate eyes. Her outfit was low key: plain dark blue jeans, a red turtleneck that matched her lips, and a trench coat that was about four sizes too big. She crooked her finger at me. "You want a reading?"

I rolled my eyes. Salem was the town of psychics. I could take my pick at any given time. I shook my head. "I don't have any money."

"This one is on the house." Her smile was warm and open, but something inside me was on guard.

"I've never seen you here before." Newbie psychics always wanted to try and make their name here.

"It's my first day, and you're my first customer."

I shook my head. "No, thanks."

I took a step to leave, and she called after me once more. "I can help you find what is missing."

Ice ran through my veins. She couldn't possibly know. I whirled around to face her with all the attitude I could muster. "How do you know what I'm missing?"

"Friend of yours?" She winked and crooked her finger once more. "Come, and I'll show you."

Was this how Piper got taken? The promise of something intriguing or someone with the answers and she stepped right into a dark tent with no question. I didn't know, but I was going to do it anyway. Besides, someone so small had no chance of taking me. I'd crush her with one hit.

"Ugh, fine." I stepped into her tent and was surprised to find two tables set up, one on the right side of the tent and the other on the left. They were small round tables with only two seats set up across from each other. Black tablecloths were draped over them and hung down to the floor.

"I'm Tilly, by the way." She motioned to the empty table to our left.

"I'm Dice."

I took a seat, but I couldn't take my eyes off the guy sitting at the other table. A dark ominous presence rolled off him, and it made me rethink ever walking into the tent. His hair was long and straight and ran down to his chin. He wore a thick black sweater and black army pants. When he met my eye, I could've sworn his eyes changed from green to milky white and back again. A set of tarot cards sat on the table in front of him, but he didn't touch them, just sat there with his hands hovering over the deck.

I continued to stare at him. Tilly cleared her throat, getting my attention. "That's Maze."

He gave me a single nod that I didn't return. Everything about that guy made me want to leave, but Tilly had the opposite effect. She was warm and sunny, almost welcoming. "You said you could help me find what I lost?"

"Oh, yes." She sat in the chair opposite me and held her hand out to her side. The tarot cards flew from his table and right into her hand.

I jumped back and looked from her to him and back again. My heart hammered in my chest. "How'd you do that?"

"Parlor tricks." She winked and began to shuffle. "What is it that you're looking for? Lost love, job, or sense of direction?"

This line of questioning was more familiar. "Let's see what the cards say?"

"Ah, lost a friend then." She kept shuffling, and a card flew out onto the table between us. "Three of Swords. You've lost something, and it wounds you deeply. It's heartbreaking. You feel abandoned, and disappointed."

"Tell me something I don't know." *Typical.*

She pulled a card from the deck and laid it down next to the other. "Six of Swords. This tells me that your friend is moving on to something new. The transition will hurt you both but, in the end, it will be for the best."

I shook my head. "She would never willingly leave me. I know Piper. It's not like that. We are devoted to each other."

Tilly arched her eyebrows. "Did you ever think she may not have had a choice?"

"That's what I'm worried about." What if she was forced into something she didn't want to do or a place she didn't want to go. I wasn't there to help her or protect her. And that was my job as her sister. That's what we did for each other. We supported, protected, and always remained loyal. This was the first time we'd ever lost touch since meeting, and deep down I was worried the worst had happened.

She pulled another card and flipped it onto the table between us. I sucked in a sharp breath. "Death? Are you trying to tell me she's dead?"

Maze snorted and shook his head. Tilly tapped the card with her long black nail that looked more like a claw. "It's a common misconception to think that the death card actually means death. It's a transition, a new beginning for her."

"How does that help me?" I crossed my arms and slouched in the chair.

Tilly leaned in. "Because I could take you to her."

"No, no. I am not going in there with you." I stood at the edge of the Broad Street Cemetery right across from the famous Pickering House in Salem. Tilly was to my left and on the other side of her stood Maze, all silent and creepy with a shovel in his hand.

Tilly shrugged. "Then you will never know what happened to your friend."

My stomach rolled and my heart sank. "Are you telling me she's buried in there?"

"Only one way to find out." She took a step onto the grass and began walking toward the back corner of the cemetery, where large trees stood tall and imposing.

This was some kind of trick. These two were going to drag me out here and kill me for a weird thing that they thought represented witches but really didn't. I was going to be the next face on the missing fliers . . .

or not. Piper was the only one who really cared about me. Would she walk into that graveyard with two complete strangers if it would help? The answer was a resounding yes. But if something happened to me who would continue the search for her? Who would make sure she got home safely? No one.

Tilly glanced over her shoulder. "If you leave, you will always wonder."

A cold shudder wracked my body and I wanted to forget this whole thing, but she wasn't wrong. I would always wonder if the little psychic from Artists' Row knew all along where my best friend was, and I didn't listen. I took a step onto the grass and motioned for her to lead the way. We wandered around old gray headstones that were still covered in a thin layer of ice from the sleet a few nights ago. The grass crunched under my feet with each step I took. I stayed a few feet back from them just in case I needed to run. But when they came to a stop under one of the trees and looked down at the freshly dug up dirt, I thought I might puke.

"Is she . . . is she there?" My voice shook, and I felt a ball form in my throat. No, it couldn't be. I shook away the thought.

"Only one way to find out." She gave a nod to Maze and without a word, he started digging.

At first, I flinched each time the shovel hit the dirt, like it was a slap in the face. But the farther down he got, the more I knew in my gut that I would find her there. My hands shook, not from the cold but from my frayed nerves. My breaths came in faster panicked puffs. I fought against the nausea and just kept on breathing the cold air. I didn't say a word to Tilly, and she didn't try to speak to me or even comfort me. Instead, we both just watched Maze get lower and lower while the pile of dirt beside the grave got higher and higher.

The shoveling continued. Thwack. Thwack. Thwack. Each time it hit the dirt, I winced like it would be the last time. Until there was no more thwacking sound. I didn't look down, didn't even dare to. My breath caught in my throat, and I fought the black dots that swarmed my vision.

"Why'd he stop?"

Maze threw the shovel out of the hole then climbed out to stand next to Tilly. When he met my eye, that harshness I'd seen earlier had left, and in its place was a silent pity. I knew that look well. It was the kind of look I got when people found out I was an orphan and had no one. But I did have someone. I had Piper and she had me. We were our own little family, and without her, I was all alone in the world, with no one to turn to.

I shook my head. "No."

"You have to." Tilly pointed toward the hole. "For her and for yourself."

Tears pooled behind my eyes and threatened to spill over. I curled my hands into fists and looked to the sky, staring at the light pink and dark blue colors that came with sunset. It would've been pretty had I not been standing here. *Please, God, don't let it be her. Don't take her away from me. She's my only family. Please, God . . . please.*

"Dice. It's time." Tilly's voice was warm and gentle.

I swallowed and let my eyes drift down to the ground and into the dark hole. My hands flew to my mouth and my legs shook. My legs went weak, and I fell to my knees. A sob ripped from my lips, and I heard myself screaming. Tears spilled from my eyes and poured down my face. There was my friend, the only person I had in the world, laying at the bottom of an unmarked grave. Her face was a pale blue-gray color, and her eyes were closed tight. Dirt covered every inch of her, but even so, I would know that face anywhere.

"Piper! No!" Another sob broke through, and I curled my hands into the grass, screaming. My heart was torn in two. The pain ripped and tore at my chest like it hurt to even breathe. "You have to help her, please."

When I got no answer, I looked up and they were gone. It was like Maze and Tilly never existed. I was alone in the graveyard, kneeling over my best friend's dead body with not a soul in sight to hear me. I shook my head no. This couldn't be happening. I-I couldn't do this. Couldn't live through this. Every breath hurt my body, and I wanted to lie down next to her and let the tears just fall.

This couldn't be it. This couldn't be how it ended. We'd come so far and had so much more living to do. "SOMEBODY HELP ME!"

I crawled to the edge of her grave. "Piper, I swear I will find who did this to you. Piper, please."

But she was too still in death. Another sob hit me and this one made my throat feel raw with emotion. "PLEASE! HELP ME!"

CHAPTER TWENTY-THREE

PIPER

*L*ight flashed behind my eyes and pain exploded across my body. Distant screaming echoed in my head, and I flinched away from it. Everything was too loud, and the thoughts were coming too fast. Voices filled my mind, and I didn't know what they were all saying, nor did I want to. But it was a rush of sensory overload. I felt everything, heard everything, smelled everything. My skin was too sensitive and so very cold. My body was ever so still. I was cemented in place on a cold metal slab that didn't feel right under my skin. The tips of my fingers rested on the cold metal beneath me.

Burning pain filled my throat and tightened around my stomach. My eyes flicked open and blinding light filled them. I quickly shut them tight.

The sound of music drifted on the air, along with the smell of something vile. I wrinkled my nose and let my eyes open once more. A single white sheet lay over my naked body, and bright light shined down on me. I could feel every fiber in that sheet and the warmth from the light. My body was smooth and clean, and my hair fell back from my face onto the table.

When the door creaked open, I kicked my legs and rolled off the table entirely too fast, and my mind had to catch up with where my body had gone. The sheet fell to the floor, and I stood there naked in the middle of a square room. The walls were made of cinderblocks that were painted a pale green color. The floor was freezing but it didn't seem to bother me, and three more metal tables were lined up next to the one I stood at. Another woman lay on the table beside mine. A little white dress lay on a rolling cart next to her. I grabbed it and shoved my arms in. It fell off my shoulders and opened all the way down from my chest.

Across from me was a silver wall filled with square doors. The word coroner ran through my mind, and I knew something had happened. I didn't know what or who I was, but I knew this place meant death. I smelled it in the air and lingering on my skin.

I walked to the desk at the front of the room and stared down at the papers there. That burning pain lanced through my chest and up my throat once more, forcing me to double over and hold onto my stomach. I reached for the half-drunk bottle of water on the desk and chugged it down. For a moment, it eased the intense burning that started to cloud my mind. Before I could take another step, the water shot out of my stomach and from my mouth like a hose, soaking everything. I pressed the back of my hand to my mouth and sucked in a breath. The burn came back. More intense than before. It was boiling like nothing I'd ever felt before. Blisters had to be filling my throat and mouth. When I darted my tongue over my lips, it felt like sandpaper.

The door banged open and a chubby bald man in a white coat strolled in. He had a set of headphones wrapped around his neck and a bag of something greasy in his hand. "What the fuck?"

It was the smell that hit me first. Something warm and divine that would soothe the blistering pain in my body. I turned toward him and tilted my head to the side, studying him. Suddenly, I knew without a doubt he was easy prey. I didn't say anything, just took a step toward him. My body moved with a catlike ease it never had before. Two little fangs popped from my teeth and stabbed my bottom lip, giving me a hit of my own blood. The burning cooled for barely a second.

"You-you're supposed to be dead." His body quaked, and his skin turned a pale shade of yellow.

I took another step toward him. Every muscle was ready to pounce on him and take what the burning in my throat so desperately needed. The sound of his heartbeat intensified and drove me into a frenzy. Blood pumped through his veins, and I licked my lips, just tasting it on the air between us. Sweat broke out over his body and he backed away and slammed into the wall behind him. He dropped the bag, and food exploded at his feet and scattered across the floor. A whimper slipped from his lips, and he took a step to the side as if debating whether to run. My instincts screamed at me to take what my body needed, to grab him and sink my fangs into his neck. The little voice in my head liked it. Liked the smell of fear and the hunt.

I licked my lips. "Run."

His eyes widened and he turned to the side. His muscles tensed and I felt a smile spread across my face. It was like watching him move in slow motion. He darted down the hall, and the predator in me purred with pleasure. I was out the door and on him within seconds. I grabbed his shoulder and spun him around. This close, he was so much bigger than me. At least a foot taller but I didn't care. I shoved him against the wall and leapt. My fangs sank into his neck like a hot knife through butter. Warm coppery liquid flooded my mouth and down my throat. The burning eased and I sighed with the next sucking pull I took from him. It went down my throat and filled my muscles. The haze of thirst receded, and flashes of a blond girl and a beautiful guy with dark chocolate hair filled my mind.

The pain doubled feeling like lava down my throat. I choked on my next sip. I extracted my fangs and shoved the guy away from me. He smacked into the wall and fell to the ground. I backed away from him and kept on walking toward the exit sign down the hall. Pain shot from my stomach and up my throat. Dizziness exploded behind my eyes, and I forgot everything else. Acid shot from my mouth, and I hunched over, vomiting up what little I had drunk. It burned like a hot poker had been shoved down my throat. I couldn't breathe. Every muscle in my chest and back was pulled so tight it felt as though my own heart might shoot from my chest. I let it go, splashing the hallways with bloody vomit until I could stand and breathe again.

I grabbed the edge of the dress and swiped it across my mouth. I took another step and the thick metal door under the exit sign was there. I shoved it hard, and it flew off the hinges and out into the dark parking lot. The sound of metal scraping across asphalt echoed through the parking lot. I ran out into the night, feeling the cool air on my skin and the icy ground under my bare feet. I sucked in sharp breaths, trying to cool my ever-burning tongue. It didn't help. My thoughts turned to only one thing . . . thirst.

Thirsty.

Hunt.

Kill.

Drink.

CHAPTER TWENTY-FOUR

DICE

"*Y*ou sit down right there." Sergeant Larceny pointed to the chair at a table in the interrogation room.

"What happened? Did you find who did this to her?"

It'd only been one night since I'd found Piper, and I still couldn't explain how to the police. I told them about Maze and Tilly, but when they went to find the tent it was gone, and no one had heard of them. My eyes were dry, red, and puffy from the number of tears that'd I'd shed for my friend. My throat was raw and still hurt from the uncontrollable sobs. If Piper was alive, I would have killed her for making me cry. I hated crying.

He stood in the doorway and glared at me. "Did this to her? You've got a lot of explaining to do."

"What are you talking about?" I sat up straight in the chair and realized it was bolted to the ground and couldn't be moved away from the single metal table.

"Yeah. You don't know what I'm talkin' about, my ass." His Boston accent was never so thick as it was right now. He jabbed his finger at me. "Don't you move."

"Masshole," I muttered to myself as he slammed the door.

When I looked up at the two-way mirror, I was a complete mess. "Oh, shit."

I tried to finger comb my hair down instead of standing up straight. I wore a ripped sweatshirt, and equally crappy sweatpants. Black makeup was smeared around my eyes and down my cheeks. I tried to wipe it away with my fingers but all that did was smear it even more. It had been a long night and it showed, but what could I do? I'd lost the only person in the world who I loved and who loved me in return. My bottom lip started to quiver, and I felt the tears threaten to spill over once more. But I sucked in a sniffling breath and forced myself to get control. I'd be damned if I let any of these cops see me cry.

The door opened and Sergeant Larceny walked in

accompanied by another detective. He pointed to the man, who was middle-aged, with gray hair, and a thick mustache. He wore a gray suit, complete with white button-down shirt and gray tie. He carried a laptop in one hand along with a Manila folder. They took the seats across from me and both glared.

I stared back. "What?"

"We are not here for stunts and games and certainly not when someone ends up in the intensive care unit." Sergeant Larceny slammed his hand down on the table between us.

I glanced from him to the detective and back again. "I'm sorry, what?"

The detective still hadn't said a word. He just opened the laptop. He clicked a few buttons, and the black and white video of an empty hallway came up. The walls were made of painted cinderblocks and linoleum flooring. Harsh fluorescent lights flickered, giving it an all-too-eerie look. It was the kind of hall I wouldn't walk down in the middle of the night. No one should: I'd seen that horror movie a thousand times.

"You watch this," the sergeant snapped. The detective pressed a couple of buttons and the video began to play.

A taller bald guy in a white lab coat walked down

the hall and into a door on the side. The angle pointed down on him, like the camera was in the upper corner between the ceiling and the wall. He held a paper bag in one hand and wore a pair of headphones around his neck. He went into the door and disappeared. "I don't really see what this is—"

The man came flying out of the room. He pumped his arms, running as fast as he could. A second later, a woman in a white dress had him in her hands. It was a blur of movement that the eye could barely track, and yet, there she was, holding him against the wall with her bare hands. He was at least a foot taller than she, but terror was plain on his face. I couldn't make out the woman's face behind her wild wavy hair. If I didn't know any better, I'd say it was Piper. She had the same long hair and the same build. But she didn't move like Piper. She was fast, and more cat-like than anyone I'd ever seen.

She leapt up on the guy, using his own height against him, and shoved her head in between his neck and shoulders. "Is she . . . is she?"

The detective looked me over like he was gauging my reactions. "Biting him? Yeah."

The woman suddenly ripped away from him and shoved him into the wall. The bald guy slammed back into the wall then melted to the floor in a heap. The woman backed away from him, clutching at her stomach. Then she heaved and a fountain of blood shot onto the floor and walls. It was everywhere. She sucked in deep breaths and used the edge of her dress to wipe her mouth.

"That's just . . . disgusting." I wrinkled my nose and shook my head. "Is he going to be okay?"

"Is he going to be okay? No! He's not going to be okay! He's lost a massive amount of blood, and it took fifty-seven stitches. His collar bones are broken, and both shoulders were dislocated. He still hasn't woken up."

I shook my head. "Is that the same person who killed Piper?"

The detective paused the movie just as the woman turned her head to the side, and they got a clear profile picture of her. "Lady, that is Piper."

I grabbed the computer and dragged it closer to me and squinted at the screen. My heart stopped in my chest. Adrenaline flooded my body. I would know my bestie's face anywhere. It was her. "What the fuck?"

"Why don't you tell us?" the sergeant snapped. "This ain't play time. There are man-hours here. People got hurt. Reporting someone missing is illegal. You think this is a game. Assault isn't a game, and you two are in a whole mess of trouble."

"What the hell?" Visions of Piper at the bottom of that grave covered in dirt and not a sign of life about her flooded my mind. "This can't be happening."

"It is. Now tell us where she is."

"I-I have no idea. I-I thought she was dead." I glanced at the screen once more. She was most definitely not dead. But was that her? She didn't move like Piper and didn't act like Piper. But she looked like her.

"Don't play with me. We need to get her off the street before someone else gets hurt." The sergeant rose to his feet and placed both hands on the table and leaned over me. His face turned beet red. "Where is she?"

I leaned back in the chair and crossed my arms over my chest. If that was Piper and she was alive, she'd need me now more than ever. I wasn't the person who would rat her out even if I knew where she was. I was the person she could call to hide the body. "I don't know and even if I did, I wouldn't tell you."

They shared a look, and the detective joined the sergeant, both of them standing over me like two big guys were going to intimidate me into talking. "Maybe we'll let her cool off here for a while until she decides to open up."

I kicked my legs up on the table and crossed them

at the ankles. I raised my chin at the two of them. "Yeah, it's going to be a long night for you ladies. Because I have nothing to say, and you can't hold me here."

"Try us."

Oh, I will. Piper was out there somewhere, and I was going to find her before they did. I pressed my lips together and stared straight at my own reflection. There wasn't a chance in hell I would give them an ounce of information. *Good luck, boys.*

CHAPTER TWENTY-FIVE

PIPER

I pumped my arms, running as fast as I could through the forest. Sticks and icy leaves crackled under my bare feet. The lingering scent of animals filled the air and yet none of them could satisfy the thirst that burned deep within my chest. I needed more, something stronger to satiate the never-ending desire. Every muscle in my body burned to move, to kill, to hunt. My thoughts turned to one thing . . . food. Branches snatched at my hair and tore the dress. I didn't care.

The smell of something warm and tangy hit my nose, and I stopped short, digging my heels into the ground and skidding for a few feet. I hooked my hand around a tree, and it snapped in my grip and fell to the side. Branches crashed around me and broke over the other trees. I held the piece for a moment, studying all the tiny fragments of wood and the way they splintered. Every color, every facet was so easy to see. The sounds of little creatures scurrying away from a greater predator filled my ears.

I tossed the tree trunk aside and sniffed the air once more. That warm copper spice called to me, and I went for it, pumping my arms harder. Trees loomed over me, and I leapt up onto a low-hanging branch to get a better view of my prey. I jumped from one branch to the next, following the scent of the most delicious thing ever.

I stopped just at the top of a tree overlooking a small lake. The moon reflected on the glassy surface along with the few clouds dotting the sky. Just at the edge of the lake, a huge black bear tipped its nose to the water and lapped at the water, sending tiny ripples outward. The thick, fatty scent was heavenly and had me on edge. I leaned toward it trying to taste its flavor on the air. Maybe the blood would stay down this time… maybe not. I couldn't remember what hadn't worked. All I knew was I couldn't stop myself. Nothing else mattered but the thirst.

A few yards behind the bear, deeper in the woods, a flickering light caught my eyes. Fire. It danced and flickered in the night, and the smell of burning embers mixed with the smell of my meal. On top of that, a scent I'd never smelled before. Something foreign, not human, and not animal. I didn't know what it was, but it piqued my curiosity.

But first . . . snack.

I dove off the top of the tree, leapt across the water, and crashed into the bear. Thick fur and the smell of earth assailed my senses. A claw ran across my skin, scraping at it, but I didn't care. Snarling broke the night as we tumbled through the trees wrestling for the upper hand. The bear was strong, but I was so much stronger. We twisted and spun across the ground, wrestling and beating each other. To the bear, this was life or death. To me, this was my next drink. When we came to a crashing halt, I pinned the bear to the ground on its side. It snapped its neck toward me, baring its teeth at me and growling. A roar ripped from its chest and drool flew from his mouth across the clearing. I bared my teeth at it and a hiss burned up my throat. I slammed its shoulders into the ground and forced its head back to the side. Even pressed to the ground, it still kicked its legs and tried to fight me off. I could feel its hammering pulse under my fingertips and smell its warm, earthy blood seeping from the scratches I gave it during our little tumble. I licked my lips. This time, I would drink him dry and quench the desert in my mouth. This time, it would stay down.

As I leaned in to sink my fangs home, a high-pitched cackle drew me up short. I jumped back from the bear and held my arms out, ready to end whatever would try to take my kill. I hunched over about to spring forward and attack. Adrenaline pumped through my veins and I wanted to spring into action, but the girl in front of me was different than humans. Her hair was pulled back tight to her head, her makeup was dark around her eyes, and she had bright-red lips. A pleather corset was wrapped tight around her body with pants that were equally as tight.

"Ohhhh, a new little baby." She sauntered out away from two other people at a fire. She kicked a log out of her way. It soared across the clearing and cracked against a tree. "See? I can do it too."

I tilted my head to the side, studying her. She was strong. It showed in the way she moved and the flex of her muscles. I was looking at another predator. She took a step toward me, and I hissed in her direction, baring my fangs. She froze and giggled at me.

"Linda, come look at this," she called over her shoulder.

"I'm busy, Mandy." The girl at the fire rose and stepped over a body lying at her feet. The heartbeat was faint and slow but still there. I licked my lips and took a step toward it, ready to sink my fangs in.

The girl stepped into my line of sight, blocking the food from me. She swayed on her feet and slow-blinked at me. "Hey, that's ours, and newborns aren't so good with the tainted blood."

Tainted what? I shook my head. I didn't care. I wanted it.

I sprinted at the first one and grabbed her by the throat and lifted her up off the ground. I held her over my head and shook her. "Mine."

The guy jumped up from his seat next to the fire and ran into me at full speed, knocking me to the side. I dropped the one I had by the throat and flew off my feet into a tree. The tree cracked and snapped under my weight. I crawled out from the wreckage and yanked the branches from my hair. A deep growl rumbled in my chest. How dare they come between me and what I wanted? I would kill them all.

The three of them rushed to line up against me just as the bear loped off.

Dinner . . . gone.

There was nothing left for me here. I didn't care to fight. The only thing I felt was the pain of hunger and thirst hitting me at the same time. And they didn't smell the least bit enticing. The human on the floor was nearly empty of everything. Mandy, the one in the middle, pulled a square object from her pocket and held it to her ear. It lit up bright against her skin, and I heard a voice on the other end.

Mandy never took her eyes off me. "Yeah, we got a feral one."

I turned and ran into the night . . . hunting for more.

CHAPTER TWENTY-SIX

ATLAS SAVAGE

Killing was an art—an art meant to be executed in the most inventive kind of ways. To some it was abhorrent, to me it was life, and there was only one way out. If I so happened to be that way out for some, then so be it. In the animal kingdom, it was kill or be killed. I had no doubt my time would come. My sins were many and my good deeds less. But if my King beckoned, I would answer every time. Because his loyalty and mercy would be answered with my own unwavering loyalty . . . forever.

Grayson had become a brother to me, and Moira had taken me in as a son. All of them accepted me for the true monster I really was. The King summoned me to his chambers, and I would go without fail. A monster on call for them all. I walked through the castle like a ghost. Courtiers scurried out of my way as I walked down the halls. They didn't even make eye contact with me. It was for the better. Attachments were liabilities. To others, the castle might've been cold, but I called it home. The gothic architecture was calm and comforting to me. The candles kept it warm and the decorations for Christmas were officially in full swing, complete with decorated trees up and down the hallways. Garland whirled around every open beam and around every window. Lights were strung through, giving it that magical twinkling effect.

When I got to the King's chamber, the guards didn't look in my eyes. They just opened the door for me to enter. I strolled in and Titus stood behind his desk. It was a large wooden piece with carvings covered in gold leaf. Papers were stacked in neat piles on the tabletop along with books and pens. He wore black tailored pants, black shoes, and a perfectly fitted vest. But the thing Titus was well known for was his crimson floor-length velvet coat. It puffed up around his neck and hung loose on his arms. He had one hand on his hip while he rifled through his papers with the other. A cup of blood sat on the corner of the table, and I recognized the vintage from the scent. O-positive with a touch of cabernet mixed in, a vintage he favored in all his donors. Titus glanced up at me and his lip twitched into a smile. Sometimes it felt as though he was looking right through me with his ghost-like eyes.

"Savage."

I inclined my head in a small bow of respect. "Your Majesty."

He stopped what he was doing and faced me fully. The thing with Titus was that he could be in a room full of people or completely alone and he still made anyone feel like they were the only one there with him.

"Something happened to Grayson while he was gone."

"Yes." I didn't lie.

He ran his hand through his long hair. "Dare I ask what?"

I hesitated. We'd never crossed the line between brotherhood and loyalty to the crown. To me, being friends with Grayson was one in the same. We were loyal to each other. "Best not."

"Anything that need be cleaned up?" He was calm and collected. I knew deep down he cared for Grayson more like a son than a nephew. They were blood of blood. Titus would step in front of death for Grayson any day of the week. Even so, if he knew how close

Grayson had come to touching the curse, it would unnerve him. And in the year of the prophecy, we needed a strong royal house.

"I've handled all things."

He gave me a nod. "He seems troubled as of late."

"Yes."

"How can I help?"

Emotions were not my strong suit. I stood there trying to offer some molecule of advice. When I stood for long moments, unmoving, he shook his head. "I'll speak with Moira."

"Better decision." Anything even remotely emotional should go to Moira. "Anything else?"

He handed me a piece of paper. "Reports of a feral just came in. I need it dealt with."

I took the paper and glanced at the location and handed it back. "Is the team ready?"

"Already mobilized and awaiting you." He paused. "If it can't be saved . . . put it down."

"Understood." I gave him a single nod and headed out the door.

"And, Savage," he called after me.

I stopped and glanced back at him. He met my eye. "Reports are it's strong. Very strong."

Interesting. "Makes the hunt all the better."

"Let me know how it goes." He waved me away and I was out the door.

I marched down the hall to my room. When I got there, I ripped my shirt off and threw it on the bed. My tattoos vibrated across my skin, waiting to be called upon. I ran my finger over my chest and Poe, my raven, emerged from my skin. I called on the blood magic that vibrated through my body and brought the nightmares pictured there to life. A fine red mist covered my skin like a sheen of sweat. The reaper on my back was next. I ran my finger over it and my body heated up, forcing all the power to that one point. Leather straps circled around my arms and neck like armor. A thick black hood went up and over my head. The sword tattoo on my arms ensured I always had my weapons with me.

I stepped up to the mirror and barely brushed it with my fingertip. It rippled under my power, and Poe cawed and soared right into it. I quickly followed and hurried down the cold hall that would take me to my destination. My footsteps didn't echo off these walls like others did. I moved silently, as though flying over the floor. At the end of the hall was the other end of the rippling mirror the team would've set up at the location. Poe dove into the mirror and soared through first. When I stepped through, I walked into a tactical deployment. The entire team was dressed in head-to-toe black army gear. Each of them was strapped with blades on their hips and ankles. Assault rifles hung from their shoulders at the ready. The guns wouldn't kill a vampire, but they damn sure would slow it down.

Jester, the leader of the assault team, smiled and nodded at me. "Savage."

We slapped hands and did a half bro hug. "Jester, what do we got?"

He was just a bit shorter than me and more muscular—the way a human navy seal might've been built. His jaw was square and bulky. His nose was flat and complimented his almond-shaped eyes.

"Nothing like I've seen before."

Interesting. "How so?"

"I sent two of my guys after it already. They never came back. This one is strong. Very strong. But it doesn't act in the normal ways." He pulled a map from his pocket and held it out to me. He ran his finger in a line over the thickly wooded area. "It's moving in zig zags all over this area."

"What does it want?" Usually, feral vampires only went after one thing . . . blood.

"It's trying to feed."

"Trying to?" I glanced up at him. "Is it defective in some way?"

"Quite the opposite. She's something to behold, but she can't seem to keep any blood down at all. It seems whatever she drinks comes right back up."

The hairs on the back of my neck stood at attention. "She?"

The guys all nodded. Jester scoffed. "Oh, yeah. *She.*"

They almost acted as if they revered or respected her wildness. This was bad. This was very bad. I rolled my sleeves up and pressed my fingers to the weapons on my forearms. The swords I had tattooed down each of my arms glowed a bright red, and again that red, blood-like mist covered them. They shot from my arms and down into my hands.

"Make a perimeter and drive her this way. I'll go from the other end, and we'll meet in the middle." I pulled my mask up over my mouth and my hood lower over my eyes.

Jester waved his hand, commanding the rest of the team to move out. They took off and the forest was clear of them within seconds. I stood there for another moment, letting my sense expand outward. Other vampires were fast and strong. But I had something extra —a sense for the hunt. All I had to do was focus on the one thing I wanted, and my body would send me in the direction I needed to get exactly that. Poe was a part of me and I was a part of him, I tapped into him using my senses as he soared overhead. I felt through Poe and knew he too was feeling the cool air through his feathers. When I closed my eyes, all I heard was the symphony of the forest. The wind rustling through the bare trees, small critters in a panic with the number of predators nearby, and the movement of my team. A normal vampire wouldn't hear them, much less a newly made one. And yet there was a sizzle across the ground, a current of danger I hadn't felt before, at least not with a feral.

Then it hit me. "No!"

Poe turned and I ran toward my desire, using my senses and him as a guide. Gunfire filled the air and shouts echoed toward me. I ran into another clearing and the men were standing back-to-back in a circle with their guns pointed up toward the trees.

"There! She's over there!"

"No! Here!"

"No! That way."

"On your left!"

"Right."

I stood on the outside waiting while they lost their minds. The girl was a hunter for sure. But how strong was she? And what would it take to stop her? Then I saw the eye reflected at me in the trees. She was there one moment and gone the next. The branches rustled, and one of the men flew up off the ground and smacked into the tree behind me.

"Behind you!"

Another one was suddenly thrown up in the air and landed on his face at my feet. I chuckled and darted to my right. I grabbed a branch and swung myself up into the tree. I landed just next to her on the branch. She was hunched over with her wild midnight hair covering her face. Her white dress was in tatters around her body, and it was covered in blood.

I gave a little whistle to catch her attention. She leapt off the branch like a startled cat and landed just above me. When I tensed to leap up next to her, she dove right for me with her little fingers shaped like claws ready to tear at my throat. Blood covered her mouth and neck, but I couldn't see the rest of her face behind that curtain of hair. The smell was a mix of animal and human. I ducked to the side at the last second and let her hands shove right into the tree. The wood splintered around her hands.

"Been hunting?"

I grabbed the back of her neck and yanked her head back. Her hair flew out of her face, and I froze.

My stomach sank and I held my blade away from her. "Holy shit, Piper?"

A feral scream ripped past her lips and she struck out with her fist, connecting with my rib cage. I flew off the branch and landed on the ground next to the others. They pulled their triggers, firing off a volley of bullets. Light blared from the tips of the guns, unleashing a deafening sound.

I shoved Jester to the side. "Hold your fire!"

All at once, firing stopped and everything went silent. The smell of gunpowder and hot metal filled the air.

Jester pulled his mask from his face. "Are you crazy? We need to put her down. She's too dangerous!"

If Grayson ever found out that she rose and we killed her, he would never forgive himself. Or me. "We capture her."

"Do you even know how to do that?" His brow furrowed.

"Piss off." I laid my swords across my arms and that glowing red mist covered them and sucked them back into my skin, then I yanked the taser from his belt and wagged it in his face. "I can bring in something alive."

"I'll believe it when I see it."

But he was right. I didn't capture. I killed. It was my way. But for Grayson, I would do this, and it would either save him or damn the kingdom completely. If she survived this and could come back from being feral, that is. Either way, Gray deserved to know, and I would deliver her to his doorstep. I turned and ran in the opposite direction, chasing behind her. There was no rhyme or reason as to why she moved the way she did. Feral vampires were all instinct and no thought. It'd be amazing if she even remembered her name.

I pumped my arms and ran harder. She was fast but getting weaker. Dawn would soon approach, and I had to get her out of here and out of the sun before it was too late and she turned to dust.

It may already be.

The second she came into view, I dove for her, wrapping my arms around her hips and taking her down to the ground. She kicked out and flipped us over. I rolled and shoved her to the ground, pinning her arms to her side. Her fangs extended as she growled and hissed at me. I shoved the taser to the side of her neck and pressed the button. The current popped and sizzled when it hit her skin. Her body jolted and shook with the high-voltage. When she went limp, I sucked in a deep breath. I rose to my feet. Her fingers had already began to twitch. *Bloody hell.* I pressed the taser to her neck again and hit her with it once more. She went completely still, and I knew I only had seconds before she would stir once more.

I needed a way to lock her up. "Over here!"

There was a rush of movement and the team had us both surrounded with all the guns pointed at Piper. Jester tossed a set of handcuffs toward me, and I caught them. I snapped them on her wrists before she woke once more. "Get the ones for the ankles too."

He shook his head. "Why keep this one?"

"None of your business," I growled.

"I hope the bastard who left their progeny to go feral like this pays for it." Jester pulled a set of manacles from his back pocket and clapped them around her ankles. "You sure the King would want this particular one?"

Definitely not. "Don't concern yourself with such matters."

He is going to kill me . . . and Grayson.

Get ready, brother. We're coming home.

CHAPTER TWENTY-SEVEN

GRAYSON

"I don't bloody well understand what I am doing here." I marched toward our holding facility and lab area.

"I was told to fetch you, Your Highness." The lab assistant was wringing his hands nervously as he walked beside me toward the stairs that would lead to the lab. He was meek, with short dark hair and small black eyes. He was much smaller than me. He barely had an ounce of muscle. Everything about him was nervous. His posture was hunched, his words were stilted and humbled, and sweat beaded his brow.

"By whom?"

"M-M-M-Mr. Savage," the man said, shuddering at Atlas' name.

I motioned for us to continue through the doorway that would lead to the depths of the castle. "Very well."

The stairs were made of that dark stone and kept winding down deep into the castle where the light of day would never touch. The stone architecture turned from dark and gothic to a light, sandy color. It reminded me of the walls of the Grand Canyon, except this was no rustic get away.

When I got to the bottom, a state-of-the-art facility was in full swing. Stainless steel beams, countertops, and equipment made up the lab. Vampire technicians in white coats buzzed around with their iPads in hand. Some sat at tall tables with microscopes and others stood in front of a sixty-inch touch screen with DNA strands on display. Our genetic research was some of the most important done in the world of Evermore. Some believed it was the key to unlocking the secrets of the supernatural. Others believed that magic couldn't be explained by a blood test. Me? I thought it made life for vampires a lot easier. The technology we developed here gave us the power to run our blood stores, our vampire police, and our tactical teams. We weren't in the dark ages in this gothic castle.

As a whole, we advanced with the times. Gone were the days of hunting humans in back alleys. Some still did that for sport, but the more refined of us called for delivery. This lab allowed for vampires to become civilized in a way that was never possible before. We were more than just a kingdom of vampires, we were a technological empire. It was a beautiful contradiction: old world values and looks with all the advantages the new world had to offer.

On the perimeter of the lab were holding facilities for the vampires who needed our medicines the most. Some had lost their minds after an infinite lifetime. Some had been born feral and left to die. We tried to help them all. Three of the walls of their holding cells were made of thick rock that was unbreakable even to a vampire. The front wall was a special kind of glass that was also strong enough to hold any kind of supernatural while also allowing our doctors to study them at a safe distance to maybe someday help them.

As I walked by the containment units, the inhabitants were in various stages of madness. One stood in the corner with his back to me, muttering to himself. Another sat on the ground drawing pictures with her own blood on the floor. Farther down was a guy strapped to the bed while a red and black mist swirled from his body and shot back into it, the muscles in his arms, legs, and neck all straining against his restraints. It was like blood magic had gone horribly wrong inside of him. But he was not a born-vampire. I could tell from his lack of heartbeat and pulse. He thrashed on the bed, bellowing in agony.

My brow furrowed. "What's wrong with that one?"

The assistant stammered for a moment, then ran his hand down his face and composed himself. "We have no idea, sir."

The young vampire paused before we reached the next holding room. He shuffled from one foot to the other and didn't make eye contact with me. "I was told to leave you here, and if I didn't leave you here, my entrails would be my dinner tonight. And I fancy my entrails right where they are."

I waved him on. "Yes, we will leave your entrails where they must be. Please let Sav know I'm here."

I'd texted him several times. Usually he answered me within seconds. This time, not one of my messages was answered. A scream echoed from the open door and the sound of metal tools crashing to the floor filled the air.

"Hold her down!"

"Grab her hand!"

"Pin the shoulder!"

Goosebumps broke out on the back of my neck, and I took a step toward the door. The lab assistant ran into the room. A moment later, he flew from the door like a rag doll and slammed into the wall. He fell to the floor in an unconscious heap, his white coat balled around his midsection and shoulders as he slouched to the side. Another scream. I had to know. Had to look.

"Give me the taser!" a familiar voice bellowed.

Sav?

"The sodding thing doesn't have a charge left in it. You've hit her too many bloody times!" a man yelled back at Sav.

"Doc, where is that needle?" Sav's voice was strained, and the sound of groaning metal filled the air.

"Just a moment, my boy," the doctor called back in a panic.

I stepped in front of the window and my blood turned cold. There on the table was a smaller vampire in the throes of feral hunger. Sav leaned over her body, holding down her arms while Jester lay across her legs. Sweat coated them both as doctors rushed around the room trying to gather what they needed to sedate her. I couldn't see her face, but everything about her was familiar.

"Here this will help!" Another assistant ran to Sav's side, wrapped a restraint around the girl's wrist, and tried to fasten it to the metal table.

Sav's eyes widened. "No, don't!"

But it was too late. The woman went into a frenzy and threw Sav and the assistant into the wall. Sav dropped to the ground, dazed and holding his head. The assistant didn't wake up. The second her arms were free, she grabbed Jester by the back of the neck and threw him into the ceiling. The crashing sound vibrated the room and made the lights flicker. Rocks and dust crashed to the floor with him. He didn't move after he fell facedown. The woman sat up straight and my heart stopped in my chest.

"Piper?"

She was covered in dirt and blood. Her hair was in knots and the little white dress was in even worse shape. She tilted her head to the side and sucked in a deep breath through her nose. She leapt up on the table and stood there staring at me for only a second.

Holy shit. She's alive. Shock flooded my body, and I didn't know what to say. I couldn't find the words to even describe the elation and terror I felt at the sight of this crazed little creature. She was deadly and wild, but not in a good way. I held my hand out toward her.

"Everything is okay. Calm down, Piper."

Sav staggered to his feet, sucking in heaving breaths, and narrowed his eyes at me. "Bloody CALM DOWN. You never say that to a woman. What the fuck are you thinking?"

"Shut it," I muttered and didn't break eye contact with Piper.

"Piper, I know you're confused."

She sniffed the air once more and leaned toward me. Her tongue darted over her lips and a low growl rumbled in her chest. She leapt off the table and dove right at me. Her body hit me like a freight train, and I slammed into the wall behind me. Piper's fingers dug into my shoulders, and I felt the material of my shirt rip from her little claws as they punctured my skin. Her mouth pressed to my neck and her little fangs pierced my skin. With the first sucking pull of my blood, pleasure and pain mixed in my body.

"Holy shit! Grayson!" Sav screamed from behind her. "Doc, needle! Now!"

The older doctor fumbled with the syringe as he handed it to Sav. He took it and ran toward us. But she'd gotten her little fangs in me, and I was paralyzed to her whims. Another pulling suck from my blood, and it was all pleasure this time. I groaned and she pressed into me.

She dislodged her fangs from my neck and for a bare second, her eyes cleared. She looked at me, then down at herself. Confusion riddled her face. "Grayson?"

Sav ran up behind her and stabbed her in the neck

with the syringe. When he pressed the plunger, her eyes turned back to that feral beast. She turned toward him and leapt forward, screaming. I caught her around the waist and pulled her back before she took his eyes out. Her body went limp in my arms, and I held her there for a moment. Just staring at her. She was alive. She was here. And she was completely insane.

Sav dropped the syringe on the ground and swiped his hand over his forehead. "Surprise, mate."

I scooped her up into my arms and carried her into the exam room. Her head fell limp over my arm and her hair dragged on the floor with each step I took. I gently placed her on the table and glared at Sav on the other side. "Surprise? That's all you've got to say for yourself? Surprise!? You could've rang me to at least let me know about her."

"I didn't know if we would bloody well make it. The entire team is injured because of her. I might've had to put her down." I flinched at the thought. *Put her down.* "And you've been walking around here like a sad sack for about as long as I could stomach. I'm not a saint."

He marched to the drawer and pulled four metal cuffs from it. Each of them an inch thick and three inches wide. They would react to the system of magnets we had installed under the table. He threw two of them at me.

I snapped one around her wrist and her arm instantly snapped down to her side on the table. Then I did the same to her ankle. "Sad sack indeed."

He didn't say anything else. He just fastened the other side of her body with the cuffs. I pointed to Jester on the floor and the two lab assistants knocked out. "Let's get them some attention."

"Right away." Doctor Stanbourn hurried over to the phone hanging on the wall. He snatched it up and hit the buttons in quick succession.

I stopped listening when he started murmuring. "What the hell is this, Sav? What happened? HOW could this happen? We waited . . . for days."

"I don't know." He pressed his lips together just as more vampires ran into the room.

It was like watching a medical show. They all hovered around Jester and the assistant. A team of them came in with a gurney to scoop up Jester. A younger doctor with blue eyes and long blonde hair pulled into a ponytail hovered over him, checking his vital signs. If he'd been a made-vampire, he'd wouldn't have any.

"Is he dead?"

She shook her head. "Not yet."

They scooped him up onto the gurney and wheeled him out of the room. Four other vampires in lab coats got the assistants to their feet and dragged them away. I turned back to Piper and brushed the hair back from her face. She was a mess. Dirt and blood were caked over her face and hands. Scratches marred her skin. I'd never seen the dress before, but it looked like something she'd stolen. Even that was nearly destroyed.

Doctor Stanbourn straightened his glasses and sucked in a deep breath. He was an older looking vampire. If he were human people would assume he was someone's father. His sire changed him when he'd hit his late fifties, and though the change made him strong and fit, he still held some maturity in his face and grey streaks in his dark hair. The wrinkles around his eyes were nearly smoothed out from the change, but even so, he looked much older than the rest of us. My way of life wasn't typical of other vampires. I was used to the violence and horrors that came with fighting and wars. The witches were a surprisingly vicious lot. Vampires like the good doctor lived a peaceful life, for the most part. Even feral vamps were easily subdued, especially by Sav and Jester. So this situation was new to him. They didn't live in a world of monsters and villains.

"Does someone want to tell me why this feral creature was brought in?" The doctor pulled a small rolling station from the corner of the room.

On it sat his laptop and mouse along with other medical supplies. He stood in front of it and plucked wireless probes from the table, then placed them on her chest and down her arms. The technology would run a full diagnostic on Piper and send all of the data to his computer within moments.

I glanced at Sav, and he looked back at me. This was not a question I wanted to answer. "Doc, can you tell me why she's so feral?"

"Any number of reasons. But mostly, the thirst wasn't sated properly, and it drove her to madness. Whoever made this one was horribly irresponsible."

I curled my hand into a fist at my side. This was all my fault. Her death. The atrocious start to her vampire life. All of it was my failing. I should've been there for her, and I wasn't. Maybe Piper wasn't wrong. Maybe her picker *was* broken, and I had just proven that tenfold. I wanted to be better. I wanted to prove to her that she could trust me *and* herself. And this was what I'd done to her. I'd taken her away from her life, her best friend, and everything she'd known.

"I agree."

Sav growled at me. "It's not true."

"It is." I glared at him. "It was irresponsible."

"Your Majesty. Do you know this woman?" The doctor folded his hands and rested them on the table in front of him.

"She's my—"

"Grayson, don't." Sav shook his head.

"She's my progeny. I sired her." I waited for him to say something, to chastise me for making such a monster. But Piper was no monster. I deserved all the yelling in the world at this point. I'd acted rashly, and these were the consequences.

His mouth dropped into a little O-shape and then he opened and closed it a few times like a fish out of water. He scrubbed his hand down his face. "But you left her."

"She didn't rise, you bloody ponce," Sav snapped and began to roll his sleeves up.

I shook my head, stopping him.

The doctor's brow furrowed. "What do you mean *she didn't rise?*"

Just the thought of it made my stomach turn. "I waited for nearly three days, and she never rose. I waited. I waited next to her the whole time."

"Hmm." He turned to his computer and began to type up notes.

"Hmm, what?" Sav glared at him. "For a man with centuries of education, you lack the words required to explain the thoughts necessary to convey the information we need."

"Much is unknown." When we didn't speak, the doctor glanced from him to me and back again. "We will have to keep her sedated until I can figure out how to clear her mind. She's severely malnourished and physically roughed up. I can't risk my staff working in such close proximity with her until her mind is right. She's just too dangerous. From there, we will know more."

He glanced down at the computer and his lips turned down in a frown. My stomach tightened. "What? What does that face mean?"

"Her physiology is off." He pressed his lips together and sighed. "She might be very sick."

"Might be?" My stomach twisted into anxious knots. How could I have bungled this up so badly?

"Her readings are all over the place. I've never seen anything like it. But at the same time, we are always learning new things about our species and its capabilities. I'll only know when we wake her, and we can't do that right now." He shook his head and pushed his glasses farther up his nose.

"Why can't we do that now?" I wanted her awake and lucid this instant. I had to know if I destroyed the little creature or if she could be saved. I'd do anything to save her.

He took his glasses off and rubbed his eyes. "We had a potion we used to clear the mind of the feral. A favor from a witch, and we used the last of it on another patient before she came in. There's only so much modern technology can do for the supernatural. Sometimes it takes a bit of magic."

Sav pressed his finger to his bottom lip. "So, it's a witch who can make potions that you need?"

The doctor nodded. "It will take some time."

I sighed and ran my hand through my hair. "I know of a witch who can do potions."

"If you could do that, it would save an immense amount of time." The computer screen lit with more information from the monitors. He pressed a few buttons, then looked up at me. "The sooner the better."

"Yeah, we're going to need more security." I glanced around at the few armed guards we had at the entrance of the lab.

Sav's brow furrowed. "What kind of witch is this?"

I sighed and pulled my phone from my pocket to call in a favor I wasn't ready to ask for. "The kind who lives by the motto *stabby stab motherfuckers.*"

CHAPTER TWENTY-EIGHT

GRAYSON

I pressed my finger to the mirror I had set up in a private room on the other side of the lab. It rippled under my touch, and I stood there for a moment holding my breath. I'd never asked the queens for anything before, nor had I planned to. Favors were meant to be used only in dire straits, and I was in one hell of a mess. I stepped through the mirror and into the long hallway. The cold seeped into my bones and yet my palms were still damp from nerves. When I woke this morning, I thought my life was destined to be one way forever. But now all that had changed. I was a sire now, and with that came responsibility.

When I reached the end of the hallway, I pressed my hand to the mirror and it moved under my fingers.

There she was, the little demon witch who could help my Piper. One of the most powerful and ruthless to ever walk the earth. And yet she had the biggest heart for the people she liked. If she didn't like someone, well, I was sure their funeral would be lovely. She lay on an extravagant bed. Holding her legs upright, she crossed and uncrossed them at the ankle. It was a four-poster bed made of dark wood. A bright purple comforter was balled in the middle of it. The rest of the room was small and lined with shelves full of supplies.

Her jet-black hair hung over the side of the bed while the rest of it was braided into a half up faux-hawk. She wore black tights and a black dress with a white collar. Combat boots and an array of knives strapped around her body finished off the outfit.

"Ughhh. I'm boredddd." She rolled to her side. "Let's go do something."

"Maze and Tilly told us to wait here," a man's voice rumbled from out of view. It was the balm to her impatience.

"I think they were wrong." She pulled a knife from a holster on her thigh and began to clean her nails with it. "You want to go train?"

"I'd like to give the shoulder a rest today."

"One little dislocation and no more training. I'll be

gentler next time." She sighed and rolled onto her back. "I gotta go do something."

"When I want gentle, I'll ask for it." He chuckled. "Until then we are to stay put just like they told us too."

I stepped through the mirror and into the room. She rolled off the side of the bed and landed on her feet with her knife pointed at my throat. I held still but wasn't afraid for even a second. Her black eyes widened, and she shoved her knife back into its holster.

"Gray! Cool trick. Mirror travel? Who would've thought?" I could already see the wheels turning. "That's like a no-warning sneak attack type thing . . . I like it."

She leapt up and threw her arms around my neck. I wrapped my arms around her tiny body and gave her a quick hug. "Ophelia."

"That's enough of that," the calm deep voice came from the shadows of the room.

"Cross." I let go of her and nodded in his direction.

He stepped from the shadows and smirked at me. Long strands of his hair fell over the side of his face and into his golden eyes. Cross was only an inch taller than me and we were similar in build, but his dark side was so much darker than mine . . . or so they all thought. We did our customary bro greeting, then stepped back from each other.

"Good to see you, man. What's up?"

I swallowed. "I'm in need of a . . . a favor."

"Ohhh, I'm intrigued." Ophelia bounced up and down. "Yes, I'll do it."

"But you haven't got the foggiest of what I'm going to ask for?" I glanced from her to Cross and back. He just rolled his eyes and walked over to a dresser drawer and pulled a bunch of knives out. He began to strap them to his body.

"Yes, that's the best part, isn't it?"

"What's with the knives?" I pointed to the fifth one Cross strapped to his body. "We're in no danger of a fight."

Ophelia rolled her eyes. "I keep telling him to stop acting like a rookie. If he wants to be ready, he should always be strapped."

"I always have one." Cross rolled his eyes.

"Like I said, rookie move. Who only carries one?" She turned to me. "Ignore him. I'll eventually teach him survival tactics."

"Okayyy." I glanced around at the shelves filled with potion bottles and ingredients. Some of them glowed bright colors, some held a smoky solution, and some had bubbling liquid within. Ophelia, aka death, was the Queen of Potions, which meant that there was no other witch better than her at potions. If I needed it, she would have it. "I need a potion, love."

"That's it?" She groaned. "You know you're all secretive about vampire life and all I want is to know what it's like to bite someone in the neck, and you won't even take me for that."

She glanced at the side of my neck where Piper had bitten me. "But apparently you are into it. First time I've seen you with something like that."

"O." Cross warned.

"Whatttt?" She wrinkled her nose at him. "Fineee. What kind of potion do you need?"

"The kind that can clear the mind of a feral vampire." I held my breath. She had to have it for Piper's sake. She'd been through enough. I just wanted her to live and be healthy.

Ophelia froze and a smile spread across her face. "You have a feral vamp. Where is it? Can I see?"

"She's not a bloody sideshow." I was going to run through the whole room and collect every bit of potion ingredients I could and leave without volunteering up Piper as a form of entertainment.

"Ohhh, so it's a she? Is *she* the *she* who did the fangy bitey bit on your neck?" Ophelia walked across the room and grabbed an empty jar.

Heat flooded my face. "Maybe."

"So, you liked it?"

"O!" Cross snapped. "Do we need to do a lesson about boundaries again?"

"Probably." She waved him away. "Besides, I was just wondering how the bitey bite feels and if we should, you know, play with it."

"You bit me yesterday." He sighed. "Just help the leech out."

"Rigghttt. Yeah, I liked that." She sauntered over to one of her shelves and grabbed two containers, both holding a blue liquid that looked exactly the same. She popped the lid and smelled each of the contents, then held them at eye level examining one and then the other over and over. After a few seconds of inner debate, she shrugged and chose the bottle in her right hand. She poured some into the jar and then paused. She took a look at it, then poured a little more.

Bloody hell. Was she guessing? "Are you sure you know what you're doing?"

She paused with three other vials in her hands and met my eye. "Hello. Queen. Of course I do."

Cross shook his head and mouthed the words, "She doesn't."

A chill went down my spine. "O, this has got to be

done properly." It was life or death, and she was everything.

"Yeah, yeah I got it." She danced around the room and picked up another bottle. She swirled the fizzing pink liquid around, then dumped half the bottle into the jar. A moment later, she dumped the rest in. The contents of the jar fizzed up, nearly pouring over, and she slammed the top down on it. "Behave yourself."

The jar stopped fizzing instantly. I arched my eyebrows at her. Did it just listen to her? Cross chuckled. "I know. Weird."

She poured a couple more things into the jar, and when it glowed a bright red, she nodded at it and tucked it under her arm. "Okay. I'm ready."

I motioned to the jar. "Great. Give it over."

She held it away from me. "No way. Imma go see the feral vampire."

"No, you're not." I shook my head.

"You want the potion?" She wagged it at me.

I pinched the bridge of my nose. "Obviously."

"Then to vampland we go." She walked over to the shelf, grabbed her potion belt from it, and wrapped it around her hips, then she grabbed a handful of vials and threw them all in there haphazardly.

I looked from her to Cross and back again. I knew Ophelia. She wasn't going to budge on this, not even for a second. I could try to use my vampire speed and steal the potion, but that would result in a fight. I would get hurt, she would enjoy it, and I just didn't have time for it. I groaned. "Fine, but if you stab anything, you have to leave right away."

"Booyah, bitch! We going to see the vampires with the fangy fangs."

"Ophelia." This could go horribly wrong at any second.

She held two fingers up. "I will not stab anything. Scout's honor." She looked at her fingers. "This is how you do it?"

"How am I supposed to know?" I turned away from her and headed toward the mirror. I pressed my fingers to the surface and then looked at her over my shoulder. "Come along then."

I pressed my way through the mirror, and it melted over my skin. I was beyond keeping my abilities a secret anymore. Piper needed a solution *now*, and I didn't have time to waste. I stepped into the hallway and waited for them. Cross came through first and glanced around.

"This is nothing like a magical portal."

He wasn't wrong. Most magical portals created by witches or warlocks were just a pure magic that you would float through. Mirror travel was a form of blood magic, but it also spoke of how different our species were. Each time I went through, I stepped into the same long hallway. It was white, sterile, and freezing. Ophelia came through next. She shook her head and brushed her arms down her dress.

"That was slimy." She wasn't wrong. It didn't stay sticky, but in the middle of the thing it felt bloody disgusting sometimes. "I'll pass next time."

My uncle was going to kill me. There was also a chance he wouldn't be surprised at all. Either way, I was screwed. Like, up shit's creek kind of screwed, but I might as well keep paddling. Piper was relying on me, and this time I wouldn't let her down. "When we get through, don't touch anything, got it?"

Ophelia wrapped her arms around herself and shivered. "I'll try."

When we reached the end of the hall, I paused. "Don't try. Do."

I pressed my hand to the mirror and walked through into the lab. Cross jumped in behind me, then held his hand out for Ophelia. When she stepped next to me, her eyes went wide. "Are you serious?"

"What did you expect? Coffins lying about and blood dripping down the walls?"

"Well, yeah. I thought it'd be all cool and creepy.

But this . . ." she looked at all the advanced technology, ". . . is so much better."

I strolled out of the room and began making my way toward Piper. Ophelia sauntered beside me, and the technicians and doctors all froze at the sight of them. It wasn't every day that a vampire saw a Queen Witch, and it wasn't every day that they felt the kind of power that rolled off them. When I'd first gotten to Evermore, it took getting used to, but these were two of the most powerful of their kind. To a vampire who'd never felt it before, it would be both intoxicating and suffocating.

Ophelia turned to the room. "You got a problem?"

I grabbed her arm and pulled her along with me. "They've never seen a witch before."

"So? Doesn't mean they stare." She raised her voice. "It's rude."

"As you were." I waved for them to go back to work.

When they fluttered into action, Ophelia gave me the side-eye. "Exactly how powerful are you among the vampires?"

"Enough." As I dragged her past the holding tanks, her mouth dropped open and she stopped. She froze in front of the vampire who stood in the corner talking to himself. "What's wrong with him?"

"He's older and is lost to the madness of the ages. It happens on rare occasion when an older vampire loses track of what age they're in and the times all blend together."

"Will he be okay?" She sounded genuinely concerned for him.

"Eventually." I kept us moving past the girl playing with her own blood.

"But wait, she looks like we could be friends. You know I love to make friends."

I didn't even acknowledge that one. Only Ophelia would want to be friends with a crazed vampire addicted to their own blood. When we got to the man strapped to the bed with the red and black particles swirling around him, she planted her feet and yanked her wrist from my hand. She stepped in close to the glass and peeked up at Cross. "Do you feel that?"

He moved in closer and whispered. "Oh yeah. I feel it."

"What? What do you feel?" When I looked at him and let my senses take over, I felt only chaos and nothing. "It's only chaos."

"Pure chaos." She placed her hand on the glass.

He threw his head back and thrashed on the bed as the mist swirled around him even faster. It shot into his skin, then ripped back out again, forcing new wounds to appear all over his body. Drops of blood fell to the ground under his gurney and he wailed in agony. Black grains seeped up from those drops and flew right back into him. Alarms blared to life in his room, and the staff began to rush forward.

Ophelia threw her arm out, blocking their path. "Don't go in there."

The blonde doctor tried to shove past. "He needs to be sedated or he will die."

"If you go in there, *you'll* die," Ophelia countered.

The doctor looked toward me. "What do we do?"

I groaned, knowing exactly what needed to be done. I stepped into the doorway and Ophelia jumped in front of me. "Stop him."

Cross slammed his arm down on my shoulder. "Can't let you—"

One second he was there, and the next he was gone. His body hurled across the room and slammed to the top of the wall. He crashed to the ground and popped to his feet. "What the hell?"

Sav stood where Cross had once been. "No one touches him."

"Unless you want your balls chopped off, I suggest you keep your hands off my soulmate." Ophelia snickered at him.

"And what are you going to do, little witch?"

She let her eyes drift down his body. "Why don't you check?"

She had a knife pressed right to where his femoral artery would be. "If I go in one direction, you bleed out. If I go in another, I'd be revoking your privilege of having children."

"Enough!" They all stopped. "Ophelia, I got this."

I stepped around her and into the doorway, just close enough that my blood magic would work. I held my hand out and a fine red mist like sparkles drifted from my hand. It wasn't like the kind of power the witches used. This was subtle, and if no one was looking, it would hardly go noticed. It was like a fine glitter drifting on the air. It touched the man and I let the command seep into my very being.

"Be still." The blood seeping from his body stopped and he fell silent. "Relax."

The tension eased from his rigid muscles, and he went limp on the table. The grainy black mist hummed over his skin, but it didn't fight to tear him apart, and that was something. I dropped my hand and the staff all stared at me. I turned to the lot of them. "Didn't you hear my friend. It's rude to stare."

They jumped into action and collided with each other trying to get back to work. Ophelia gave me the side-eye. "You've been hiding a lot of things, king daddy vamp."

"Don't ever call me that again." I turned away from all of them and walked down to Piper's room.

I felt them all trailing behind me, and it was exactly what I wanted. The doctor sat beside her bed, taking frantic notes on his computer. I walked to her other side and stopped beside her. I was relieved to see that someone had taken the time to clean her up and get her into a hospital gown. When she woke up, I didn't want that gore to be the first thing she saw. Like this, she looked like she was peacefully sleeping. Her hair fell back from her face in wild waves. Her skin was perfectly smooth, even her eyelashes looked thicker. I couldn't believe it possible, but the change suited her. It made her features more defined, her lips fuller and a cherry-red. Even her muscles looked stronger. She was utterly lovely.

Ophelia sauntered into the room and smiled. "Ohhhhh, don't we have a pretty pet here."

The doctor glanced up from his computer and smiled. "Who's this?"

"Doc, this is Ophelia, Queen of Potions, and Cross, Malback heir to the Malback line."

The doctor shot to his feet. "Ophelia as in daughter of . . . of . . ."

"Alataris. The evil king." She offered him her hand. "That's right. But you know he's dead now."

"Indeed, my girl. Indeed." He swallowed and wiped his hand down his jacket before taking hers. "It is an honor." He dropped her hand, then offered his hand to Cross. "To you both."

She extended the jar out toward him. "Here you go."

He took it with both hands like it was the most precious thing in the world. "But the last batch took months to brew."

She shrugged. "Yeah, not everyone is as good as I am."

"Modest, isn't she?" Cross rolled his eyes.

She jabbed a finger in his direction. "Hey, it's not cocky or ego when it's the truth. Besides, every woman should own her awesomeness."

"I wish to change my opinion on the witch. After further consideration, I have decided she is of the blood and standard to which I fully approve of." Sav nodded in her direction.

"So glad you approve." I rolled my eyes.

She winked at him. "Sorry, Mr. Bitey, but I'm taken."

Sav glanced to Cross. "I wouldn't dream of interfering in such a union, but I rather like the thought of friends."

Ophelia nodded. "I'm always in the market for more best friends."

"I was under the impression that one could only have one best friend." Sav chuckled. "How many have you collected?"

"36! I include the lunch lady because she gives me extra brownies." Ophelia leaned over Piper and whispered, "And they are delicious."

I waved my hand between the two of them. "Can we focus here! Ophelia, how do we have to give her the potion."

"Oxygenated face mask is best," she and the doctor said at the same time. She gave him a thumbs-up. "Breathing it in will hit her hard and fast."

Just then a guard knocked on the door and faced me. "Prince Grayson, the King has summoned you to court."

Bloody fantastic, that is.

Cross' eyebrows rose, and he shook his head. "Prince? I knew there was more to you, Leech."

Ophelia sighed. "We all did." She turned to the doctor, completely uninterested in me. "Now, you want to put three drops into the nebulizer and let it run for like thirty minutes."

He took frantic notes on his computer. "Anything else?"

"Yeah, what are you going to do with that guy invaded by black magic?"

His eyes widened. "Is that what it is?"

"And then some." She plucked at an invisible string on her sleeve. "I could stay and help you with that . . . for a price."

"Ooooo," Cross chided.

I couldn't take much more of this. "I've got to see the King. Doc, do fetch me the moment she wakes." I nodded toward the door. "Sav, shall we?"

The doctor turned back to Ophelia. "What's the price?"

I turned and walked out the door with Sav by my side. And then I heard Ophelia muster all the excitement she had to offer.

"Well, I'm looking for best friend 38, and I think blood-girl will fit the bill perfectly."

CHAPTER TWENTY-NINE

GRAYSON

"*Y*ou did what!?" Titus shot to his feet and marched off the dais in the throne room. His face went from placid to bright-red with fury.

"Right. So this is going well," I muttered under my breath.

"At least there is no one to watch," Sav whispered back.

He was right. At least none of the other courtiers were present to watch the King literally tear me to pieces. In all fairness, rightfully so. Even so, his words echoed off the stone walls and high ceilings.

"Of all the daft things I've ever heard of, *this* is what you've endeavored to do?" He threw the length of his crimson coat out of the way and put his hands on his hips.

"If I may—"

"—No, you may not!" Titus cut me off. "You are a Prince of The House of Shade."

"Indeed." I nodded.

"And The House of Shade does not make progenies! We do not bore made-vampires." He ran his hand through his hair and began to pace. It was never good when Titus paced.

"It's never good when he paces," Sav leaned in and whispered in my hear.

"I know."

Titus paused and faced us. "I can hear you."

I cleared my throat. "Uncle, let me explain."

"Oh, so now it's *Uncle* when you've made a complete balls up of everything!" He turned away from me. "And this, the year of the prophecy."

"I know it's bad timing, but—"

"Bad timing?" He seethed. "There is no time for a progeny in this house. How will you care for her? Do you even care for her, or was this some whim of a child?"

"I am nearly two hundred years old. The time for childhood has long since passed."

"And yet you strive to remain so in your actions."

He walked over to the blood fountain and grabbed one of the crystal glasses.

The sound of trickling water filled the room as he filled it, then he reached into his inside pocket and pulled a flask out. He took his time unscrewing the top, glaring at me, then poured a dark brown liquid that smelled like whiskey into the blood.

"It was not a childish pursuit to save an innocent who would've died because of me." It was true. If I had shown up like I promised, none of this would've happened.

"You've spent too much time among the witches. Death comes to us all. Ask him." He waved his glass toward Sav. "He's death incarnate."

"He only speaks in truths." Sav shrugged.

"Not this time. She wasn't meant to be there, and I acted on instinct to save her." Just recalling the sound of the car crashing into her, the snap of her bones, and the blaring horn nearly made me want to vomit.

He walked past us both and climbed the dais. His coat fanned over the arms of the throne as he sat down. "Instinct you say?"

"It happened, and I acted." There was no denying that Piper was mine. Nor did I want to. I would live with the consequences of my actions.

"And then you left her to rot alone?" His tone was

riddled with disappointment. "If it wasn't bad enough to make a vampire, you just left her to go feral. She nearly killed a human."

I fought not to curl my hands into fists. "Right, because leaving her to rot seems like something I would do on a normal basis."

"Are you saying you didn't?" He leaned forward on his throne. "According to all reports, she is as feral as they come."

I wasn't surprised in the least. Titus had a finger on the pulse of everything happening in Evermore. Even more so when it came to dealings within the castle.

"I would never," I said through gritted teeth. "I might've been out and about dodging responsibilities here, but I am not a lout. Nor do I faff about with the ways of our world. I stayed. I waited. For three agonizing days, I waited for the dirt to budge and it never did. Oh, yes, I was there and she did . . . not . . . rise."

It was the most painful three days of my life. Titus groaned and took a deep drink of his blood. "And yet here she is."

"Yes."

"And what's this I hear about a witch and warlock in the castle?" He motioned to the walls surrounding us.

I held my chin up, even though I knew I was so screwed. No other supernaturals were supposed to be in The House of Shade unless given specific permission from the King. "I needed the potion to clear her mind and see if she could be saved. We didn't have any, so I made a call and got some."

"You made a call?" He narrowed his eyes. "To whom?"

Sav and I shared an *oh shit* look, and I squeezed my eyes shut tight. "Ophelia."

"The deadliest Queen of Potions to ever walk the Earth is in my castle right now because of your feral little vampire and you didn't think it would be important to let me in on this information?"

When you put it like that. I flinched at the connotation of my complete lack of respect for the crown in this matter. Was he wrong? No. Did I regret it? Also, no. "My apologies, but I called in a favor."

"We did up the security, I might add," Sav stepped in, but when Titus hissed at him, he snapped his mouth shut.

"Like that would matter." He leaned back in the chair. "Now tell me, were you involved with this human before you turned her?"

"Yes." I wouldn't lie to him, even if it would save me the tongue-lashing I deserved.

"And you cared for her?"

"Yes, but I was leaving to return home the night of the accident and her transformation. It was never the plan to turn her or stay." It was never in the cards for me to stay with Piper or make her a vampire, but fate had other plans.

"Women are never the plan." He sighed. "Men fall hard and often for tiny little things. But let me remind you, you and I aren't afforded that luxury."

"I know."

"No, you don't know!" he snapped. "Your mother is the loveliest creature. It is easy to see why your father fell in love with her, but the curse took him. You are not invincible, and it will take you too."

"I was trying to avoid that." If only he knew how much I tried. I didn't want Piper to become a vampire. I wanted her to live out her human life, get married, have kids. Not walk the night like some cursed creature. But that was exactly what I'd damned her to.

"And yet she now lies in the bowls of this castle as a newly turned vampire." He narrowed his eyes at me. "I'm sure that wasn't part of the plan either."

"Clearly not." Guilt riddled my whole body and a dull ache started in my chest. I'd messed up. "I had no other choice."

"Death was the choice. It was the natural way of life."

She was too young to die, and I couldn't let her go. "Something in me just wouldn't, and I saved her."

He finished off the rest of his drink. "Very well."

"Very well?" My guard went up. Titus was always calm, but when he was this calm in the face of the mess I'd created, all kinds of warning bells went off in my head. There was a cunning side to him that I didn't want to see or cross, and yet I knew damn well I'd crossed it.

"Then she will go to be with her own kind."

"Surly you can't mean . . . Marius?"

Marius fancied himself as the ambassador to the made-vampires, or Night Spawn as we liked to call them. He encouraged their breeding and even more so their loyalty to him. Titus worked with Marius cautiously. It was clear the man had ambitions, but for now Titus held all vampires under his rule.

"That wannabe posh bastard?" Sav shook his head.

"Something you'd like to add, Atlas?" Titus rose to his feet and looked down on the two of us.

I shook my head, already disgusted by the thought. "You can't send her to *him*. He'll turn her into one of his cronies with the slicked-back hair, looking like common movie vampire garbage."

"I'll strike a deal with you then." People wondered where I got my deal-making, convincing nature from. This right here. I'd witnessed Titus do this a million times. Give only two options, but they were two options that he himself could live with.

I arched my eyebrow. "Interesting. What is the deal, Uncle?"

"Your progeny can either go to live with Marius or you will take on the full duties of what it means to be a sire."

"I'll do it."

"Let me finish." He wagged his finger at me. "In doing so, you will stay under this roof. You will participate in the coming prophecy, and you will assume your role as Prince of The House of Shade."

I could already feel the chains tightening around my neck, like I was being strapped here. "And if I refuse?"

He waved my question away. "Then she goes, and you continue on your path of destruction and merriment along with your magical friends."

"I'll do it." The moment I tipped my blood into Piper's mouth, I'd already signed this deal. I wouldn't leave her in a life that I forced her into. Selfish bastard was not a title I wanted added to my name. I gave him a bow and turned for the door, praying that she would wake.

"Oh, and Grayson, one last thing," he called after me.

My stomach sank. I knew it couldn't be that easy. "Yes?"

"Once you've raised your progeny to be self-sufficient you will leave her and never see her again."

The thought of not seeing her shot a jolt of pain right through my chest. Piper was a ray of light in the darkness, and now I'd forced my own darkness upon her. But to stay with her would end me because I would fall. I need only hold off long enough to make sure she was okay. I'd do anything in my power to ready her for the world. She'd never have to work or toil again. Two hundred years of life afforded me a fortune I would lavish upon her for all her days, even if only from a distance.

When I said nothing, I felt his impatience and anger grow. "Do we have a deal?"

My shoulders hunched. I felt deflated. "We have a deal."

Love would always be pain for a Shade. This I knew well.

CHAPTER THIRTY

PIPER

The world was a hazy place, at least at first. My head pounded like I'd been drinking cheap tequila all day on the beach and didn't even bother to have a sip of water. My mouth was dry like a desert, and my entire body ached. It was the kind of ache that came from throwing up all night long. Yet I didn't remember drinking that much or even going to a party. My eyelids felt heavy, like they didn't want to open at all. Even my body felt heavier, and not in a *I ate too many tacos and now I'm boated* kind of way. It was more than that. It was deep in my muscles. I tried to move my arms, but they were stuck to my sides.

I forced my eyes open and everything was blurry. There was a mask over my face, pumping air into my lungs. The flavor didn't feel like that crisp, clean cold oxygen. It tasted more like the bubble gum flavored medicine they used to make me take when I was a kid. An older man hovered close to my face. He shined a bright light into my eyes. I squeezed my eyes shut to block out the prickling light. I turned my head away from him and memories of flashing headlights filled my mind. A blaring horn. Then pain. So much pain.

"Where . . . where am I?" My words were muffled by the mask over my face. Even so, the breath felt weird in my lungs. It was lighter, like there was no burning to breathe, only that it was a habit and my muscles kept on doing it.

He turned to some people in the room. "Best if you give us some space."

Footsteps hurried from the room, and he turned back to me. "Now, if I take the mask off, you're not going to bite me, are you?"

Bite him? What the hell? I shook my head. "No."

He gave me a warm grandpa kind of smile and pulled the mask from my face. I glanced around the room, and this place was like no other hospital I'd ever seen. The walls were a thick, rough rock like the room had been carved from the side of a mountain. Stainless steel counters and equipment lined the room like a super modern hospital.

"You hold very still so you don't hurt anyone else." He moved very slowly as though trying not to startle me. He lifted his head and spoke in a very low, calm tone. "Go get him. Now."

"Go get who?" I pulled at my wrists. They didn't budge an inch. "What's going on?"

I pulled harder and the metal table below me bent ever so slightly. The doctor looked down at my wrists. "Fascinating."

This was it. I was going to die on some psycho's table. He was going to carve me open like a serial killer and bleach my insides before lighting me on fire. I fought against the restraints and kicked my legs, but they too were restrained.

There was a blur of movement at my side and then Grayson appeared. "Piper, shhhh. It's okay. Everything is okay, love."

"Grayson?" What the hell was happening? Was he part of this too?

"Yes, it's me." I'd never seen him have a full smile. But this was a genuine one of relief and happiness.

I held still for a moment. "Please tell me what's going on."

He looked to the doctor and motioned to the restraints. "Let's take these off."

"I'd prefer a bit longer to ensure she won't hurt

anyone." He glanced from me to Grayson and back again.

"Now, Doctor." He kept his position bent down low beside me. He ran his fingers through my hair the way he did on the nights we'd spent together. It always calmed me before and it calmed me now. "You're not going to hurt anyone, are you?"

"Noooo, why? Why would I hurt someone?" I began to panic again, but Grayson shook his head and shushed at me.

"No, you'd never hurt anyone. I know you, Little Creature. All the flies are safe around you." The doctor handed him a remote and he pressed the button. The restraints around my wrists and ankles fell away, and I scrambled to sit up so fast I made myself dizzy.

I pulled my legs to my chest and wrapped my arms around them. I waited for my heart to hammer, but it never came. "I don't feel right."

"I know." Grayson took my hand. "I'm so sorry."

"What happened to me?"

"I need you to stay very calm." He sat down on the table next to me. "What do you remember?"

I shrugged. Everything was so hazy. "I remember walking in the street, then I think a car came and I-I think I got hit." I looked around the room. "Am I in some kind of hospital or something?"

He shook his head and tightened his hand around mine. "Piper, you died in that accident."

My mouth fell open and I shook my head. "No, but I'm alive. Just as much as you."

"I tried to save you, Piper, as best as I could. I tried." His voice broke for a moment, and he cleared his throat. "But your injuries were too extensive."

Tears pricked at my eyes and confusion riddled my mind. None of this made sense. I was here talking to him. I couldn't be dead. "No."

"I want you to know you're still you. Totally and completely you." He met my eye. "Just a bit stronger."

"What are you talking about?"

The doctor took his glasses off and rubbed his eyes with the back of his hand. "Sometimes you just have to come out with it."

"Piper, you're a vampire now." He held his breath, waiting. His face was deadly serious.

A burst of laughter came from my chest. "You're kidding, right?"

He opened his mouth and two fangs popped down. He stayed like that for a moment, then he popped them back in. "I'm sorry, love. It's true."

I sat there for long moments just shocked. I remembered getting hit, the pain over my body, the slow cold that took it over . . . and then nothing. My body was stronger now. I felt the thrumming power through my body. I looked at the doctor. "Are you one too?"

He gave me that kindly grandfather-like smile again, then his two fangs popped right out. "Yes, I am."

I pointed at Grayson. "I had my tongue in your mouth, and I never felt those."

He chuckled and shook his head. "Yeah, I behaved myself."

"I mean, we both know that's not true." My mind raced with a million questions and not even one could be answered before my brain moved on to the next.

The doctor cleared his throat. "My dear, I have to ask you some questions. And if you remember anything, I'd love to know. It could help future newly feral vampires."

"Feral?" How could I be feral? I was calm and collected. "I'm not feral."

"You were for a short time, but you're doing great now, love." Grayson nodded toward the doctor. "Just try if you can."

I pressed my lips together and gave him a little nod. This was the most surreal thing that'd ever happened in my life, or should I say my death. But I was glad I got a second chance. The chance to maybe live just for a moment longer.

The doctor pulled a rolling station closer to the table and perched his glasses back on the end of his nose. "Did you eat an animal?"

I shook my head. "Ew. Not that I can remember."

"Did you have a human?" His fingers flew across the keyboard.

"Oh my God. Grayson, did I kill someone? Did I hurt them? Is that why you all had to tie me up?"

"Piper, calm. Also, ouch." He pulled his hand out from mine and shook it. "Gentle, love."

"Did you have one with alcohol?"

My eyes widened. "Like a person with alcohol?"

He paused and looked up from his computer. "Precisely."

"Um, no? Is that a thing?" I lowered my voice and leaned toward Grayson. "Is that really how vampires get drunk? They get a human to drink and then, you know, kill them?"

"First, we don't kill humans. Second, kind of yes." He nodded.

"Oh, I don't want human blood. I want to do the vegetarian animal thing." I shook my head. I couldn't wrap my mind around biting someone's neck and drinking them down like that.

"Freaking Twilight." Grayson rolled his eyes. "Listen, love, that's not an option. Animals do not provide the right nutrition for Vampires. You'll only make yourself sick and go completely feral from the thirst. It has got to be human blood."

"But what if I don't want to bite anyone?"

The doctor chuckled. "My dear, not to worry. Your sire will teach you all you need to know to thrive and live in this new life of yours."

"Sire?"

He pointed to Grayson. "He's your sire, and he will teach you."

I chuckled and waved his comment away. "Oh, I'm not into that daddy dom thing."

Grayson looked to the doctor and then burst out laughing. The doctor's face turned a bright red and he fumbled with the mouse to his laptop for a few moments before composing himself. He straightened his coat and took a breath. "A sire is not for, um, how do I put this, sexual play. A sire is the term we use for the vampire who made you."

I froze. "You made me?"

Grayson nodded. "I had to save you, Piper. It was the only way I knew how."

"So, what do you call me? Baby vamp? Newbie? Rookie fanger?"

"Well, you're my progeny."

I didn't know what to say about that. It was all so unreal and confusing at the same time. Everything was too much all at once. Shock took over my body and a numbness settled in. I didn't know how to react or if I should react at all. Everyone was so calm like turning into a vampire was a natural thing. Until I knew how to feel about it all I'd do what I normally did. Bottle it up until it exploded out. I'd never relied on someone before, let alone asked them to teach me how to live. I'd always just figured it out. To have to rely on Grayson now was a lot and asked for a lot of my trust, which I didn't give easily. But he did save me, and I was here now. There was no other choice but to get myself up and dust off. I had to learn to live in this world and Grayson would be the one to teach me. Unless I went crazy again, then I would end up being locked up back here.

"Okay. First lesson, sire. How do I not go crazy? Where do we get blood? And how many times do I have to drink it?"

The doctor chuckled and started taking the sticky probes off my skin. "I think that's enough for now. I'll send Martin in to introduce her to the rest."

"Who's Martin?"

"He's the one who will do your vampire orientation." He smiled and rose to his feet. "You'll love him. Everyone does."

The doctor pushed his cart into the corner of the room. "I'll be here, and we'll have an appointment in a few days to check your progress. It was lovely to meet you, Piper."

"Thank you." For some reason, I didn't want him to leave. He was the first person I met in this life, and I knew better than to get attached, but at the same time I liked the older vampire.

Just as he left, another Vampire sauntered right in. He was just a bit shorter than Grayson, with bright-blue eyes and slicked-back blond hair that was parted on the side. He was slim and tailored to perfection in a burgundy three-piece suit, with a pressed white shirt, navy-blue tie, and polished brown shoes. He held an iPad in the crook of his arm and a canvas sack hung from his shoulder. Even his skin was perfect. It was so glossy it nearly shined.

"Hiiiiii, I'm Martin. Not Marty, I hate the name Marty it sounds like the name of a candy. I am both sweet and sour but never Marty. Welcome to The House of Shade and your new vampire life." He gave his best customer service telephone voice.

"Um, thank you?"

Grayson moved to the other side of the room and took a seat on a rolling stool. He leaned back in that casual, confident way he always had about him. "Good to see you again, Martin."

"A pleasure as always, Your Highness."

"I'm sorry, your what now?" Not one time had Grayson ever mentioned royalty. I held my hand up, stopping him from answering. "You know what? Just hold up a second. We have A LOT to talk about. One thing at a time."

"Good idea, love." He smirked and gave me a wink.

I turned back to Martin. "Hi, I'm Piper. It's so nice to meet you."

"Ohhh, I love the take-charge dynamic we have going." He motioned between Grayson and me. "I can totally work with this."

He handed me the canvas bag. "First things first, clothes. I'm sure you'll have closets full to choose from, but for now let's do away with the hospital gown look. It's so . . . Girl, Interrupted."

I peeked into the bag and pulled out a single black dress. It was long-sleeved with a deep V-cut neckline that would go down to my belly button and a high slit that would show a whole lot of thigh. "Is this going to fit?"

Martin pressed a few buttons on his iPad. "Perfectly. I got your measurements from the doctor."

He pulled a pamphlet from the inside pocket of his suit coat. "Now, there are some really great options for blood from the Royal Reserves of Practice Blood, or the RRPB as we like to call it. You can choose your blood by flavors or even favorite blood type. And for our fun party vampires we totally have spiked blood."

"I'm sorry, what?" It all sounded like gibberish to me.

He opened the pamphlet and handed it to me. "Every vampire can order whatever kind of blood they require to survive from our stores, and it'll be delivered right to your door."

"I can order a human?"

He chuckled and shook his head. "No, we prefer no unwanted guests. The blood comes in these very discrete bags." He pointed to a line of swatches. "And you can pick the color bag you like. Kind of like a juice box for any time. Either on the go or at home."

"How do I know what kind of blood I like?" This was the weirdest conversation I'd ever had in my life.

"Oh, that gets even better. For our newly turned vampires, we have a sampler starter set. For the next four weeks, we will send you a sample box of all the different blood types and flavors we have to offer, and you can pick from there. And there is no obligation, you can change your order at any time."

"Why does this sound like an infomercial? I thought you all were going to have to teach me to hunt?"

Grayson pressed his hand to his mouth, fighting a smile. "We've come quite the long way since the old *hunt and kill in alleys* days. Everything is made in our world to keep both humans and vampires safe."

I pursed my lips and turned the pamphlet over. "Efficient. I like it."

"Excellent! So I'll sign you up for the samplers, and when you figure out what you like, we'll just tailor it to your taste." He winked and lowered his voice. "I'll add the spiked side samplers just for fun."

My cheeks heated. "That sounds like fun."

He pulled a phone from his back pocket and handed it to me. "This is your new phone. It has all the vampire apps set up in it. The alarms for sun-up and sun-down are already present and connected to our mainframe, so they'll automatically update no matter the season. There's also an app for vamp-friendly bars, restaurants, and entertainment."

I swiped up and the phone opened for me right

away. It looked like an iPhone but way more advanced. "Is this an iPhone?"

He scoffed. "Honey, no, where do you think they got that technology? Not from humans, I can tell you that."

"Wow. Okay."

"I also have my number and Prince Grayson's programmed in there. So, any time you'd like to hang out, I am around. Because all of *this*—the wild hair, bright eyes, and zero fucks attitude—is just fabulous," he motioned to me, "and I am here for it."

"I have to call Dice and let her know I'm okay."

Silence.

"What?"

They exchanged a look and Grayson readjusted himself in the chair. "Love, you can't call Dice. As far as she knows, you died in that car accident. It's imperative that our world remain a secret from humans."

"Oh, but she wouldn't tell anyone." I shook my head. "I swear she wouldn't."

Martin placed his hand over mine. "Humans cannot know about our world. It's illegal, and if she did find out, it could end up costing your friend her life. It is best that you both grieve each other and then continue living your lives. You wouldn't want to put her in danger, would you?"

"No." I hung my head and tears pricked at the back of my eyes. "I would never want to hurt her."

Martin gave my hand a squeeze and offered a sympathetic smile. "I know it's going to be a transition, but I am here to make it as smooth as possible for you."

I fought back the emotions I would let go later. I needed time, on my own, to mourn the life I'd lost and the friend I would never see again. I couldn't think of her right now. If I did, I would surely lose it. *One thing at a time.* I forced a small smile. "Thank you for that."

His iPad pinged and his smile faltered for a second, then he forced it firmly back in place. "Well, I will have your order placed now and delivered to your chambers."

"Umm, where am I going?"

Grayson rose to his feet. "In the castle. You'll be staying in the suite next to mine."

Heat rose to my face. "Okay."

Martin hit a few more buttons. "Excellent. I'll make all the arrangements."

His iPad pinged once more, and this time he kept his smile firmly in place. "And on that note, the King has commanded your presences. He wishes to meet you, Piper."

I'd never met any royalty before. Nerves gathered

in the pit of my stomach. I grabbed the edge of my hospital gown and twirled it. The fabric tore as easily as if I tore a piece of paper. "Then, of course, I will be there. When would he like to see me?"

Martin looked up from his iPad and met my eye. "Right now."

CHAPTER THIRTY-ONE

PIPER

The dress was too smooth, too airy, too expensive. I felt naked under it. Which I kind of was. There was only a small set of black panties to allow for some coverage, but everything else on me was out . . . all the way out. The dress was a light silky material that flowed around my body with each step I took. The V-cut stopped just above my belly button and exposed all the cleavage my curvy little body had to offer. The sleeves clung tight to my arms, and I let my hair flow free and wild down my back. Changing my clothes and looking in the mirror was an adventure. My skin was only slightly paler, my muscles were more well-defined, and I didn't need an ounce of makeup. My lips turned to a cherry-red. My lashes were so thick I looked like I had black eyeliner on, and even my cheekbones looked high and sharper all on their own. No makeup for eternity. Being a vamp had its perks.

Grayson walked beside me with that smooth, confident glide he always had. He too had taken the time to change, though he was gone and back in seconds, never leaving my side. He wore a double-breasted black suit with a white button-down shirt under it. He'd forgone the tie and left his collar open, exposing that perfect smooth skin. Two little punctures marred the side of his neck, and a memory flashed in my mind of my teeth in him. I flushed with embarrassment.

"Did I do that?" I pointed to them.

"A small price to pay." He pulled his collar up higher, hiding them. "A first for me."

"So, I'm your first?"

"For a lot of things, actually." He smirked.

I tried to play it cool as we took our time walking through the castle. But it was a freaking CASTLE. Never in my wildest dreams did I think I'd even see one of these up close and personal. "You said you were in private security, not a prince."

"When one is trying to maintain a low profile, one tends to omit things to keep them simple. Though it wasn't a lie. I am part of a small group of chosen warriors deemed worthy by fate to protect the Witch Queens of the world."

I stopped walking and my voice rose. "Wait, there are real witches?"

He turned on his heel and moved in closer to me, catching my eye. "All the things you thought were only fairytales are true. The myths are true. The world as you know it is about to become a much bigger place. Are you ready for that, Piper?"

This both excited and terrified me at the same time. "I think so."

He held his hand out toward me. "Then, shall we?"

I placed my hand in his and let him guide me down the hall. I'd never seen anything like The House of Shade. The castle itself was built from a cold dark stone that reminded me of slate. Thick wooden beams arched up the walls and met in carved pointes on the vaulted ceilings. Dim lights twinkled up and down the halls, giving that dark slate stone a warm, gothic feel. Pine garland wrapped around each of those beams and was decorated with winding red and gold ribbons. Christmas trees lined the halls and were adorned with sparkling ornaments.

Vampires milled in the halls like the castle was a social place to hang out. As we walked, they all stopped talking and stared at us. Suddenly, I was self-conscious of my dress. The others were dressed in a more traditional type of ball gown, complete with dress all the way to the floor, sleeves down to their wrists, and collars that cut across their breast the way they did in the history books in old England.

"Are you sure I'm dressed appropriately to meet the King?"

"You look lovely." Grayson slid a group of onlookers a sideways glance and they looked away from us, falling back into their conversation. "The King will be gracious as always."

"If you're the Prince, doesn't that make him your father?"

He pressed his lips into a hard line. "My father died. That wasn't a lie. Titus is my uncle."

"And this is the family business you were running from?" We paused outside a set of carved, wooden double doors.

His lips turned up in a half-smile and he glanced down at me. "Not anymore."

Two guards dressed in crimson uniforms reached for the handles and yanked them wide open. "Presenting Prince Grayson and Piper Santiago."

An entire room of vampires all turned and faced the door at once. I squeezed Grayson's hand, trying to steady myself. Had I still been human, my heart would've raced in my chest and sweat would've covered my palms. As it was now, I felt only my own balling nerves in the pit of my stomach. I wasn't used to being the center of attention, and I was very much at the center of things now. I'd gone from bartender to vampire overnight, and it was all a bit too much.

"Piper," Grayson whispered. "Gentle, love."

"Right. Sorry." I eased my grip and let him escort me into the throne room. Even more vampires lingered around the perimeter of the room. They all froze and watched as we slowly made our way to the dais. There was a stillness to vampires that was unnerving. Humans fidgeted and moved around constantly, even when sitting. But vampires were like living statues.

I wasn't used to my heightened sense, but even I could tell *some* of these vampires didn't have a heart-beat and that others did. I wasn't sure what that meant or how it worked within this strange new world, but I was curious to find out. In old movies, they were portrayed as pale, skinny, bloodsucking demons. It couldn't have been further from the truth. There were all different ethnicities from around the globe here. Yet each of them dressed in that regency-era clothing. It made me wonder, did vampires wear sweatpants? If not, that was about to change really quickly.

Blood fountains were spread through the room and only added that trickling sound to the silence. On the dais sat a huge throne carved from a dark mahogany wood that reminded me of Grayson's eyes. The King sat perfectly still, with one arm resting on the arm of his throne and his elbow leaning on the other while he rested his hand under his chin. I expected a crown . . . he did not wear one. Instead, he had perfectly straight hair that fell just past his shoulders and ghostly light-blue eyes that tracked my every movement, with a light goatee that matched the color of his hair perfectly. The resemblance between him and Grayson was clear in their chiseled features, full lips, and the *I own the world* attitude that just seeped from them naturally.

I expected some kind of royal uniform, but I couldn't have been more wrong. He wore a tailored vest with embroidered crimson swirls that matched the floor-length velvet coat that flowed loosely from his shoulders and over the arms of his throne. A smile spread across his face as we approached.

"Ah, and this must be the Piper I have heard so much about."

Grayson held my hand up and pulled me forward.

He gave a small bow and I tried to follow suit by bobbling out a curtsey. "Indeed it is, Uncle."

"You are a vision. I can see why my nephew chose you for his progeny." He rose from the throne and spoke to the crowd of onlookers. It was all so grand, so opulent, and such a show.

"Thank you, Your Majesty." I felt like I was on display for all to judge and see.

"I told you she's exquisite." Grayson dropped my hand and motioned to me. "Is she not?"

The King walked down the two steps and was face-to-face with me. He looked down on me, and his smile didn't reach his eyes. "More beautiful than I could've imagined."

Why did I get the feeling that wasn't a compliment? He turned to a gorgeous woman standing off to the side. "Isn't she, Moira?"

"Piper, may I present my mother, Moira Shade." Grayson's voice turned warm and adoring at the sight of the woman.

She was lovely to the point where I felt almost connected to her instantly. Absolutely beautiful with dark chocolate, wavy hair that fell all the way to her slender waist and big round eyes that were the same color as Grayson's. Her dress was Old World magnificence. It had a sweetheart neckline that fell off her shoulders. The sleeves started low on her arms and bunched around her wrists. The top corseted tight around her torso and was inlaid with gold embroidery. The rest of the dress flowed to the floor in smooth layers of shining black material. It was simple yet completely stunning.

She gave Grayson a warm smile and reached out for him. He bent lower so she could place both hands on the sides of his face. A faint red glow came from below her fingers, and the two little punctures on his neck disappeared in an instant. She placed a kiss on both of his checks.

"There you are, dear. All cleaned up." Her voice was low and gentle.

"Thanks, Mom," he muttered under his breath.

He stepped away from her and gave her the space to get closer to me. I gave her my best curtsy and lowered my eyes to the floor. "Your highness."

She gave a light chuckled and took both of my hands in hers. She tugged me up and dropped one of my hands to cup my cheek. "It is lovely to meet you. And please call me Moira."

There was an instant connection I felt deep in my chest, like she could be trusted with anything I could ever do. Acceptance rolled off of her in the most motherly way I could imagine. "I am so happy to meet you. Grayson always speaks so highly of you."

She winked at him. "It's a mutual love."

"That we all feel." The King stepped in and took my hand from hers. He spun me toward the rest of the court and stepped to the side. "With my blessings, I present to you . . . Piper of The House of Shade."

A round of dignified applause broke the silence of the room. It was all so proper. There was no hollering or whistling. It started gently and ended just as quietly. I didn't know what else I was supposed to do. Did I bow? Did I give a speech? Was I a princess now or just the little beast he created?

A voice boomed from the back of the room. "And that concludes the introduction of the newest progeny of The House of Shade."

Without any fanfare or hubbub, the members of the court all moved toward the double doors, leaving the four of us to stand there alone. When the doors sealed shut, Titus took in a deep breath and let it go on a sigh. "That went about as well as to be expected."

Grayson removed his coat and tossed it aside, then rolled up his sleeves. "Indeed."

"Now, my darlings, don't fret. All will be well." Moira stood between the two of them like the sweet white frosting in the Oreo cookie between the two hard sides.

Gone was the perfect picture of serene royalty, and in its place were three visibly stressed vampires. I couldn't help but feel it was my fault. "Have I done something wrong?"

"No, my dear."

"Of course not."

"Not in the least."

They all answered at the same time. I glanced around at the three of them in their overly proper clothing and their perfect British accents. It was clear I was not up to that standard of royalty. I was an orphan from Salem, not a debutant in London. "I'm sorry to say so, but you all don't seem very happy about this."

King Titus sighed. "It's not that we aren't pleased to have you with us, Piper. You are quite lovely indeed. But there are certain things within our society that are taboo, and a royal making a progeny is one of them."

I turned toward Grayson. "You were supposed to let me die?"

He straightened his shoulders. "I've never been one to follow the rules, love."

"Well, if that's not the understatement of the year." Titus put his hands on his hips.

This whole thing confused me. "But aren't all vampires made this way?"

Moira gave me a gentle smile. "No, some vampires are born much the way a human would have a baby. They are the natural born vampires. And others are made, like you. The catalyst is death."

Why did that feel so awful? "But I feel so alive."

"You are no different than us." Titus was adamant. "All vampires are created equal."

The double doors flew open and smacked into the walls with an echoing bang. A man stood in the middle of them looking very out of place among the royal beauty. He was tall and slim with dark hair cut close to his head on the sides and spiky on top. His face was strong and angular, with plump lips and a thin goatee around his mouth. Though the rest of us were in gala attire, he wore tight, dark gothic pants, a loose knit black sweater, and a modern trench coat that stopped just at his ankles. "That's what I always say, aren't we all the same?"

"I don't recall inviting you, Marius." Grayson took a protective step in front of me.

"I did," Titus groaned. "Though you are late."

Grayson glared at him over his shoulder. "*You* did this?"

"It is the law, and I must uphold it. Because I'm the

one who bloody well made it." Titus waved to Marius. "Enter."

Marius motioned to someone in the hall. There was a blur of movement, and a younger vampire joined his side. Grayson growled. "Lovely. He's brought his pet."

The *pet,* as Grayson called him, was clearly a made vampire but had been turned in his late twenties. Straight, sandy blond hair fell all around his face. This guy was beautiful in an intriguing kind of way. Like a nineties heart throb with his perfect face, bow-shaped lips, and strong chin. He had a sleek, muscular build that fit perfectly in his dark blue jeans and black turtleneck sweater.

"Tut tut, we both have progenies now. Not pets, Grayson." Marius wagged his finger at him. "Respect for all vampires, remember?"

"You may call me Your Highness or Prince Grayson." Grayson didn't step from in front of me. "And of course I remember. I bloody well wrote that law, you daft—"

"Grayson, dear, manners." Moira lightly placed her hand on his arm, silencing him.

The vampire waved to me. "Hey, I'm Theon . . . the pet."

"Hey." Grayson shot me a look and I stepped out from behind him to offer Theon my hand. "I'm Piper."

A smile spread across his lips, and he took my hand. "It's nice to meet you. Good grip you've got there."

I quickly dropped his. "Don't know my own strength just yet."

"I like it." He chuckled.

"What do you want, Marius?" Grayson grabbed my elbow and escorted me to his side.

"To meet our latest Night Spawn. As per the agreement we have made with the crown, all Night Spawn are to be registered with us in London and then reported to you." Marius moved in front of me and extended his hand toward me with his palm up. "And aren't you just a lovely little one."

I glanced at Grayson, and he gave me a little nod of encouragement. I laid my fingers in Marius' palm, and he tugged me close to him. I stumbled forward, and before I even stood straight, Titus and Grayson were beside me like two guard dogs. They hissed a warning at him, but he didn't let go of my hand. Instead, he held on tighter. Marius chuckled and bent low over it and pressed his clammy lips to my skin. I shoved my hand forward and yanked it back hard, knocking Marius to the ground at my feet.

"Oops." I wiped the back of my hand down the side of my dress. *Gross.* "I'm really having a hard time getting used to this whole *super strong* thing."

He popped to his feet and gave me a little bow. "Difficult when you're new."

"Riighhtt. That's what it was." This guy reminded of all the skeevy ones who came to the bar and hit on me. I knocked them on their asses too. I guess there wasn't that big of a difference between vampires and humans after all.

Theon chuckled and shook his head. "That's a first."

"I'm sure it won't be a last." I narrowed my eyes at him. I didn't need this on my first night as a vampire. I wasn't some toy to be tugged on between both sides of some odd vampire hierarchy I didn't understand.

"Marius." Titus waved his hand and the vampire stood straight and faced him as though following a silent command. "Do not forget you are a guest in my castle and can be easily replaced. As stated, we have other ambassadors who would love your job."

Sweat beaded his brow and his muscles shook like he fought whatever hold Titus had on him. His eyes bugged from his head and the muscle in his jaw ticked with annoyance. "Yes, and give my regards to your sister, will you?"

Another waved of his hand and Titus released him. Marius stood straight. He pulled at the collar of his sweater. Titus turned his back to Marius and walked up the dais toward his throne. "And you have the job of ambassador by my will alone. Next time, decorum is necessary . . . and perhaps a tie."

"Yes, my King." If ever a man had gotten knocked down a peg or two, it was Marius in this moment. He gave him a deep bow, and his cocky attitude was held in check, though it visibly pained him to do so. This was a vampire who owned his own little piece beyond these walls. I'd seen gang leaders like that. But there was always a bigger fish, and Titus was the megalodon to Marius' little minnow.

Titus whirled around and sat down on the throne. He crossed his legs, then waved him away. "Next time be on time. I will see *all* vampires are well. You are dismissed."

Without another word, Marius and Theon darted from the room in a blur of movement.

Grayson rounded on Titus. "He's a bloody fucking halfwit, he is."

"I don't disagree." Titus sighed.

"We need a new ambassador, Uncle. The crown has been working toward advantages for all vampires. Is he really the right choice in this matter? You did not have him in mind when you started to change our world."

"Indeed, I did not. But that is a problem for another day." He waved toward me. "Just go register her."

"I will." Grayson grabbed my hand and pulled a handkerchief from his pocket. He rubbed it over the spot where Marius kissed my hand. "Disgusting sack of piss."

"Tonight." Titus seethed from his throne.

Grayson opened his mouth to argue, but Moira stepped between the two of them. "Sometimes it's better to just get things out of the way. Would you not agree?"

I could see Titus and Grayson butted heads even if they did love each other. "I've never been to London. It might be fun to see some of it."

Grayson sucked in a breath through clenched teeth. "Very well. Tonight it is."

Titus glared at him. "This is what happens when you have to clean up the mess you've made."

Grayson looked me up and down. "Or my greatest accomplishment yet."

CHAPTER THIRTY-TWO

PIPER

"*S*top staring at me."

"I can't help it." I didn't take my eyes off Sav. "I *knew* you were a vampire."

He didn't look at me. He just kept on walking down the hall. "I don't think when one sees a person, they think vampire right away. I'd be lying if I didn't say I doubted your abilities to judge me so in your human life."

"Oh, yes I did. You're too . . ." I wrapped my arms around myself and pretended to shiver, ". . . like, cold and creepy."

"On the contrary, I'm quite warm-blooded." He arched an eyebrow at me. "Creepy?"

"Totally, you've got stone-cold killer written all

over you. How many people *have* you killed?" I kept turning my head to look at him even when he didn't dare look at me. There was something so pokable about Sav, like he was so serious but in a way that begged to be bothered.

"Countless." He stopped at the mirror at the end of the hall and pressed his fingers to it. He didn't bother to wait for us before he shoved himself through.

I hiked my thumb at him. "That's your best friend?"

"For as long as I can remember." Grayson motioned for me to step through the rippling mirror.

It was surreal to be in this position. I couldn't believe I was dating a vampire as a human and now was one myself. This world was unbelievable. When things stopped being crazy, I might actually get my bearings. For now, I went with what they said and asked me to do. They'd been vampires for . . . I paused before I stepped through.

"Um, how old are you?"

He pressed his hand to my back, nudging me forward as he chuckled. "Worried I'm an old man?"

When I stepped through the mirror, a shiver went down my spine. It felt cold and gooey over my skin, like I'd fallen into a bucket of slime. As I stepped through to the other side, the mirror peeled off my skin, leaving none of the stickiness behind. I looked down at my dress expecting glittering piece of the liquid mirror to still be there or to be a little damp. But no, I came out exactly how I went in. I dusted my hands off and faced him as he came through.

I scoffed. "I think it's too late to worry about old. But I was curious. Are you a thousand?"

"Though I am wise," he walked to stand beside Sav, "I am not old, love. I'm one hundred and ninety-nine to be exact."

"So, you are totally old."

A bark of laughter came from Sav's lips, and he crossed his arms over his chest. "She's not mistaken."

"Good to see you two have reached an agreement on something."

We stood in an abandoned building. There was a lone mirror in the back corner of a room with broken down walls covered in graffiti. Pieces of ripped plastic tarp hung from doors and exposed ceiling. It was a half-finished construction project that'd been long since abandoned. Broken, exposed pipes and beams hung low everywhere. The cool wind whipped through the building and made goosebumps break out over my skin.

"Where are we?"

"Tower Hamlets. It's a borough in London." Grayson walked in front of me toward a broken window.

It was a stark contrast to the royal opulence of The House of Shade. After everything I'd seen there, this was a severe down grade here. Grayson kicked the rest of the glass out from the window, then climbed out of the building onto a ledge. When I made no move to follow, he peeked his head through.

"Come on then." He nodded toward the outside.

I kicked one leg through the window and placed my foot on the small ledge. The wind whipped past us, sending my hair and dress flying around my body. I stood there looking down at a dark street at least six stories below. This part of London was like nothing I'd ever seen in pictures before. It was rundown and dangerous-looking. The buildings were in disrepair and covered in graffiti. Boarded up windows were a staple in the area. Multiple barrel fires were spread up and down the back-alley streets and disheveled-looking people gathered around them warming their hands against the winter night. There was no merriment for Christmastime here. It was sad and violent. They were all so far away, yet with my vampire eyes I could see everything perfectly. I clung to the side of the building, holding myself on that narrow ledge.

"Now what?"

Sav chuckled. "Are you scared?"

"I'm hanging off the side of a building. Any normal person would be scared." My fingers dug into the brick exterior, and it crumbled under my grip.

"But you aren't normal, and you aren't a person. You're a vampire." He let go and leaned back. He fell off the side of the building with his arms spread wide. His hair whipped into his face and he closed his eyes. His echoing laughter filled the air and faded away as he disappeared.

"Oh my God. He's insane!"

Grayson smirked and winked. "He's not wrong. Trust your instincts and let's have a little fun."

He let go and stepped off the side of the building, falling into the darkness behind Sav. I held onto the building tighter. I closed my eyes. "Oh shit, oh shit, oh shit."

My mind told me this wasn't possible. That old saying, 'if a friend told you to jump off a bridge, would you?', came to mind. Reason told me not to. But it also told me vampires weren't real, and yet I was one. There was no *reason* behind any of this. But it was a new world and a new way of life, and I was going to live it. I let go and leaned forward.

I dropped from the ledge and let gravity take me.

My stomach went up into my throat and my hair whipped back from my face. The slit of the dress opened and my legs were exposed to the crisp air. One moment I was free falling with panic riddling my body and the next I felt in total control. My instinct took over and I rotated in midair. I wasn't a kid about to do a belly flop into a pool. I was a cat finding my feet no matter what distance I fell from. My legs pointed down as the street rushed toward me. I hit the ground and it was like stepping out of bed. My legs bent, taking the impact, and my dress fell into place around me. There was no pain. I even caught my balance right away.

Grayson and Sav melted from the shadows of the building. Sav crossed his arms over his chest and fought a smile. He gave me a nod and walked down the alley. Grayson didn't bother to hide his smirk. "Very good, Little Creature."

I looked him up and down. "Pshh. And I did this in heels. How are your nice flat shoes?"

"Sassy, I like it." He crooked his finger at me, then turned and walked away.

Excitement flooded my body and I wanted to run and play all night long. It was all so new, and I might've been dead, but I'd never felt so alive. I jogged to catch up to him, which only took a second. We wound our way through people huddled on the streets, broken down cars, and crumbling buildings. Had I been human, this whole scene would've freaked me out and had me holding my taser at the ready, but I wasn't and it made me feel completely empowered. No one could hurt me anymore. I was strong and I felt it in my bones.

Sav stopped in the middle of the street and look up at an old hotel. It took up the whole corner of the street. The outside was tan with cracked red trim. Dark, dirty stains ran over the entire place like at one point a fire had gotten a little too close to the outside and scorched it. A bank of doors ran across the entrance. Where the glass would normally be was covers with sheets of plywood. They opened every few minutes and someone would slip out and disappear around the corner. Had I come across this place in Boston, I would've thought it was a crack hotel.

Sav nodded at it. "I'll wait here for you."

"We'll be quick." Grayson motioned toward the doors. "Shall we?"

"We shall." I didn't hesitate. I stepped in front of him and marched toward the doors, feeling all the confidence in the world.

I'd just stepped off a building and landed like a superhero on the street below—in heels and a dress.

One little registration office was no big deal. I reached for the door and yanked it open. The metal hinges groaned and snapped right off.

"Oh shitttttt." I held the whole door, metal frame and all, with the plywood in one hand.

I turned to Grayson as he stood there laughing his ass off. I waved it at him. "Be good or imma throw this at you."

Two maintenance men came running out of the hotel in their long sleeve blue coveralls and matching hats. "Don't worry, ma'am. Happens all the time."

They each grabbed one end of the door. One held it in place while the other pulled new hinges and a handful of screws from his pocket. They moved it to where it'd been before I'd ripped it off. The guy didn't even pull out a drill, he just held the hinges in place and quickly punched the screws in, then did the same on the door. He swung it back and forth, giving it a test run.

"See? Good as new."

I pointed to the guy and gave Grayson a thumbs up. "You should tell your uncle these guys are super efficient."

"Noted."

It was only then that the two men noticed him standing there. They both froze with their mouths hanging open, staring at him. Grayson met their eye and gave them a half-smile. They didn't move. He took a step toward the door. They still didn't move.

"Lads, do you mind if we just . . ." He motioned to the door and the two men jumped into action. They collided with each other, then both of them scrambled to open the door for us. At the same time, they yanked the door right off the hinges again.

I pressed my hand over my mouth and forced myself not to laugh. Grayson gave them a smile and then pressed his hand to my back. "Let's continue."

He patted both the men on their shoulders as we passed. "It's alright."

The inside of the hotel was shockingly different from the outside. I expected an old rundown interior with bad lighting and disgusting furniture. But I was learning that in this world nothing was as it appeared. The interior was chic, clean, and very London Punk. The walls were painted a matte-black finish, but there were brightly colored paintings everywhere. The floors were black wooden planks laid in a herringbone pattern. Bright, funky furniture was spread throughout the lobby and there were vampires lounging everywhere. I thought this would be a den of humans lying around and a bunch of ugly-faced vampires feeding off them while a woman in the corner threw stacks of papers around. What I got was a sleek-looking lobby complete with a front desk and a little rope to guide people to the proper line.

The female vampire behind the desk was a character all by herself. Her outfit was everything punk and amazing. She wore blue denim shorts, fishnet stockings, black combat boots, and a ripped black t-shirt that showed her hot-pink tank top under it. The whole thing was topped off by a leather jacket with silver zippers everywhere. The makeup around her eyes was dark and dramatic, along with her dark-red lips.

When I approached the counter, she gave me a warm smile and leaned on the desk in front of her. "Hi, my name is Amanda. And welcome to the Night Spawn headquarters. How can I assist you today?"

"We're here to register her properly with the Night Spawn." Grayson rested an elbow on the high counter in front of us.

She gave him a glance, then did a double take. She straightened her stance and messed with her thick dark hair. "Gra . . ." She cleared her throat. "Grayson Shade."

"That's right." He gave her a little wave. "Nice to meet you."

Her eyes widened when she turned back to me. "That means you're Piper Santiago."

"News travels fast," I muttered.

"In this world, always, Little Creature." He winked at her. "Amanda, love, I'm wondering if we might be able to do this quickly. She's had quite the night already and I feel a bit of rest is in order."

"Absolutely." She pulled an iPad-looking tablet from behind the desk and laid it on the countertop. If you would place your finger on the circle for a sample, we can get started."

I pressed my finger to the circle and a quick pinch pricked my skin. I jerked my hand back. "Ouch."

A drop of my blood rested on that little circle. It seeped into the tablet, and she took it back behind the desk. Her brow furrowed in confusion, and she pouted her lips. "Hmm, I think it's broken." She gave it a little shake. "It says *unclassified*."

"What does that mean?" I wrinkled my nose. "Last I checked, I'm totally a vampire." I leaned in and let my fangs pop out, then I whispered, "I just jumped off a roof and landed . . . in heels."

Grayson held his hand out for the tablet. "May I?"

Amanda hesitated for a moment and then handed it over to him. He took it and ran his hand over the screen for a moment, then handed it back to her. "All fixed."

"How did you know how to do that?" She shook her head. "What I mean to say is, thank you, Your Highness."

"Grayson is good, Love." He gave her that dazzling smile and I swear I witnessed another person falling under his web of charms. "And I just overrode it. She's Night Spawn, not a Day Walker."

"Right. Of course." Amanda shrugged. "I have no idea why it did that. The rest of the stuff is working properly."

The screen lit up and the blue light illuminated her face, reflecting off her glittery eyeshadow. "Okay, first things first. Is your death a clean one or do you require a cleaning crew to make it so?"

"A cleaning crew?" That sounded so *men in black*.

"In the event of a disappearance, we would fake your death to give any living relatives closure and ensure no one will be searching for you. There is a thirty-day period with this as we have had some, dare I say, messy deaths to clean up as of late." She glanced up from her tablet, waiting for my answer.

My thoughts turned to Dice, and a dull ache started in my chest. I couldn't imagine eternity without her. Sadness assailed me and I was lost in thoughts of all the time we'd spent together. And now I was going to live forever . . . without her?

"Yes, Atlas took care of everything." Grayson's words pulled me from my thoughts and back to the present, but the dull ache remained the same.

"Atlas . . . Savage?" Amanda glanced around the lobby and down the little hall right behind her. "He's not here, is he?"

"He's waiting outside, why?" I was genuinely curious why she seemed so nervous.

"I've heard things about that guy." She shivered. "He's terrifying."

"Indeed, he is, love. But I promise he's of no dangerous to you tonight." Grayson caught her eye. "So shall we continue?"

Dazzled, she blinked at him for a moment before jumping into action. "Right. Okay, so no cover-up?"

"Not at all."

"Right this way." She picked up the tablet and waved for us to follow her.

She sauntered down the hallway and I followed quickly behind. The hall was long with multiple doors. Each of them was made of frosted glass and thick black metal. The doors slid opened and closed automatically as vampires walked in and out. We stopped at the first door, and it slid open. An entire salon flashed into view. It was modern and chic with black chairs, black counters, and bright hot-pink walls. But there weren't hairdressers. Instead, men and women all stood behind their clients with magic swirling around them. With a flick of the wrist, magic of all colors flew from their fingers and around the heads of their clients, changing their hairstyle completely.

"Cool!" I wanted to walk in and sit and watch for the rest of the day.

"Will you be needing a new look to hide your old identity for a while?" She motioned to the salon. "Short and blonde might suit you."

"Absolutely not." Grayson shook his head. "You don't mess with perfection."

"Moving on." The girl walked farther down the hall and another door slid open to reveal a small bar.

It looked so cool, like an underground punk bar, with dark furniture and wild colors on the wall. Vampires sat at the bar, each of them had one of those mini-sampler cup trays in front of them. Music drifted out toward us, and it reminded me of a trendy beer bar in the heart of Boston. Except these vampires were sampling blood. It was all so much fun. They laughed and sipped just like they would have if they'd been alive.

"Would you like to set up for a blood delivery service? We have samples."

Martin had already done so when I was in the castle. I gave her a smile. "I think I already have."

Grayson nodded. "Already taken care of."

Amanda typed on the tablet. "Housing? There's usually a three-month time when new vampires will stay with us. Would like to be relocated to a different part of the world?"

"Taken care of," Grayson said.

"Clothing?"

"Done."

"Classes?"

"In process."

Amanda pressed the tablet to her chest and sucked in a breath. "I'm not feeling very helpful here, Your Highness. If everything is done, then what is she doing here? She's essentially a royal."

I was beginning to wonder the same thing. Why bring me here when everything was taken care of? Grayson chuckled. "First, it's the law. Second, she needs proper identification."

"Ah, right." She turned and led us back down the hall and into the lobby. But I wasn't done exploring. I wanted to see more of the building, meet more of the other vampires, try the bar. It was all so cool. I wasn't ready to leave just yet.

We stopped back at the counter, and she reached below the desk and handed us a sealed manila envelope. "Everything you need for your new life."

When I opened it, three IDs fell out: a vampire identification that looked strangely similar to a New York driver's license, an actual human license for Great Britain, and a single human passport. "No vampire passport?"

"Mirror travel doesn't require a passport." She winked and handed me her card. "Piper, anything you might need, you can always contact me right away."

I slid the card back into the envelope along with the IDs "Thank you so much."

Grayson gave her a little nod. "Well done, love."

"Anytime, Your Highness." She beamed at him with her little fangs showing.

I gave her a small wave and then we both walked out the door, and I felt a little more at ease . . . for just dying. Grayson stood beside me on the street. I sucked in a breath, taking in the cold night air and the strong smell of something delicious. "Oh, I miss pizza already."

"Don't worry. It won't be all blood all the time." He nodded toward the Pizza Hut across the street. "Your body will start to adjust and food will become a thing again."

I stared at the glowing sign and my mouth watered. "I want it."

"Not a good idea."

"How bad could it be?"

"Badddd."

I took a step toward it. "Imma do it."

CHAPTER THIRTY-THREE

PIPER

"I shouldn't have done it." I lowered myself to lie on the cold bathroom tiles. The bathroom was far too beautiful for this. White marble tile wasn't meant to be used as a cold compress for vampires heaving up pizza they never should've eaten. I eyed up the shower with like eight hundred heads, wondering if burning myself under an onslaught of hot water would make me feel any better.

Grayson placed a towel under the tap, soaking it in cool water. He gave it a little squeeze, then laid it over my forehead. "Fledglings don't handle food well. You'll be on mostly blood for a while."

My stomach rolled and I rushed to sit up, waiting for the heaving gags to take me. I rested my head on the toilet seat, but nothing came. Maybe I was done?

Forgotten memories flashed through my mind: running in the woods, hunting, the burning thirst. I shook my head and squeezed my eyes shut.

"Piper, are you well?" Grayson hovered close by, and I wanted to tell him to leave me here to rot in the things I'd done to myself. No girl wanted the guy she liked to witness this.

"Yeah, I think so." But I wasn't. It was coming back in pieces. Animal blood in my mouth, the taste of vomit, the driving need to hunt.

I flopped back down on the ground and rested my head against the side of a huge bathtub. Grayson handed me the damp towel. "Right, blood from now on. You're a vampire and have to accept that."

"I've been a vampire for like a day. Well, only one day that I can clearly remember, and really all I know is I'm strong and drink blood."

He sighed and sat down next to me. "You're rather fast as well."

"I sound like Superman." I swiped the towel over my mouth.

"Not quite. You can't go out in the sun." He gave me a sad smile. "It'll take time getting used to it."

I sagged even more. I would miss the warm sun on my skin and the way it smelled on the flowers in the summer. But if I was being truthful with myself, I was a night creature way before I actually became one. "I'm going to miss the beach, but it's still beautiful at night. And truthfully, I used to sleep most of the day anyways. What else doesn't apply? What about garlic?"

"Myth."

"Will I light on fire if someone hits me with a cross?"

He chuckled. "No. Myth."

"Glow like a diamond in the sun?" How cool would that be?

"Oh, if only. I wouldn't need half my charm if I did." He rose to his feet and offered me his hand.

"Holy water?"

"Myth." He stuck his fingers under the water, then sprinkled me with it. "You can bathe wherever you'd like.

"Silver bullets?"

"Myth, and I believe that's werewolves, but its also a myth for them. They're quite difficult to put down, actually." He opened a drawer and pulled out a toothbrush and toothpaste then handed them over to me.

"Do we also have dentists?" I teased before loading up the toothbrush and scrubbing away.

"You're a funny one, you are." He handed me a dry towel.

I wiped my mouth on it and stood there for a

moment staring at the white towel smeared with red. Flashes went through my mind, and I was back in a forest hunting. The pain in my chest was nearly unbearable. I sucked in a breath and bent over. Another memory hit me, and I tried to push it away. Blinding headlights, screeching tires, and metal hitting my body. I leaned into him and wrapped my arms around his midsection, pulling him closer. I snuggled into his chest and stood there for a moment, trying to find comfort in him from the craziness of the day.

Grayson stiffened against me. I loosened my hold on him. "Too hard."

"It's not that." He disentangled himself from me. "Piper, we can't."

I glanced around the bathroom. "Can't what?"

"This." He motioned between the two of us.

WHAT?

Then the memory hit me all at once. I froze. I'd been waiting for *him*. I'd gone looking for him the night of my death. He said he'd be there, and he never showed up. I went to find him, to confront him. I took a step back from him. "That night . . . you weren't there."

"Yes." His face turned deadly serious.

"Then why?" I motioned to the opulent surroundings. "Why all this?"

"You'd gotten hit. I wasn't fast enough to stop the car. I couldn't let you die."

"You couldn't show up either." I shoved him and he flew back, skidding across the floor.

"Piper," he warned.

It was all becoming so clear. I was pissed at him that night. We'd been perfection. He'd been warm and loving. The trust was there. Then he hadn't shown up. "Typical guy. Got too close, got scared, and bailed."

He held his hands up. "It's not like that."

"Then tell me, Prince Grayson, what was it like?" I put my hands on my hips.

"I don't have an explanation."

I knew something was weird. He hadn't tried to touch me, or kiss me, or even hold me close. Sure, when I first woke, he'd held my hand and tried to calm me. But besides that, it'd been all formal distance. I thought he was giving me space to adjust. But nooooo, he was putting distance between us. "The freaking picker strikes again."

"Don't say that." His hands curled into fits. "There is nothing wrong with you or your choices."

I rolled my eyes. "Yes, as proven by this situation. And you want me to live here with you? That's gonna be a *no* for me."

A low growl escaped his lips. "You are my progeny, you will stay here for as long as I say so."

Oh, this was an ugly side of him that I didn't want to see. Grayson had made me believing in romance again, in something more. But *this* . . . this was not that. This was complete bullshit. "Right, because what you want matters. I think you've gotten exactly what you want all the time, Prince."

"You. Will. Stay," he hissed, and I could feel the anger rolling off him.

I waved his words away. This was not a side of him I was willing to tango with. Either he'd get it together or I was out. Pretty bathrooms be damned. I was strong now, and I'd like to see him freaking try to keep me here. "Why did you change me? If you were just going to be a coward, then why? Why take the time to make me feel good? Or start a relationship with me? Was this your plan from the start? Find a girl, make her love you, then *wham*—turn her into a vamp. Keep her forever or until you get bored?"

"I was gonna break up with you!" He turned away from me and groaned. He ran his fingers through his hand and pulled at the strands. He sucked in a few deep breaths, and when he turned back, he looked like a completely different Grayson. Gone was the cocky, *come what may* attitude, and in its place was one stressed-out vampire.

That drew me up short. "What?"

"That night . . ." He paused and cleared his throat. ". . . the night you died. I was going to end it with you, then I saw you get hit."

Speechless, I looked around the room for something to say. Some way to escape this very moment. Tears threatened to spillover, but I held them back. There was no way I'd let him see me cry. I'd been right the whole time.

Stupid picker. "You are a coward. You should've let me die."

"Not in my nature to let the wonders of the world die."

Charming bastard. "Gee, Piper, I'm going to break up with you but also at the same time turn you into a vampire for eternity. Oh, and by the way, I'll be your sire and linked to you forever, making this the most awkward ex situation possible!"

He lowered his voice to make it sound *sooo* calm. "Only if you make it so."

Two could play at that game. I put on my pleasant customer-service voice. "I want you to listen closely, and I mean this in the nicest possible way, go fuck yourself."

I stormed past him and right for the door. I didn't know where I would go or who I could ask to take me back to the Night Spawn headquarters, but that seemed like a good place to start. This was bullshit. He was going to break up with me and then on a whim decide *nah* I'll make her immortal instead and take her away from everything. Who knew if I was even going to die in that street or if he'd just made the decision. Grayson Shade couldn't be trusted and neither could my damn picker.

I opened the door and stormed out into the hallway of the castle. Everything was so Gothic, so pretty, and it all looked the damn same. Grayson flew out behind me. "Piper!"

I froze and didn't dare turn around. A group of vampires who'd been meandering in the hall stopped to look at us. "Get used to your surroundings. Because you're stuck in this palace for a year."

"The hell I am!" I whirled around, ready to go head-to-head with him. His princely ass was about to meet my bartender boot.

"What's this now?" Moira's gentle voice interrupted our little spat. And by spat I meant me being so right and him being so wrong.

I took a deep breath and turned to face her. I forced myself to curtsy and schooled my features so as not to offend her. It wasn't her fault her son was an ass. "Your Highness. With all due respect, I need to leave . . . now."

She smoothed her dress and then motioned for me to move closer. The moment I started walking toward her, she crooked a finger toward Grayson, and he too began walking toward her. We met in the middle, and I refused to look at him. Anger, frustration, and hurt warred within my body. I trusted him. I wanted him. He offered me hope when he shouldn't have. I was fine on my own, working my job and hanging with my best friend. Life was fun and yet when he came along, I reached for that something more in my life that I shouldn't have. I wanted to trust him, to have a love that no one else did, and yet he'd broken my heart worst of all.

Moira lowered her voice, "And what is this about?"

How could I tell his own mother, whom I'd just met, that her son hurt me. "Your son is an ass. And I'd like to leave, please."

"Tell her she is not to leave." Grayson's face turned a bright red. His hands curled at his sides, and the muscle in his jaw ticked.

"Grayson, darling, why don't you go find Sav?" He opened his mouth to say something else, but she cut him off. "People are watching."

He pressed his lips together and his nostrils flared. "Fine. I leave you to this."

"What a lovely idea, darling. Give us some time to get to know each other." Moira moved to my side and took my hand. She hooked it in her elbow and gave it a little pat. He glared at our hands but said nothing else and then stormed away.

Moira lifted her chin and looked at our audience. They jumped back into conversation as quickly as they'd stopped to watch us. Everything about vampire court was intrigue and secrets. There was an undertone to all of it that I couldn't put my finger on. It was like I didn't know the rules to a game I'd just became a major player in. There were so many things I felt Grayson hid from me, and the rest all kept those polite smiles.

"Have you ever engaged in girl warfare?" Moira guided us down another hallway away from onlookers.

Girl warfare was a nicer way of saying *dealing with mean girls without losing your mind and winning at the same time*. "Who hasn't?"

We turned up a wide stairwell and she picked up the end of her dress as she walked up each step like she was floating. I'd never seen a woman so elegant and gentle in my life. But one look at those courtiers and they shied away from her. It made me wonder what lay beneath the perfection that I found so enchanting. Did I want to be her when I grew up? Totally. Would it ever happen? Not a chance.

"Vampire court is like this. Don't ever let them see something they can use against you or gossip about later."

My cheeks heated. "I'm sorry about that."

"You mistake me, my dear. Any time you feel the need to hand my son his bollocks on a platter, you do so." She stopped in front of a beautifully carved wooden door. "Grayson is gifted at many things and has a way of getting exactly what he wants. It's good for him not to."

My lips pulled up in a smile. "Consider it done."

"Good." She opened the door and pushed it wide. "In the meantime, perhaps you'd consider staying here. A progeny is supposed to stay with their sire for a year according to law, and I'd hate to see either of you in trouble for breaking it."

Great. Not only is Grayson keeping me here, but so is the law.

She walked into a room and waved her arm around the huge space. The king-size bed sat against the opposite wall. The headboard was made of metal twisted into floral shapes and covered in a bright red comforter that matched the walls perfectly. A huge chandelier hung over the bed and a warm glow filled the room. On the other wall, a wide-open door revealed a huge bathroom with a soaking tub. Moira gave me a warm smile.

"This is your room."

It was beautiful and dark but comfortable all the same and like nothing I'd ever dreamed. Even if I did stay, this was too much for me. "I can't accept this."

"Oh, dear, but you can."

I spun around in a circle, taking in all the amazing details. Then I walked to a door on the other side of the room and pulled it open. A closet the same size as the main bedroom was packed full of brand-new clothes. An entire wall was dedicated to the most perfect shoes with red bottoms and purses from every designer I could name. The closet itself was a mirror of my bedroom with bright red walls, a red ottoman, and a small chandelier.

Maybe just for a little while. "It's too much."

"I don't think it's enough." Moira sighed and sat down on the edge of my bed. "Things with my son are complicated. *He* is complicated."

Deep down, I wanted to know more. I cared more than I wanted to admit. But if there was one thing I learned at an early age, it was if they didn't want you, then you damn sure didn't want them. I saved myself a lot of hurt over the years with that mentality. I always believed a man when he said he didn't want a girlfriend. That wasn't about to change now. He hurt me deeply and changed my life forever. I didn't know where to go or what to do. This new world was alien to me, but somehow I had to figure it all out and get on my own two feet like I always did. Which would take time. It was difficult to admit things, but Moira was the kind of mother I always wanted. Tears formed in my eyes, and I felt that awful cry-lump start in my throat.

I sucked in a breath to fight the aching in my chest and told her the truth. "I don't know what I'm going to do. He broke my heart."

CHAPTER THIRTY-FOUR

GRAYSON

"If one is endeavoring to pout like a child, spy like a stalker, and take on the vestige of a mule, you have mastered this state perfectly." Sav walked into my room and stood at the foot of my bed.

"Piss right off."

I lay there with my arm over my head staring at the ceiling. I'd made a right mess of things and now was the time of contemplations and some self-loathing.

He crossed his arms over his chest and snickered at me. "I do question things with you often. Had I stopped you from making her, you would've hated me. Had I put her down when she was feral, you also would've hated me. And yet I did both things to your liking, and you hate yourself. Quite the quandary I'm in."

I threw my arm down and sat up in the bed. "You're quite long-winded if you don't mind me saying."

"As if this isn't information I've heard before." He walked to my closet and opened the door. Without even looking, he grabbed something and threw it at me. "Get dressed."

I let the trousers fall on the bed. "Why?"

"You can't leave her locked up for days like this. It's not proper." He grabbed a shirt and threw it at me.

"What business is it of yours?" I flopped back on the bed. "Playing matchmaker, are we? Shall I add that to your list of skills?"

"Sour git isn't something I thought I'd add to *your* list of skills, and yet here we are." He moved back to the foot of my bed and yanked the blankets down. "And I've been cleaning up your business for ages. We've got a small problem and the bigger problem."

"Small one first."

The truth was that I didn't care. I wanted to be alone for a few hours and not think. I didn't want to think about the curse, or the prophecy, or the fact that I'd done the exact opposite of what I'd set out to do. I'd hurt Piper, and for that I deserved nothing less than to lie here like a sad sack until I figured something out.

"Dice. The hot, crazy friend."

That got my attention. "What of her?"

"She's missing." Sav scrubbed his hand down his face.

I jumped out of bed and grabbed my cell phone from the side table. "So, what the hell are you doing here? Why aren't you out looking? You've got to make Piper's death smooth for the human."

"I've got Jester on it." He was so calm.

If I lost or hurt Piper's best friend, she'd never speak to me again. Not after the last few days. "I'm calling in reinforcements."

"Oh, the faith you have in me and my men. Warms the places in my cold, dead heart," he groaned.

I glared at him while I searched for the number. "So, what are you doing here, fretting about me and my progeny?"

"You must take her out. Go to London, see the lights, do something simple," he moved to the bookshelf in my room and pulled a book off it, "instead of acting like a stroppy cow."

Cocky little git. "Why exactly are you concerned about this?"

It was no secret that Sav didn't show love or concern for anyone. Yet here he was worrying about Piper and her well-being. He shoved the book back on the shelf. "*She* doesn't bother me too much."

"So?" I wasn't leaving this room.

"So, she can't stay locked up here. It'll drive her mad, which will drive you mad, which will drive me mad. In truth, I'm just saving myself here."

I found the number and hit send. It barely rang before it was answered. "Sup, Leech?"

"Kylian," I greeted him.

Sav waved his arm at me to get my attention. "You're calling the Dark Elf Prince to find a human?"

I placed my hand over the bottom of the phone. "So?"

"That's a horrible idea. Pull your head from your arse and stop this."

I was going to kill him. "Since when do you care?"

"Since now."

I uncovered the phone. "I've lost something I need finding."

"This is a mistake." He shook his head. "You need to go with Piper."

"You're so concerned with Piper, you take her then." I waved him away. If I didn't make sure Dice was okay, Piper would never speak to me. As it was now, she might not anyways. I'd messed up royally. For that I had to set everything else right, and it would start with her bestie. The one person she cherished above all others.

"Fine. I will." He spun on his heels and marched out the door, slamming it behind him.

Kylian sighed on the other end of the line. "Getting bored now."

"Right. Yes. I need you to find a girl."

CHAPTER THIRTY-FIVE

PIPER

"*A*re you sure you want to do this?"

"No."

"Then why are you?" After three days stuck in my room, I'd been getting antsy for something to do. There were only so many days of binge-watching Criminal Minds a girl could take before everyone around her became a serial killer in her head.

Atlas Savage, the last person I expected to see at my door, had appeared there ready to take me out. He was already dressed in boots, jeans, a long winter coat, and hat. He'd handed me a pair of gloves and said, "Let's go." Let's go. And that was it, we were out walking the streets of London. I'd always wanted to experience London during Christmastime. It was only a few days away, and the decorations were in full swing. White lights were strung from one side of the street to the other. They dripped down like glowing icicles, lighting up the whole street in warm twinkling lights. Every storefront was adorned with Christmas decorations—golden ornaments, bright red ribbon, garland, and lights. It was all so magical.

"I thought you might want to burn some energy off. Being trapped in the castle can be quite the experience." He didn't look down at me or even try to impress me in the least. Atlas was, at his core, whatever he wanted to be. He didn't put on airs or a show. People either accepted him for what he was, or they didn't. Either way, it looked like he didn't give a shit.

"It's nice of you." I swallowed around the ache in my throat.

His brow furrowed and he scoffed. "Nice is not a word I'd use to describe myself."

Flurries twirled down from the sky, and I could see every facet of each snowflake as it fell to the street. There was a buzz about this city. It wasn't like New York in the sense that everything was all-go and no-play. It was more uplifting and happier, like an uber posh Christmas. Everything was elegant and tasteful. Music drifted from down the street and people smiled as they too sang along while walking by. Everyone was bundled in their scarves and hats. People stood next to red buckets, ringing bells as others dropped money in. I could smell each of them as though they were individual meals. Everyone had different blood, and it all appealed in some way, especially the ones that'd had too much hot cocoa.

It was curious to me that Atlas would want to take the time to do something like this. It was all so human and cute. "How would you describe yourself?"

"I'm a rather puzzling specimen." He paused and turned to face me. "Do you plan on asking so many questions?"

"Do you plan on avoiding them?"

He glanced around as if not knowing what to do with himself. "Do females always talk this much?"

I could've been offended but I wasn't. "So I see your experience is limited with the opposite sex. Good to know. It'll help when I try to find you a girlfriend."

"Oh, if love ever dare find me, I will do my best to go the other way." He chuckled.

That was just sad to me. I may have gotten my heart broken, but if I was being honest with myself, I still wanted it. From the right guy of course. But I did with every fiber of my being. "Why?"

He shook his head. "Because love is a curse."

"How would you know?"

"I've seen the effects enough. I think it's something

to be avoided at all costs." He motioned to me. "Case in point. You love him, but does he love you?"

"Um . . . ouch, Atlas." I gave his arm a little playful shove.

He looked down to where I'd pushed him. "No one has ever done that before."

"What?"

"Pushed me." He motioned to his arm.

I shrugged. "You deserved it . . . Going after my love life like that. Or the lack thereof."

"You went after mine, which makes yours fair game." He chuckled.

I sighed. "Fair point. But if you change the subject, then I will too. Deal?"

"Deal." He pursed his lips and looked around. "Soooo, are you hungry?"

"No, I'm good." I lied. Truth was, I'd tried almost all the blood samples that'd been sent to my room. I could only manage a few sips before my stomach turned and I wretched it all out. I knew I had to tell someone, but Atlas didn't seem the sort for health confessions. When we got back to the castle, I would go see the good doctor. Until then, I'd be fine.

"Good. Then let's have some fun." He jerked his chin toward a tall white building with a black awning surrounding it. The building was three stories tall and looked like an old theatre with white columns running from one floor to the next. A glass dome sat on the top of the building, with an archways on either side of it. A huge line extended from the front door and wrapped around the corner.

My stomach burned and cramped, but I forced a smile. I wasn't going to miss time exploring London because of a little stomachache. "Let's."

Atlas bypassed the whole line and headed straight for the door. The bouncer took one look at him and opened the rope to let him in. He walked by and right into the club. My vampire senses went into overload. Neon lights flashed across the room, blinding me. The walls were a bright red with golden trim. I tipped my head back, looking up at the three other floors all looking down on us. Lights blared from the stage, and the music filled the whole club. It was all too over-whelming, too much. People flooded in around me and I could feel the blood pumping in their veins.

Atlas melted into the crowd, and I felt the music take me. My body moved of its own accord to the beat of the music. Smells filled my nose, and the heat of the living called the predator in me. Starving didn't even begin to describe how I felt. My fangs ached to come down and sink into the flesh. My throat burned and I needed to end the scorching pain. I spun around in a circle and danced my way through the crowd. I threw my hat and gloves to the floor and let my jacket fall off, revealing my tight black sweater dress. My hips swayed and my shirt rode up, exposing my stomach. I threw my hands over my head, letting my body move however it wanted.

People next to me began to stare and I let them. I could smell their attraction and feel their eyes on me. I would be that deadly flower. So beautiful I needed to be touched, but if they did, they'd get hurt. Something in me liked knowing how dangerous I was, and I gave myself over to the feeling.

A guy came up to me and began dancing. "Hey."

I didn't say a word. I just got closer and placed my hand on the side of his neck and pulled him to me. I let my hips rub against his in time with the music. In the distance I heard my name being called, but I ignored it. I was here. I was hunting. The burning would end soon.

He moved his hands to my hips and smiled down at me with that silly frat boy look. "You're hot."

"Am I?" I met his gaze and held it. Atlas called for me again, but he was so far away on the other side of the room. He couldn't get to me without drawing attention to himself and that was a no-no in vampire land.

"So hot." He was dopey-looking with short black hair, brown eyes, and a too tight royal-blue shirt.

I ran my finger over the side of his cheek, and he leaned into it. "Want to get out of here?"

Without a second of hesitation, he nodded. A smile spread across my face, and I leaned into him. "Oh good."

I knew this wasn't me. I knew I was hunting. But the hunger drove me forward. I needed blood and I needed it now. In my mind, I knew this was bad, I knew I shouldn't be doing it, but the desire was too great. I sniffed the air and found the back way to the outside. I hurried my dinner through the crowd before Atlas could get to us. I shoved through a metal door and out into the cold night air. The guy followed blindly after me. The door slammed shut behind us and I pulled him down the alley in the back of the club and behind a dumpster. With a little kick, I sent the dumpster skidding in front of the door, blocking it completely.

"Strong. I like that." He dug his hands into my hips and pulled me close. He leaned down low and tried to force his lips to mine.

I tilted my head to the side, avoiding his lips. Instead, I licked up the side of his neck, tasting his skin. I flinched back. Something didn't taste right.

But the burn in my throat demanded I taste. I peeled my lips back and let my fangs drop down, ready to strike.

"You don't want to be doing that, Princess."

I jumped back from the guy. My eyes widened and I popped my fangs back into my mouth. "Theon?"

"At your service." He melted from the shadows and smiled at me in that perfect way of his. Strands of his blond hair fell around the sides of his face to his chin, and even in the dark of night his sage-green eyes were visible. He sniffed the air and shook his head. "Something off about that one, there is. Can you not smell it?"

I took a whiff and recoiled. "What is that?"

"Drugs." Theon sniffed the air. "Ecstasy, to be exact."

The man looked from me to Theon. "Look, back off, lad. She chose me."

"If you'd like to keep your bollocks firmly intact, I suggest you leave . . . now." When the man made no move to leave, Theon got in his face so fast he was a blur. Then he bared his fangs and hissed. "Leave."

The man tripped as he ran away down the alley. "Freaks!"

We were completely alone, and I contemplated biting Theon and seeing what he tasted like. He chuckled and shook his head. "I'm not going to taste good to you either."

"How did you know I was thinking about it?"

"When one is being circled and sniffed at, one gets a hint of what's to come." He strolled to the side and leaned against the wall, completely unafraid.

I froze and straightened my stance. "I didn't realize."

"Of course you didn't. Looks like someone hasn't been taught anything yet." He shook his head. "Tsk tsk. I can teach you."

I hesitated.

He offered me his hand. "Come with me, and I'll show you a world you haven't seen yet."

A banging sound came from the metal door. "Piper!"

Atlas was nearly here, and if he found me, it was back to the castle I went. But the animal in me didn't want to be caught. It wanted to be free and hunt. Hunger tore at my insides and up my throat. It wasn't the madness from before. No, this was the controlled need to drink. I could be smart about it. I took his hand, and he yanked me closer to him, wrapping his arm around my waist. He bent his knees and we shot into the air and landed on the roof of the building. Theon pulled me down behind a ledge and pressed his finger to his lips just as the dumpster flew across the alley and dented the wall. Atlas marched out the door. "Fuck."

He pulled the phone from his pocket and dialed. "Gray, we've got a problem. Yeah, I lost her."

He sniffed the air and groaned. "There's a familiar scent with her . . . Theon."

The called continued as he marched out toward the street and took off in the opposite direction.

A wide smile spread across Theon's face and a deep chuckle rumbled in his chest. He lowered his mouth to my face and his breath fanned across my ear. "Time to go, Princess. It looks like I've been a bad boy."

CHAPTER THIRTY-SIX

PIPER

Theon was suave in a street-savvy kind of way. He didn't hold the same panty-dropping charm as Grayson, but his talents were obvious. Charisma was a strength of his. It showed in the way he moved and how other vampires reacted to him. As we walked down a dark back alley, I noticed other Night Spawn lingering about, just hanging out and chatting. When Theon passed, they stopped to give him a nod of respect, like he was royalty of the night.

Here the merriment of Christmas was left behind and the sound of a club filled my ears. Music, laughter, and the familiar smell of liquor occupied my senses. Theon stopped at a door and gave a little knock. A peephole slid open and a set of dark eyes looked him over. A moment later, it slid shut and the door swung wide open. Theon motioned for me to join him, and I moved to his side. The hall was long and dark with a faint red glow.

"I suppose the royals haven't mentioned any of these places to you?"

"No." It was difficult to think with my mind occupied by the burning up my throat and aching pain in my chest.

The hallway opened into a larger industrial-looking room. The lights weren't as bright in this bar. They were calm and dim, easy on the senses. The bar itself ran the entire length of the back wall and had every blood type on tap. The wall behind it was covered with shelves of high-end liquor. While the place was packed, it wasn't bodies grinding on each other. The music was light and subdued so everyone could talk over it. Lounge areas were decorated in dark leather with burgundy tables. Candles of varying shapes and sizes sat on the center of each table and along the many shelves on the walls. An array of lounge areas were spread throughout the entire place and were occupied by vampires all dressed in their normal human clothing to blend in with the world outside. Glasses of blood sat in front of everyone, and my mouth watered.

"We have all the options to offer." He motioned to

the taps. "You can have anything you like that isn't spiked with drugs. They tend to mess with the minds of the vampires. It's no good for the newly made. Though all our top-shelf liquor is there for your liking as well."

None of that held any appeal for me. I groaned and turned away from him, heading back for the door. This place was cool, and maybe I'd come back later, but something in me called to a deeper purpose. My hunt would continue. I felt it in my bones. That driving need to satisfy the thirst was paramount. My thoughts weren't as muddled as before, but it was taking over. I could feel it.

Theon grabbed a glass of blood from the bar and handed it to me. "This is my favorite vintage. Perhaps you'll like it too, Princess."

I took the offered glass and held it to my nose, smelling it. My stomach rolled. "Pass."

"Picky, aren't we?" He chuckled and took a sip from the glass,

"Obnoxious, aren't we?" I didn't have time for this. I needed to feed now.

"It's okay, Piper. I like a woman with some bite." He gave me a dazzling smile, and I turned away.

"I'm rather tired of dazzling men." I started walking away.

He grabbed my arm and spun me back to face him. He licked his lips and smiled. "Am I dazzling?"

"Get over yourself." I rolled my eyes. "Cute British accents no longer have an effect on me."

"Oh, is sass foreplay for you too?"

I pulled my arm free. "Thirsty and leaving."

He handed me another glass, and this time I didn't even smell it. I just put it to my lips. I tried to take a drink, but I couldn't even swallow. I spit the blood right back into the glass. "That was awful. I think my throat closed."

He crooked his finger at me, then turned and walked away. "Come along."

I groaned and followed him. He stopped in a dark corner of the bar and backed into the shadows. He leaned against the wall and gave me a devilish grin. "I have what you want."

"Oh yeah, what's that?"

Theon lifted his hand and ran his sharp nail down the side of his neck. Blood welled and my eyes locked onto it. He studied my face. "Oh yeah. That's what you want . . . take a taste."

I licked my lips and my fangs ached to sink into his skin. I was so hungry. I needed it so badly. But did I possibly dare?

CHAPTER THIRTY-SEVEN

GRAYSON

"How do you bloody well lose a sodding newly made vampire? You! A two-hundred-year-old assassin who hunts people down like a rabid dog." Angry, frustration, and worry all warred within me. There was no telling which one would win out.

"First, I'm not that old—"

"In five years. We're so old we round up, which doesn't matter because right now I'm rounding on kicking your arse." Piper was lost in London as a newly made vampire. "I knew I should've just gone. I knew it."

"And yet you didn't."

I stopped on a dime and turned to face him. "Don't put this one on me. You. Lost. Her."

We were following her sweet honey scent through the back streets of London. She'd walked away from the beauty of the Christmas decorations in favor of traveling with Theon. Of all vampires, she picked *him*. Theon Bailen, the git, going about licking at the boots of those in power, all the while playing cool. He was a leech upon leeches and now he had my Piper. I debated in my mind what kind of pain I would inflict upon him. It was a toss-up between castration or evisceration. I'd let my mood decide. I growled and began walking once more.

"Would you have preferred I made a scene to get to her in front of humans? Because I'm sure alerting the Fallen or bringing the King down on us both would be a wiser course of action." Sav walked beside me on the cold streets.

He had a point. "They're of no consequence when she's out alone."

"Technically, she's not alone."

"Right, you're looking for a thrashing, aren't you?" My blood boiled. I was angry at Sav, but I was angrier at myself. Things with Piper were so messed up that I avoided her, and now she was gone.

"Not particularly. Wasn't on my list of things to do today." He was so untroubled by all of this, but I was in turmoil.

"Is there a reason you'd like me to punch you in the throat this evening? A little concern would be welcome, man."

Sav chuckled. "Have you seen your woman. She's formidable. I saw her take out an entire squad of my guys without a weapon. Not to mention throw Jester and me across the room. You think a little shit like Theon stands a chance . . . hell no. I'd be surprised if his bollocks are still intact, and if they are they won't be for long."

We turned down the alley that led to one of Theon's frequented hangouts. Vampires lingered about chatting and laughing. But the second they saw me and Atlas, they gave a quick bow and scurried away. I motioned to the scurrying vampires. "I see you still have an effect."

"They're not running from me." He stopped at a thick metal door and banged on it three times. "If only you could see your face."

The peephole to the door slid open and two dark eyes peered out at us. They widened for a moment, then the peephole slid shut. I didn't hear any movement on the other side. Savage sighed, and I had about two seconds before I lost my patience.

One . . .

Two . . .

I planted one foot and kicked out with my other. The door ripped off and flew into the opposite wall. A big dent sat in the middle of the door. A huge vampire lay sprawled out on the floor next to it. Sav stepped over his body. "Extreme but effective."

"This coming from the moodiest sod around."

I walked down the hall and into the bar area. Her honey scent was near. I would know it from miles away. Sav was silent as ever beside me. Vampires all around the bar stopped what they were doing to look at the two of us. A reluctant Prince and the right hand of the king both standing here searching for a baby vamp that might not want to be found.

"Touché." He scanned the crowd, then pointed to a dark corner. "There."

I was in that corner in a flash, standing right behind Piper. Rage, hot and heavy, flared through my entire body. My arms shook and every instinct in me screamed MINE. "What the fuck?"

Piper was up on her tiptoes with her cute little fangs buried in that asshole's neck. She jumped and dislodged her mouth from him. "Grayson!" Her eyes widened but she leaned into him like she couldn't stop herself from trying to go for more.

I grabbed her shoulder, pulling her back from him. At the last second, she turned to the side and gagged, spitting blood on the floor at his feet. Theon didn't bother wiping the two little punctures in his neck. He just stood there wearing them like a badge of honor. He gave me a cocky smile and I was debating whether I should rip his fangs out with a sword or not. Violence or diplomacy, that was the question.

"Don't be like that, Piper darling." He smiled down at her. "It was good for me."

Violence it is.

"Moron." Atlas shook his head and stepped to the side just as I wrapped my hand in Theon's shirt and jerked him out of the corner.

His legs dangled off the ground, and he clawed at my hand. I yanked his face close to mine. "You. Don't. Touch. Her."

"Other way around, mate. She touched me."

Motherfu . . . I threw him. His body spun in midair and slammed down on a table across the room. It splintered under his weight, crashing to the ground. Vampires rushed for the door, clearing out from the bar in a stampede.

I grabbed Piper's hand and pulled her toward me. "We are leaving."

She yanked back on it. "I can't."

Another heaving gagged wracked her body but

nothing came up. I bent down and caught her eye. "How much have you had?"

"Barely anything." She shook her head. "What's on the floor. I couldn't swallow it."

Theon popped to his feet and dusted himself off. "Come now. I know I taste good."

I took a step toward him, and Atlas stepped in front of me. "It would be my utmost pleasure to handle this for you."

"I'm going to kill him myself." I was about to step around him when Piper lost her balance and stumbled into me.

"Your progeny is hungry. You're going to let her starve?" He raised his eyebrows, challenging me.

As bad as I wanted to knock Theon for a loop, Piper needed me more. "Fine. Give me a mirror."

Atlas pulled a disk out of his pocket that looked like a silver frisbee. He tossed it at the wall and it stuck there. The disk expanded and grew to the size of a full-length mirror. I threw her arm over my shoulder and supported her weight on my side. Her hair fell over the side of my body, bathing me in that honey scent of hers. I helped her to the mirror and pressed my hand to it. In no time, we were in the cold hallway heading toward my room.

"I can't believe you did this, Piper. Of all the things

. . . Theon." I was angry, hurt, and disappointed all at the same time. I knew we weren't in the best of places, but to bite someone else . . . we reached my room in moments. I stopped at my bed and let her sit on the edge. She hunched over with her hand pressed to her stomach.

"I'm just so . . ." her head snapped up and her eyes locked on the pulse in my neck. Her tongue darted over her cherry lips, ". . . thirsty."

"You can't let yourself starve like this. It's not right. What about all the samples I had sent to your room?"

She rose to her feet and sauntered toward me in that slow hypnotic way she always had about her. The dress was too tight to her body, drawing my eye to the way her hips swayed and her hair fell all around her. She was too beautiful, too fiery, too tempting. She leapt toward me, wrapping her arms around my shoulders and pressing her body against mine. Her fangs were buried deep in my neck so hard and so fast I slammed into the dresser behind me. With the first pull of blood into her little mouth, I felt all anger melt away. She groaned at my flavor and held me tighter as if not wanting to let her prey go. I wrapped my arms around her and tilted my head away, giving her exactly what she needed.

Her hips ground into me and my body stiffened

against hers. When she reached down between us and cupped me, my hips flexed of their own accord. "Piper, we can't."

She popped her fangs from my neck and licked her lips. Breathless, she tossed her hair to the side and smiled up at me. My blood had an instant effect. She was stronger, brighter, and infinitely more seductive. "Why not?"

"We just—"

"—Screw it." She leaned in again, this time on the other side, and buried her fangs deep in my neck.

When she went to fumble with my belt, I didn't stop her. I didn't stop her at the zipper or the fly of my pants. When they dropped to the floor, I kicked them away. I couldn't fight her, fight this, I didn't want to. Not even for a second. I craved her with every fiber of my being. I always had, and no amount of reasoning could deny it . . . I was hers.

She hiked up her skirt and slipped her panties down her legs, kicking them off of one foot and letting them hang from the other. She hopped up and wrapped both of her legs around my hip. When she gave another gentle suck with her lips, I was nearly undone. I reached between us and slid myself over her, readying us both for what was about to happen. She pulled away and lapped at the little marks on my neck.

"Do it. Do it now." She ground her hips down on me and took us both exactly where we needed to be. Her dress rode up around her hips as I held her there.

All the problems, all the angst, fell away and then it was just me and her. I splayed my hands across her ass and held her up as my hips smacked into hers. Everything about this moment was perfect. How well her curvy body fit against mine, the excited sounds that she made, her tongue on my skin, and her honey scent completely enveloping me. But the most perfect of all was the connection I felt between the two of us. She and I were always meant to be like this. I felt it deep in my bones.

I stumbled forward with her in my hands and we both fell to the bed. She threw her hands over her head and grabbed onto my headboard. Her head thrashed back and forth, sending her wild hair flying in all different directions. My name was like a prayer on her lips, and I bent down low, taking her mouth with mine. The taste of her sweetness flooded my mouth and drove me wild for more. My need for her was overwhelming, and it drove me wild. Everything moved so much harder and faster.

Her body tightened around mine and her legs pulled my hips in closer. Sweat dripped from me onto her. Neither of us cared. It was just her and me. A moan broke past her lips, and she threw her head back, arching into me. I felt her tighten around me and I could no longer hold back. I fell into ecstasy with her, and I never wanted to it to end. Every muscle in my body tensed and released. Light exploded behind my eyes and there was nothing for me but Piper.

"Grayson." She cupped the sides of my face and smiled. "Don't ever stop doing that."

"Not sure I could, Little Creature." I pressed a kiss to her lips and let our excited breath mingle together.

A giggle rumbled in her chest. "I meant, like, right now."

"Give us five minutes, love. And nothing will stop me."

CHAPTER THIRTY-EIGHT

GRAYSON

*W*armth covered my chest and small puffs of breath tickled my skin. Yet something wasn't right. Something was off in my room. My eyes flashed wide, and there stood Titus at the foot of my bed, looking down on me covered by a very naked Piper. She lay face down with only her back exposed to him. I knew what the bed looked like. It was completely torn apart. There were pillows on the floor and one on top of a beam overhead. Claw marks marred my mahogany headboard and every bit of clothing had been ripped to shreds at some point during our hours-long bout of lovemaking. Bite marks covered my neck, wrists, and arms.

I didn't know what time it was, but when I looked outside the sun had either set or still hadn't come up.

My guess was the former. The muscle in his jaw ticked and he balled his hands into fists and released them repeatedly. "Outside. Now."

Without another word, he marched from my room. I ran my hand through my hair and pulled at the strands. "Oh shittttt."

Piper lay fast asleep, sated from my blood . . . and other things. I reluctantly disentangled myself from her and slid out of the bed. I grabbed the first pair of trousers I saw and shoved my legs into them while making my way toward the door. I had the button done up just as I opened the door and stepped into the hallway. Titus barely let me get the door shut before he got in my face.

"Are you out of your bloody scenes," he hissed under his breath.

I scrubbed my hand down my face. "No."

"Have you forgotten all that we spoke about?" He turned away from me and took a few steps.

I knew he had a right to be angry. I was playing a game where the odds were not in my favor. "No."

He turned around and charged forward, getting so close to me that the velvet from his jacket brushed my arm. "Do you want to end up like your father?"

"No, I don't bloody well want to end up six feet under a headstone. Thank you very much." Why did they all keep asking me like I was going to say yes I wanted to end up dead?

"You're toying with things you should not be." He shook his head and sucked in a deep breath. "Have you forgotten our deal? Because I will send her away from here for good."

It was a night of passion. One I didn't not regret in the slightest. "I haven't forgotten."

"I will do everything in my power to stop the curse from taking you, but it seems I am the only one."

When I said nothing, he glared at me and continued.

"Mark these words, avenge thy crime,
Bound by blood in space and time.
From kin to kin one wretched vine,
A wicked curse seals a shaded line.
What was denied shall now be taken,
For when thee love thee turn forsaken.
Deep in thee veins thy soul will burn,
Forever more thy thirst shall yearn.
Breath by breath thy mind unwound,
To madness now thy life is drowned.
And if fate shall deem thy love requited,
Don't speak the words or curse the blighted.
For if on the wrist thy souls entwined,
Death shall call and forever find." ."

Those words rang through my mind constantly. "I know the bloody curse."

Titus waved toward the door. "Well, someone had to remind you. The deal was one year with her to teach her how to become a vampire. Not to become besotted. That display in there is not part of the deal and can never happen again or we will all lose you. Even her!"

"You don't think I know that?" The thought of one measly year with her just didn't seem like enough. The mere thought of it pained me. It tore at my chest and pulled at my heart. Piper was everything. She was . . . life.

Titus leaned into me. "It is better to admire from afar than to lose everything. Now, you can have your one year if you agree to uphold your end of the bargain. I will overlook this one night. You may teach her . . . but you may never have her again. What say you, Prince Grayson, do we have a deal?"

The saying deal with the devil *always came from The House of Shade.*

WOULD TITUS TEMPT YOU? Deal or no deal? Find out what happens next to Grayson and Piper in Wicked

Bite the second book in the The Royals: Vampire Court.

All power is bound to The House of Shade...

Click here to pre-order Wicked Vampire

IF YOU WANT FREE SCENES, more content, or just to chat about all things wicked come join my FB group Megan Montero's Wicked Readers.

Click here to join the Wicked Readers

DON'T MISS OUT ON THIS FREE BOOK!

THIS POWER CHOSE *ME*...

Within the supernatural world of Evermore everyone prays their child will be born with the Mark of the Guardian for they have unparalleled strength, intelligence, and *power*...but they have no idea what it's actually like. I didn't wish for this *gift* and I definitely don't want it. I was born a prince, I already had it all. This Mark on my neck stole all of it from me and forced me into a dangerous life I'd gladly trade away if I could...

But now the Witch Queens have ascended and it's time to try and defeat the evil King once and for all. For over a thousand years his cruelty has spared no one as his torturous power grows stronger. He must be stopped now, before his reign destroys everything and anything in his way. So I must push aside my dreams of returning home to the family that cast me out. I must step up and claim the power that chose me. I *must* enter the Trials and become a Knight in the Witch's Court.

There's only one way to prevent the tyrannical king from destroying everything I love...I must become the one thing he can't beat.

Click here to get your FREE book now!

INCASE YOU MISSED the first season of The Royals: Witch Court check it out now!

CLICK HERE TO GET YOUR WITCH COURT BOXSET

It's time to claim my power...

ALL MY LIFE I've lived under lock and key, always following the strict rules my mother set for me. A week before my sixteenth birthday I sneak out of my house and discover why. Turns out I am not just a normal teenager. I'm a witch blessed with a gift someone wants to steal from me.

And not just anyone...the evil King Alataris.

For a thousand years the people of Evermore have suffered under his tyranny. The Mark on my shoulder says I am the Siphon Witch, one of five Witch Queens fated to come together and finally destroy him. The only thing keeping Evermore safe is the Stone that shields the witch kingdoms from Alataris's magic... and now he's found a way to steal it. Suddenly, I'm sent on a quest to find the ancient spell to protect the Stone. My only hope for surviving is through my strikingly beautiful and immensely powerful

Guardian, Tucker. The laws of Evermore state that love between us is strictly forbidden, and it appears I'm the only one willing to give in to the attraction…

When the quest turns more dangerous than expected I realize I have absolutely no idea what I'm doing. I was raised human. But I have to learn my magic fast because If King Alataris gets his hands on me he'll steal my magic and my life…but if he gets his hands on that Stone we all die.

THE MAGIC CONTINUES in the second season of The Royals: Warlock Court Now in this completely set!

CLICK HERE TO GET WARLOCK COURT

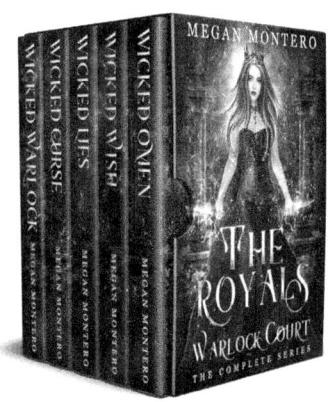

THERE'S no such thing as magical powers. . .

All my life the only kind of magic I'd ever seen was the sparkling jewels on fifth avenue. On the night of my sixteenth birthday all hell breaks loose, and by hell I mean me! I never felt power like this, so dark, so tempting, so out of my control! No one is safe around me. And now I'm being thrown into Warwick Academy.

An academy for the darker side of magic. . .the warlock side.

My captor, my savior, and the bane of my existence, Beckett Dust insists on keeping me here even though we can't stand each other. I don't care how drop dead gorgeous he is or that he rules the school like he owns it, I need to stay as far away from him as I can. His deepest desire is to turn me into a weapon in the great war to come. My deepest desire is . . . him. There's a thin line between love and hate and right now I'm walking it.

IF YOU'RE all caught up on The Royals don't worry there's more to come. In the mean time check out The Night Realm: Magic Marked my awesome co-written series with Chandelle LaVaun.

CLICK HERE TO GET MAGIC MARKED

He put a spell on me...

Or at least he *must* have, because none of this makes any sense. None of this can be *real*. I'm not a mage with magical powers...I'm just *me*. Ellie Sutton. Your average, everyday seventeen-year-old high school *human* student. My biggest concerns are bullies, failed exams, and missing the express subway twice in one day.

Magic is something I read about in comic books, it's not real. People don't move things with their minds or summon lightning with their hands. I don't care what Stellan Wentworth says. It doesn't matter that he's breathtakingly beautiful or that his eyes sparkled when I challenge him. He's the kind of hero found in romance novels, not my real life. I'm dreaming, I have to be.

Because if I'm not, then what he's telling me is true. This gorgeous, terrifying world is in turmoil...and if I don't learn how to use my magic overnight...they'll all die.

Midnight Mage

Marvel Mage

Master Mage

Court Marked

Fatal Fae

Christmas Marked

Bite Me, Santa

Jingle My Bells

For Nick, Thank you for all your help along the way with this one and being my guide to all things British over the years.

Xoxo- Megan

MEGAN MONTERO

WICKED BITE

THE ROYALS: VAMPIRE COURT BOOK ONE

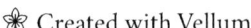

ABOUT THE AUTHOR

Megan Montero was born and raised as sassy Jersey girl. After devouring series like the Immortals After Dark, the Arcana Chronicles, Harry Potter and Mortal Instruments she decided then and there at she would write her own series. When she's not putting pen to paper you can find her cuddled up under a thick blanket (even in the summer) with a book in her hands. When she'd not reading or writing you can find her playing with her dogs, watching movies, listening to music or moving the furniture around her house… again. She loves finding magic in all aspects of her life and that's why she writes Urban Fantasy and Paranormal.

Learn about Megan and her books by visiting her website at:

Www.meganmontero.com

Printed in Great Britain
by Amazon

40167311R00253